I0822711

INTERSTELLAR RUSE

Book Four of the Oracle of Light

Cil Gregoire
Alaska Sci-Fi Queen

PO Box 221974 Anchorage, Alaska 99522-1974
books@publicationconsultants.com, www.publicationconsultants.com

ISBN Number: 9781594339936
eBook ISBN Number: 978-1-59433-893-9

—First Edition—

The events, people, and incidents in this story are the sole product of the author's imagination. The story is fictional; any semblance to individuals living or dead is purely coincidental.

Dedication

To my brother Dudley
Who knows Louisiana's beautiful
Swamp lands
By heart.

Books by Cil Gregoire

Oracle of Light series:

Crystalline Aura
Book One of the Oracle of Light

Anthya's World
Book Two of the Oracle of Light

Elemental Forces
Book Three of the Oracle of Light

Interstellar Ruse
Book Four of the Oracle of Light

Acknowledgements

Thank you so much Renamary Rauchenstein for your editing and guiding hand. Also Herman Thompson, Becky Smith, and Dawn Rinehart. I couldn't do it without you.

I express sincere thanks to my fellow authors at Author Masterminds for their help and support. They are: Evan Swensen our great leader and publisher, Carl Douglass, Gordon Parker, James Y. Qeqe, Irene Petteice, Lyle O'Connor, Magdel Roets, Mary Ann Poll, Mary Flint, Nancy Shaffer-Perez, Rich Ritter, Robin Barefield, Steve Levi, T. Martin O'Neil, Valerie Winans, Victoria Hardesty, Rebecca Wetzler, and Walter Grant. These authors span the genres and I highly recommend that readers check out their great works.

Characters

Earth

Alice	–	A high school student in South Louisiana; Seth's twin sister.
Angela	–	Works at the gift shop owned by Elaine and Ilene.
Adele	–	Melinda's widowed aunt; she has four sons and lives in Ketchikan, Alaska.
Crystal	–	Daughter of Vince and Maggie Bradley. Rock's twin sister.
Elaine	–	Ilene's mother. Owns a gift shop that sells locally made items.
Greg	–	Adele's son, Melinda's cousin; owns his own fishing boat.
Grumpy George	–	A recluse; Rahlys' nearest neighbor in the woods to the south.
Ilene	–	Daughter of Theon and Elaine.
Jack Faulkner	–	A widowed, retired Bristol Bay fisherman; long-time friend of Vince Bradley.
Justin	–	A high school student in South Louisiana; friends with Seth and Alice.
Leaf	–	Son of Vince and Maggie Bradley. Rock and Crystal's older brother. Melinda's little brother.
Maggie	–	Vince Bradley's wife; mother of Leaf, Rock, Crystal and Melinda. Rahlys' closest friend and closest neighbor in the woods to the north.

Melinda – Vince and Maggie's adopted daughter. Big sister to Leaf, Rock, and Crystal.

Officer Gerald LeBlanc – Retired Louisiana police officer; once investigated mysteriously disappearing items.

Rahlys – A free-lance artist living in a remote cabin in the Alaska woods; possesses the Oracle of Light.

Raven – Once an ordinary raven; Raven became Rahlys' familiar after plucking the Oracle of Light from the Susitna River and taking it to her. Enhanced by the Oracle, Raven can communicate mentally through pictures.

Rock – Maggie and Vince's younger son; Crystal's twin brother.

Seth – A high school student in South Louisiana; Alice's twin brother.

Aaia

Brakalar – Former Head of the Academy and Councilor of the Runes of the Crystal Table. Escaped the Devastated Continent through an energy field in the Crystalline Landscape bringing the deadly Rod of Destruction to Earth.

Caleeza – Second in command of the lost expedition to the Devastated Continent. Once transported to Alaska's North Slope by forces in the Crystalline Landscape; now a founding colonist of the secret valley hidden in the Crescent Mountains.

Captain Setas – The only resident of Limitation Island; ferries expeditions sanctioned by the High Council to and from the Devastated Continent.

Clova – High Councilor of the Runes of the Crystal Table.

Councilor Anthya – A councilor of the Runes of the Crystal Table, Anthya was named after Sorceress Anthya who nurtured her after her mother's death during the Dark Devastation. Anthya was present during the great sorceress' forging of the Oracle of Light and is connected to the crystal in Rahlys' possession.

Cremyn	–	A member of the lost expedition; The Cremyn valley is named for her.
Drak	–	An independent historian not recognized by the High Council; Drak inspired Kiril's interest in history and gave him a map of a hidden valley in the Crescent Mountains.
Droclum	–	An evil sorcerer who invoked the forbidden spell that led to the Dark Devastation that nearly destroyed the planet Aaia.
Edty	–	Once a member of the Band of Rogues; now a founding colonist of the secret valley hidden in the Crescent Mountains.
Inventor Sulyan	–	A recluse living and working in a hut behind the Academy in the Community of the High Council. He invents gadgets of convenience for those weak in the ability to draw energy from the elemental forces.
Kaylya	–	A rogue explorer of the Devastated Continent; Rojaire's love of his heart. She disappeared in the Crystalline Landscape shortly after she and Rojaire discovered the vast expanse of crystals arriving on Earth; years later Councilor Anthya brought her back to Aaia.
Kiril	–	An aspiring explorer and student of the Academy; Kiril's interest in history was honed by Drak who gave him the map of the hidden valley in the Crescent Mountains.
Ollen	–	A member of the lost expedition; now a founding colonist in the secret valley hidden in the Crescent Mountains.
Quaylyn	–	A councilor of the Runes of the Crystal Table; trained Rahlys in using the powers imparted to her through the Oracle of Light to defeat Droclum. Rahlys' love of her heart.
Rojaire	–	An independent rogue explorer of the Devastated Continent; led the mapping expedition that rediscovered the hidden valley in the Crescent Mountains.
Sarus	–	Leader of the lost expedition. Through metamorphosis, Sarus' mind is absorbed by the Crystalline Landscape.

Sorceress Anthya	–	The great and powerful sorceress who fought Droclum on Aaia until his escape from death that led to the Dark Devastation. Anthya died creating the Oracle of Light to protect Earth from Droclum's evil.
Tassyn	–	Once a member of the Band of Rogues; now a founding colonist in the secret valley hidden in the Crescent Mountains.
Thayla	–	A warrior princess from the planet Twaka.
Theon	–	Once a follower of Droclum; went to Earth seeking the Dark Orb; has a daughter, Ilene on Earth; now a founding colonist in the secret valley hidden in the Crescent Mountains.
Traevus	–	A member of the lost expedition found by the expedition sent to find them; was on the mapping expedition that rediscovered the hidden valley in the Crescent Mountains.
Vestan	–	Drak's great grandfather.
Wessid	–	Kiril's chosen father, a provider by trade.
Zaloka	–	Kiril's chosen mother, a ceramist by trade.
Zayla	–	A councilor of the Runes of the Crystal Table; second in command of the expedition that searched for the lost expedition; killed by Brakalar with the Rod of Destruction in the Ruins of the Temple of Tranquility.

Table of Contents

Chapter 1 Earth 13
Chapter 2 Aaia 31
Chapter 3 Earth 46
Chapter 4 Aaia 57
Chapter 5 Earth 67
Chapter 6 Aaia 76
Chapter 7 Earth 88
Chapter 8 Aaia 100
Chapter 9 Earth 109
Chapter 10 Aaia 120
Chapter 11 Aaia 134
Chapter 12 Earth 146
Chapter 13 Aaia 157
Chapter 14 Earth 168
Chapter 15 Aaia 178
Chapter 16 Earth 190
Chapter 17 Aaia 202

Chapter 18 Earth 213
Chapter 19 Aaia 220
Chapter 20 Earth 224
Chapter 21 Aaia 228
Chapter 22 Earth 239

CHAPTER 1

Earth

A red fox scampered lightly over crusty snow through boreal forest of spruce, winter-bare birch, and alder. The fox cast a sharp shadow under the full moon unveiled by fast-moving broken clouds. Seeking cover from the moon's watchful eye, it paused in the shadow of a spruce tree, sat on its haunches, and sniffed the air testing for a whiff of the subtle but alluring scent that led him here.

At first the fox picked up only the ubiquitous aroma of spruce needles and sticky resin, oxygen-rich ice crystals and pungent crusty leaf mulch newly exposed in broadening circles around trees, tiny islands of bare ground exposed by spring snow melt and the heat of rising tree sap. Another chilly breeze rustled through the trees, ruffling the fox's reddish-brown fur fluffed out against the late night chill.

And there it was again, the alluring aroma of living flesh and the fetid scent of manure and ammoniated urine. The fox's nose pointed out the direction as overhead scudding clouds chased by the wind once again momentarily obstructed the moon's view from its actions.

The frantic hectic cackling in the hen house was heard first by Keiluk, sleeping protectively by her young master, her canine senses instantly alert. In nearly the same instant, five-year-old Leaf bolted upright in his bed, his tousled carrot-orange hair and emerald green eyes as charged with energy as the intensely focused expression on his youthful face.

"The chickens are in trouble," he whispered to Keiluk. Leaf loved the chickens; the big black hen that ruled the coop, the little white one that was her closest follower, the two red hens who were somewhat down in the pecking order, but so clever and spunky, and the ten hens covered in little black and white jagged stripes that filled out the flock. Every day he helped feed and water the hens and sometimes he was even trusted to collect their eggs.

The cacophony of cackling and fluttering hens reached manic proportions, spurring Leaf into action. Without another thought, Leaf teleported to the hen yard barefoot and dressed only in his super hero PJ's. Left behind and unable to follow her master, Keiluk barked alarmingly in protest, rousing Vince and Maggie to wakefulness.

The fox continued scratching purposefully at the hen house door unaware of Leaf's sudden appearance. Leaf also loved the red fox. The cunning, beautifully cloaked red fox with his fluffy white-tipped tail was a favorite character in his story books. But it was obvious from the hens' cackling, they did not share his sentiments. He had to do something fast, before Keiluk woke Mom and Dad.

Raising his hand, Leaf extended it toward the fox still intently clawing at the wood of the chicken coop door. At that moment, Vince rushed out the door with a shotgun in hand ...just in time to see the red fox vanish and his little son, barefoot and dressed for bed, standing boldly triumphant in a rush of moonbeams newly freed from the obscuring cloud that had scudded on.

Vince dropped his gun on the porch and rushed out to the hen yard to his son, plucking him up into his arms and hugging him tight. Leaf's body was warm to the touch despite the cold night air and crusty ground.

A mile and a half away, the red fox yelped sharply–startled and disoriented by the sudden change in its surroundings. It stood in boreal forest much like before with dark patchy clouds still scuttling raggedly across the moonlit sky, but there was no sign of the anticipated dinner that had been so close at hand. The scent of wood smoke, usually associated with humans, drifted in the breeze. Although all was quiet, the fox quickly distanced itself from the small, squat, dark log cabin it spotted quietly nestled in the trees.

Another chilly breeze ruffled the fox's fur and sent the bare tree branches clacking overhead. Then the fleeting scent of a ground squirrel alerted the fox's senses. Still intent on dinner, the red fox scampered off into the forest after new prey.

"Leaf...!" Maggie cried out in alarm, following her husband out onto the porch into the frigid moonlit night. Her left hand clutched close her unzipped coat, while her right hand maintained a firm grasp of Keiluk's collar. The somewhat large four-legged bundle of white fur and muscle quietly strained to reach Leaf even though he was in her line of sight and she could see that he was all right.

"Leaf, you can't go rushing out into the night at the first sign of danger," Vince lectured, his concern momentarily outweighing his relief.

"I had to protect the chickens," Leaf explained.

Holding his son, Vince could feel the aura of warmth Leaf projected around them. "Where did you send the fox?" he couldn't help asking.

"I sent him all the way to Grumpy George. Grumpy George doesn't have any chickens."

Not a permanent solution Vince reasoned, but it would probably do for tonight. Keiluk eased her tugging as the chickens quieted down and Vince approached carrying Leaf. Seeing no further reason to control him, Maggie released her hold on Keiluk's collar and the dog darted down the steps to meet them. Jumping up and down in joy, Keiluk licked Leaf's bare feet.

"Don't you ever dash out into the night, barely dressed, like that... ever again," Maggie cried out, her disheveled red hair and glaring green eyes only a tone subtler than Leaf's. In contrast, Vince's homogenously brown hair and brown eyes were a quiet background to his family's stunning color. "You're grounded," she added shivering in the chilly breeze, her heart chilled with fear despite the rushing warmth of overwhelming relief over her son's safety.

"I'm sorry," Leaf said as contritely as he could. He wasn't sure what being grounded meant, but he understood he had upset her. For that he was indeed truly sorry. Vince wondered how she expected to ground a child who could teleport.

What's going on out here? Melinda asked telepathically, hugging a blanket around her while stifling a yawn. *Why were the chickens upset?*

Melinda's warm brown skin, straight black hair and almond eyes contrasted sharply with the rest of the pale-skinned family. A native of Southeast Alaska, Melinda lived with her father on their fishing boat until he was killed and she was taken captive by Droclum. Terror had stolen her ability to speak, but under Droclum's dominance she acquired the ability to communicate telepathically. Eventually she was rescued by Rahlys and adopted by Vince and Maggie into their growing family.

"A fox was trying to get in the hen house. It's gone now; everything is all right; back to bed everyone," Vince explained herding them back inside.

Good night, then. A young woman of nineteen, Melinda didn't hesitate in heading for her room. She had been involved in enough of Leaf's escapades over the years, sometimes willingly, most of the time out of necessity, to know when to take an easy exit if it was offered. She felt for Maggie and Vince, how they worried over Leaf; Maggie struggled even more than Vince at accepting their son's unusual abilities. But Melinda knew that if Maggie and Vince were aware of everything Leaf did that they didn't know about, they would go ballistic with fear.

Hoping to escape from further reprimand, Leaf also dashed off to bed with Keiluk following at his heels. Incredibly the twins had slept soundly through it all.

"The incident is over; let it go," Vince whispered to his wife. He unloaded the gun and locked it up. "It's one a.m. and all is well. Leaf thought only to save the chickens."

"I know," Maggie said taking a deep breath. "It just scares me so."

Vince took his wife gently into his arms and when she dropped her head onto his shoulder, rubbed her back soothingly. Maggie responded gradually, allowing the tension to flow out of her body.

"Everything is going to be all right," Vince reassured her. "We both know that Leaf is an incredible little fellow. He did what he felt was right. Despite how much we fear for his safety, we have to at least be thankful for that."

By the time Melinda returned to her room, the chill morning air had ushered her to full wakefulness. The house was quiet again with everyone back in bed. Outside a mighty gust of wind brushed against the log wall, playing the chimes hanging outside her window.

Unable to go to sleep, she sat on her bed in the dark room and watched the shifting patterns of moonlight trickling in through the wind-rattled trees. Two year old Crystal slept peacefully in her own bed a few feet away while Crystal's twin Rock shared Leaf's room on the other side of the plank wall that divided the log addition into the girls' room and the boys' room. Soon Crystal would have the room to herself. She hadn't told anyone yet she was leaving, but her decision was made. At nineteen it was time to reclaim her true identity, come what may. She glanced at her little sister realizing that Crystal would grow up without her, but with two brothers, the day would definitely come when Crystal would appreciate having her own room. Melinda smiled wistfully at the thought.

Sitting in the quiet darkness alone with her thoughts, Melinda felt the slight tug of the mysterious key she kept tucked away hidden in a little musical jewelry box buried in a drawer. The strange sensation was very subtle and only noticeable when there were no distractions. Reaching from where she sat, Melinda pulled out the bottom drawer of her nightstand and dug out the jewelry box, jostling the release of a single musical note from the movement that blended in perfectly with the faint tinkle of the wind chimes outside. She sat with the box in her lap for a long hesitant moment without opening it. The object's strange tug became more perceptible with the box in her lap. Slowly she opened the softly padded blue lid, colorless in the dark, and removed the numerous pieces of costume jewelry she had collected or made over recent years. This facilitated lifting the bottom lining, tearing from the sides due to wear. Reaching in with her fingers, she retrieved the mysterious key from its hiding spot. The flat metallic artifact acquired through a nightmare didn't reflect the moonlight, but seemingly drew in the darkness. In her hand the urge to leave her home of six years and seek...seek what she didn't know...became even stronger. In a way it spoke to her heart, for she had already decided to pick up her life in the outside world...the world that extended beyond the confines of the forest of the northern Susitna Valley.

It was not a rash decision; Melinda had given this move a lot of thought over the past few months. *I am ready to reclaim my identity. By leaving I can protect the Order of the Oracle from exposure. No one will ever have to know I've been living up here all this time.*

Her decision finalized, Melinda stashed the strange key back in its hiding place and slipped under the covers on her bed, bringing the coverlet up to her chin. Soon the warmth lulled her into deep, peaceful sleep.

☆☆☆☆

In the spring awakened end-on-the-road village along the Alaska Railroad Ilene walked to the nearby train station. A silent sigh of relief made room for a blissful sense of freedom as Ilene, a backpack filled with delectable goodies slung over one shoulder, reached the nearly empty local train platform. After a long and uneventful winter with few distractions Ilene and her mother were definitely in need of a break from one another. Her mother seemed to grow crankier and harder to please by the day. Thoughts of her constantly grumbling, less-than-happy mother were already growing fonder as the distance increased between them.

Perhaps I've been a bit cranky lately myself. I know Mother means well, but I'm a grown woman; I need more space to breathe. And she needs to develop more interests; something or someone other than the gift shop...and me.

Ilene embraced the day, surprisingly sunny and clear...and remarkably still...after such a blustery night. *Has spring finally arrived?* Warm sunshine glared blindingly off what remained of open areas of white snow, while the snowpack along the roadway, darkened by a winter's accumulation of road grime, dripped with snow melt. Brilliant sunlight reflected off Ilene's dark gray eyes; the warmth of the sun allowing her to pocket her knitted hat exposing an abundance of curly mossy brown hair that refused to be tamed. A trip into the wilderness to visit Rahlys relieved tension. Rahlys didn't know she was coming, but Ilene had an open invitation. Probably the guest cabin would be available, although since Kaylya and Quaylyn left a year ago, Ilene has been staying with Rahlys at the main cabin, both women preferring company to help dispel the loneliness.

The quaint little local train clanged merrily as it approached the platform, surprising everyone by being on time. Classic and with character, the local train bore no resemblance to a rocket or a silver bullet but rather the old antique passenger cars nostalgic of the old west. Upon boarding, Ilene glanced around; there were a few travelers occupying seats toward the front of the railcar, so Ilene chose a seat further back on the side of the aisle she knew offered the best views of the mountain and the Susitna River along the way.

As the train began to move forward, a new conductor ambled toward her to collect her ticket. Ilene allowed herself to relax and enjoy the anonymity that the change in conductors afforded her. For once she would not be interrogated with questions she didn't want to answer concerning her father. With the ticket transaction quickly completed and her mile post destination duly noted, the conductor moved on. A vista of the mighty Susitna River, still mostly encased in ice with only a few open leads, winked in the sunshine with Denali and the Alaska Range towering majestically over the frozen river.

Heading up the tracks naturally drew her thoughts toward Theon. The rhythmic clacking of the train wheels on the rails lulled her into deep reminiscence; she barely noticed the awakening boreal forest flicking by her window. Two years have passed since she has seen her father. Theon, known as Half Ear by the locals, had been notably unusual even by Alaska standards, his mysterious disappearance never accounted for. Only Ilene and the members of the Order of the Oracle knew the truth. Theon returned to Aaia, his own world, to die...at least in his own mind. Nevertheless, the holographic crystal from Rahlys' painting assured Ilene her father was still alive, despite his unbelievably advanced age. Her heart longed to see him again, but Ilene knew that was unlikely with the vast expanse of the Milky Way galaxy effectively separating them.

Aaia! What a strange and fabulous world Aaia had proven to be! She relived in her mind the fascinating journey she, Rahlys, her father, and Raven had undertaken with Rojaire, Anthya, Zayla, Quaylyn, and Brakalar across the Devastated Continent searching for a lost expedition. The product of an Aaian father and Earthling mother, Ilene had felt a connection to the mysterious continent that Rahlys didn't share. *Will I ever have a chance to claim my Aaian ancestry? It will probably be up to the High Council of the Crystal Table.*

Sooner than she expected, the conductor returned to announce the approach of her destination.

"Oh...thank you," Ilene murmured jostling her awareness back to the present. Slowly she followed the conductor to the exit, her body swaying gently to the rocking of the slowing train. The train stopped with a gentle lurch in front of a packed snow trail that led into the woods.

"Are you sure you will be all right?" the conductor queried showing some concern over dropping off a young unarmed woman alone into the wilderness.

"I'll be fine," she reassured him with a smile and stepped down the steps to the rail bed below.

"Will you be taking the train back this afternoon?" the conductor asked. The train crew would know to look for her on the return trip if she answered in the affirmative.

"No, thank you, I'll be staying for a while."

"Take care, then," he said and radioed an "All Clear" to the engineer. The train pulled away leaving Ilene to relish the soft murmur of the open lead in the icy river across the railroad tracks from Rahlys' trail. The sun reflected blindingly off the pristine snowpack bringing tears to her eyes as she donned her pack properly and headed for the trail leading into the woods.

It was a half mile hike to Rahlys' log home over a meandering trail that wove up and down hills. The bare birch trees did little to shade the trail but the shadows they did cast helped greatly in reducing the glare. A flock of song birds recently returned from their southern migration flitted about the trees filling their bellies with the abundance of birch seeds still clinging to the branches. She hadn't gone far when the exertion forced her to pause long enough to drop her pack and remove her jacket. "It's warm," she said to no one.

"Aaaarrrk!"

Raven's unexpected piercing cry startled Ilene. She hadn't seen him arrive. Perhaps he had been there all along. Knowing Raven, he sat in wait intending to startle her. And since Raven knew she was here, so did Rahlys.

Ilene! Do you want me to meet you on the trail? Rahlys' telepathed message arriving instantly.

Thanks Rahlys, but that won't be necessary. Raven is watching over me and I'm enjoying the hike.

Then I'll see you when you get here.

Raven flew short distances ahead relating mental pictures to Ilene of the trail and surrounding woods. It was fascinating having a bird's eye view of her surroundings along the way. She became so engrossed in Raven's telepathed images, she forgot to watch where her feet were going and tripped on an exposed tree root sticking up in the trail, barely catching her balance in time to prevent a fall. Then of course, Rahlys couldn't resist meeting her part of the way on the trail and soon the two women were greeting each other warmly.

"Aaaarrrk!" Raven cawed as he flew off. Rahlys immediately relieved Ilene of her pack, teleporting it up ahead.

"Careful with that," Ilene warned. "The makings for our stay-up-all-night-and-chat party are in there."

To Ilene, Rahlys looked pallid from lack of spirit and exposure to sunshine. Her long graying straw-brown hair lacked luster, her pale blue eyes lacked their usual gleam of contentment, and her strong, slender body had shed unnecessary weight. There were twelve years difference in their age, Rahlys close to pushing forty, but their bond of friendship had been forged through deeply shared connections and incredibly dangerous adventures.

"I'm so glad you're here!" Rahlys exclaimed with true delight. "What a neat surprise! I'm in need of a distraction."

"I'm so glad to be here," Ilene sighed just as truthfully. "It was definitely time for a mother/daughter separation."

"How are things at the gift shop?"

"Business is picking up, but Mother and Angela can handle it easily. They don't need me there. I thought we should have Maggie over too; leave Vince with the kids," Ilene said turning the conversation back to partying.

"Oh, girls' night out; sounds good," Rahlys laughed softly, breathing some spirit back into her.

One more rise in the trail and they arrived at Rahlys' cabin shimmering warmly in the sun. The accumulation of snow around the cabin had barely been disturbed through the winter except for the well-defined trail in and subsidiary routes to the woodshed and outhouse.

Entering Rahlys' once spacious log home was now the equivalent of walking into a large but crowded rustic live-in art studio. Colorful vivid renditions of moose, bears, foxes, ravens, flowers, berries, ice formations, auroras, children building snow people, children sledding, chickens.... Finished works in acrylics and watercolors crowded all available wall space and lay stacked on furniture, while makeshift easels displaying works in progress limited navigable floor space. Tubes of water colors, acrylics, paint spotted rags, brushes both dry and soaking in water in canning jars, and dried out makeshift pallets, along with empty and partially full cups of cold coffee covered every bit of table and counter space.

"I don't have to ask what you've been doing," Ilene gasped soaking it all in. "Do you ever come up for air?" she asked genuine concern flavoring her words.

Rahlys hunched her shoulder, "Sometimes."

Rahlys' focus on her work had been intense now for a long time...to the point of self-neglect. Ilene was certain the single-mindedness was her effort to fill a void left from Quaylyn's departure nearly a year ago. With a sympathetic sigh she let her concern rest for now; there would be plenty of time to talk later. "Where's my pack?" she asked suddenly remembering it.

"At the guest cabin; I thought we would heat it up and have our little party there." Rahlys said waving her hand apologetically over the art clutter. Plus I could use the change in surroundings; and that way I won't be taking furtive studying glances at my work all night if it's out of sight.

"That makes sense...I guess." On that note, Ilene quickly urged Rahlys back out into the warm spring sunshine.

After a few moments of simply basking in the warmth of the sun, they headed out through the trees toward the guest cabin several hundred yards away, stomping down the snow to set in a trail. After a few yards of this Rahlys called a halt. "Let me take care of this." Realizing Rahlys had something in mind, Ilene stepped back to get out of the way.

Rahlys stood tall, her concentration intense, as she studied how she wanted to direct the force she would release to achieve the desired result. When she felt she was ready, she stretched out her hands before her, bringing her fingertips together like the prow of a ship or a snowplow and drew deeply on the abundance of elemental energy all around. Suddenly an invisible force gouged a three foot wide pathway through the snow, spewing it off to the sides, all the way to the door of the guest cabin.

"Nice...," Ilene nodded impressed. "And you didn't even need to pull up the crystal for help."

"Since Quaylyn's been gone, sometimes I forget I still possess these amazing abilities." Ilene was surprised to hear Rahlys speak Quaylyn's name out loud. She hadn't done that in a long time.

Rahlys was the Guardian of the Light, in possession of the Oracle of Light, which gave her incredible powers. The title carried great meaning on Quaylyn's world, Aaia, but was unknown on Earth beyond their tiny circle. "I might as well send some firewood while I'm at it," Rahlys decided and in moments had transferred an abundance of kindling and split pieces from the woodshed to the doorsteps of the guest cabin for easy access for tonight's party.

After building a quick small fire in the stove to take the chill out of the cabin and setting up for their get together, Rahlys and Ilene dropped in on Vince, Maggie, and the kids surprising them with a knock on the door, which set Keiluk, who had been sleeping by the stove, to barking.

"Rahlys...and Ilene!" Maggie exclaimed upon opening the door over Keiluk's excited barking. "Oh hush," she admonished Keiluk, "fine guard dog you make...waiting till someone knocks to bark." Keiluk stopped barking, but continued vying for attention with tail-wagging joy.

"Hi Keiluk, it's so good to see you too," Ilene assured her petting the rambunctious over-grown year-old white puppy vigorously. Then like a volcanic eruption, children spewed out of the boys' room led by Leaf.

"Who goes there?" Leaf exclaimed taking a warrior's stance and brandishing a cardboard sword. Rock and Crystal took positions beside him, each child boasting a different shade of red hair and green eyes. Crystal's strawberry blonde curls, wildly framing her delicate heart shaped face, blazed in the afternoon sun streaming in from a southwest window; her hazel green eyes flashed with excitement. Rock resembled Vince the most of all the children. A small but brawny sentinel beside Leaf and Crystal's delicate features, Rock boasted a strong, sturdy frame topped with thick luxuriant reddish-brown hair and a strongly chiseled face alight with green-flecked brown eyes. Standing above the others, Leaf's flaming orange hair and emerald eyes were the most striking, making Maggie's coloring dull in comparison. The visitors greeted all three children enthusiastically, giving each child a big hug.

"Look...my robot," Crystal cooed holding up her favorite toy.

"Why aren't you children outside playing?" Rahlys asked. "It's a beautiful sunny day." She didn't mention that it had taken Ilene's arrival to get her outside.

"We've been out in the woodlot," Maggie explained her own red hair in disarray. "I just got them fed and changed into dry clothes. I was thinking about putting them down for a nap, but it's getting a bit late," she added glancing out at the setting sun.

"Good, so they should sleep well tonight, because we have plans for you," Ilene said glancing around. "Where are Vince and Melinda?" she asked.

"Bringing in another load of firewood; they should be zipping in with another sled load any minute now. They were getting ready to quit for today."

The children had turned their attention back to each other and the women had barely settled in with coffee and tea when Melinda and Vince came in covered with woodchips, their outer clothing damp from snow melt. Their arrival created a new wave of greetings.

"So Ilene, how are things in town?" Vince asked after stepping out of his overalls on the porch and shaking them out.

"Town is starting to wakeup; spring is in the air," Ilene said while giving Melinda a little hug. When Ilene was away from the group she generally thought of Melinda as a young girl still, but standing before her was a young woman.

Vince and Melinda gratefully accepted the glasses of iced tea Maggie offered them. "Thanks, honey," Vince said taking a seat at the table while Melinda went to her room to change.

It wasn't long after everyone had settled down again before Ilene brought up the purpose for her visit. "Well Vince, Rahlys and I want to take Maggie away for the night, stuff her with junk food and wine, and make her reveal her inner-most secrets. Do you think you can handle the kids for tonight? We would like to have Melinda join us too."

Melinda could hear the conversation at the table from her room, and the last part of Ilene's declaration took her by surprise. She had been included with the adult women.

"Of course, take them," Vince responded with just a little hesitation. "Maggie deserves a break...Melinda too. I can handle three little children on my own for one night."

"Are you sure?" Maggie asked with uncertainty.

"Yes," he reassured her. "I think it's a wonderful idea. You two have a good time; it will be a piece of cake."

"Well if you're certain. The children haven't had a nap so they should be tired early," Maggie persisted. "They have recently been fed so you should be able to get by on healthy snacks from now to bedtime and there's soup and sandwich makings in the refrigerator." Vince and Maggie had given up on the root cellar for their day-to-day use and had invested in a propane refrigerator.

Vince shook his head and waved his hands protesting her fretting. "Go...have a good time...don't worry about a thing. I'll scramble up some eggs for them later, put them to bed, and then write." Vince was finishing up work on another novel, the first since Leaf was born, and Maggie knew he was anxious to write.

"Okay, thanks my love," Maggie conceded running out of issues.

At that moment a screaming match, accompanied by Keiluk's excited barking, erupted in the boys' room. Maggie leaped to her feet and arrived quickly on the scene where Leaf pointed out the obvious. Vince and Rahlys were right behind her; so of course Ilene and Melinda couldn't resist following them.

"Crystal and Rock both want the robot," Leaf explained supposedly an innocent by-stander as well as an intrigued spectator. The screaming and barking continued as brother and sister tugged determinedly on the desired toy with Keiluk seemingly cheering them on. Rock's greater strength won out eventually giving him possession of the prize. Crystal, red-faced with rage, screeched in dismay and then converted to being cunning. As soon as Rock relaxed his hold on the robot, Crystal snatched it out of his hands and the struggle ensued all over again, at which point Maggie took action.

"Let me have that," she said firmly, gently taking possession of the toy. "Toys are for sharing not fighting over." Her action, while perhaps justified, did nothing to stop the flow of youthful tears.

"Well, ladies, I think it's time for us to go, don't you?" Rahlys announced. "Vince can take charge from here, right Vince?"

The women enjoyed only a momentary glance at the look of consternation on Vince's face before Rahlys teleported the four of them with a wave of her hand to the warm and quietly inviting guest cabin, the toy robot still cradled in Maggie's arms.

☆☆☆☆

"Where are we going?" Seth asked brushing back long sandy hair from his flushed freckled face.

"I don't know. Let's at least make it to those woods before someone spots us." Justin strove on ahead, setting an aggressive pace despite the heat. Seth could see the circle of sweat growing on the back of Justin's shirt, but his thick dark hair remained unruffled by the exertion.

"Did you talk to Alice?" Justin asked.

"Huh...," Seth bowed his head hesitantly, "no....why do I have to talk to her?" he asked. In truth, Seth had avoided doing so. It sickened him to see lust in Justin's eyes when he mentioned Alice's name. He didn't want Justin preying on his twin sister.

The truant boys stalked through newly planted cane fields, over bramble-choked headlands, jumping muddy crawfish-filled drainage ditches, distancing themselves from the evaded school classrooms. Skipping class was turning out to be harder work than Seth expected. The heavy heat beat down brutally hot for April, even for south Louisiana.

"I just wanted you to mention it to her and get her reaction."

"You bring it up to her and get her reaction. I don't want anything to do with it. Besides, I don't know if I like the idea of you going out with my sister anyway."

Justin wasn't usually shy about approaching girls, a trait Seth was envious of, but of course the girls Justin usually hooked up with were rather bold themselves. Now Justin wanted to take Alice to the prom.

He obviously feared rejection or he wouldn't ask Seth to intervene. Alice knew Justin all too well from the three of them hanging out together.

Seth quietly followed Justin across another field, perspiration dampening his shirt. Finally the headland turned into damp woods of palmetto and cypress. Once under cover, Justin and Seth stopped for a brief rest, but having nothing else to do Justin was eager to explore. Seth readily agreed, so bending palmetto fronds and scratching trees with their pocketknives to mark the way back out, they ventured deeper into the woods keeping the sun on their right.

Gradually the moist ground under their feet rose a little, offering drier footing for willows and oaks. Seth stumbled to keep up with Justin's greater stride while glancing behind them to affix landmarks in his mind as clouds began to move in blocking the sun. He was just about to complain about the distance they had gone and his concern over getting lost when Justin came to an abrupt stop, Seth almost crashing into him.

"Look...," Justin said pointing ahead.

At first, Seth didn't see anything noteworthy, but upon closer scrutiny he saw it too. There before them, nearly consumed by the surrounding woods, stood a house so old and weathered and colorless it was barely discernible from the ground and the strangling trees concealing it.

"Let's go check it out." The boys eagerly worked their way through the tangle of trees and vines to the remains of a dilapidated porch that led to the door-less front entrance.

"Wow...it looks so old...," Seth gasped in wonderment.

"It's big too," Justin noted sizing it up. Cautiously navigating a safe route over the broken down porch, they entered the time-forgotten structure.

They expected to find rat nests and animal droppings and the like, and as they walked through the rooms they did indeed find plenty of those things, but they didn't expect to also find a large flat screen TV, computer, tools, furniture, and a wide variety of modern household items.

"Where did all this loot come from?" Justin wondered out loud. "It looks like someone lived here for a while, but I don't think anyone has been around for a while, that is if the moldy chewed up bedding is any indication." Most of the furnishings were in the two large center rooms connected by a collapsing double fireplace.

"Wow...what's that?" Justin exclaimed as they reached the fourth and final room of the shotgun house. The object in question was large filling the added on back room, the worn planked floor sagging under its weight. The base was at least four feet across and eight feet long, too large to have passed through the door.

"It's a laser cutter," Seth realized after some inspection. The boys could hardly walk around the room, the fit was so tight. "There's one at the shipyard where my dad works."

"How did a laser cutter get here?"

Seth shared Justin's confusion. "Perhaps the real question should be, why is it here?" The house was obviously older than the existence of laser cutting machines as were most of the trees concealing it and there was no road leading in. As though looking for answers they exited the house by a rear door. Most of the dark clouds had moved on, the expected shower avoided.

Outside, a large live oak, the spread of its branches dwarfing the rambling house, dominated the overgrown yard. Near the back door a crumbling structure of brick and concrete once served as a cistern for collecting rain water.

"Alice would love to see this; she loves old things...especially old houses!"

"Then why don't we show it to her?" Justin suggested. "Tomorrow is Saturday. We could pack a lunch, make a day of it. Then she would see I'm not a bad guy."

Seth knew Alice didn't care for Justin, but all he said was, "Maybe, we'll see."

☆☆☆☆

"This is great," Maggie sighed with pleasure sipping her third glass of wine, "no kids, no chores, and no interruptions...what a great idea you ladies had!" Maggie, Rahlys, Ilene, and Melinda had pushed all the meager furniture to one end of the little cabin and filled the open space in front of the wood stove with pads of foam rubber, sleeping bags, pillows, and blankets to provide comfort and room to stretch out. Offerings of cheese, crackers, smoked salmon dip, olives, grapes, strawberries, and chocolates, as well as the confiscated toy robot, circled the perimeter and the Oracle of Light, the crystal that had transferred incredible powers from the ancient sorceress Anthya to Rahlys, hovered above them, providing them with soft multi-colored light. With tensions relaxed and inhibitions lowered, all except for Melinda who stuck with apple cider, the conversation was taking on an increasingly personal turn.

"Do you think Quaylyn will ever return?" Maggie asked Rahlys, bringing up a topic Rahlys usually avoided.

"I don't know," she answered honestly, "I hope so," the last part just a whisper.

"You could go to him," Ilene suggested.

"No I can't. I still need to find the Rod of Destruction." Brakalar had been captured and returned to Aaia, but the whereabouts of the dangerous Rod of Destruction, another product of Droclum's evil remained at large.

"But the key is on Aaia. We saw it melt into the rubble in the ruins of the Temple of Tranquility," Ilene pointed out.

"I don't know. Maybe. That may only be a ruse," Rahlys said. "We can't let ourselves be fooled by what we think we saw and want to believe is true. I need to find the Rod of Destruction before anyone else does."

"Do you ever think about going back to Quaylyn's world?" Maggie asked. Rahlys hesitated in answering, but Ilene spoke up.

"I want to return to Aaia," Ilene said. "I want to train at the Academy, and explore the Devastated Continent...and see my father again."

"Perhaps one day you will," Rahlys said encouragingly. "I will relate your wishes to the councilor...if she ever contacts us again."

"Kaylya and Rojaire promised to deliver my letter to Father and speak to the High Council in my behalf."

"I'm sure your mother's wishes are different. She took it pretty hard the last time you left," Maggie reminded Ilene. "I took it pretty hard myself; with you and Rahlys both gone...it was pretty lonely here."

I was here.

"I know, Love, and for that I'll be eternally grateful," Maggie said giving Melinda a hug.

"But I should be allowed to return to Aaia," Ilene stated emphatically. "Aaia is as much a part of my heritage as Earth."

"What about you, Melinda, what is your heart's desire? You must have plans?" Rahlys asked. Six years had passed since she rescued the frightened young girl from Droclum's clutches.

Melinda had listened quietly to everyone else's hopes and dreams, contributing little about her own aspirations. The direct question caught her off guard, surprising even her when she answered.

I'm ready to go home and pick up my true identity.

"Oh, Melinda," Maggie cried putting an arm around her. They all knew the day had been fast approaching when Melinda would want to leave. Ilene and Rahlys inched closer also giving her a supportive touch.

"When?" Ilene asked after a moment of silence.

As soon as I can. I just need help getting back down to Ketchikan.

"I'll be able to help you with that," Rahlys offered gently.

"I'll miss you," Maggie teared up.

"We all will," Ilene added.

Throughout the rest of the night and well into the morning the four women strategized a plan to help Melinda re-enter her previous existence, or at least the remnants that remained of that life left behind.

CHAPTER 2

Aaia

"Stop fidgeting," Rojaire breathed softly to Kiril tapping Kiril's foot with his own to make sure he heard. Communication by telepathy was strictly forbidden in the High Council chamber. Kiril and Rojaire were seated at the formidable Runes of the Crystal Table. Rojaire was no less agitated than Kiril but the strong chiseled contours of his face, handsome when relaxed, were taut with anxiety.

Kiril made a barely concealed effort to appear quietly in control ... with minimal success. He felt dwarfed sitting in one of the large ornately cut crystal chairs, the silver-padded armrests of his throne-like seat too far apart to rest his arms on comfortably. Never before had he been summoned to a session of the Runes of the Crystal Table. He was still a new person, a student of the Academy, many cycles of seasons away from being assigned his First Mission to become an Accepted One. He stared fearfully at the ancient Water Rune etched before him in the enormous oval crystal table, the rune's dull metallic glow subdued by the room's bright crystal dome ceiling. This was not a joyous occasion ...the councilors were here to pass judgment on him. If the stern expressions of the four councilors sitting opposite him were any indication, the outcome did not bode well. Kiril's wild tannish hair and pale golden-gray eyes sparked with charged nerves. The report he had turned in to the High Council ...that is the report he and Rojaire and Traevus wrote to replace the purloined journal of their mapping expedition... had caused quite a stir among the establishment. Now the true repercussions would be revealed.

Just when Kiril was certain he couldn't endure the stress and tension any longer, High Councilor Clova entered the large crystal-domed council chamber. Traditionally the group seated at the massive oval rune-etched crystal table would respectfully go silent when the High Councilor entered the chamber, but the group summoned here today couldn't be any quieter. Tall, stern, and sleek the High Councilor crossed the dark marble floor of the chamber to a crystal throne on a raised crystal dais overlooking the assembly. Her long silky black hair bound in jeweled ties and flawlessly smooth dark skin glowed in the sleeveless form-fitting gown she wore in council colors of silver and green. Kiril couldn't take his eyes off her. High Councilor Clova gracefully stepped up onto the dais and stood before her seat to face the council.

"I welcome you here today, Councilors, Accepted One Rojaire, and new person Kiril, that we may seek together purpose and direction for the greater good of all." High Councilor Clova spoke the words with true conviction, placing all her faith in the power of the Runes of the Crystal Table to guide them to a wise decision. She was the most powerful member of the High Council, but her main role was to officiate. Her demeanor was unbiased, neither steeped in compassion nor devoid of it. If no agreement can be reached on an issue by the Councilors, she would rely on the power of the runes to guide her in a decision.

There was no small talk, High Councilor Clova went directly to business. "The topic up for discussion today: Should the Devastated Continent and Limitation Island's original names be adopted once again, and should the continent be opened for colonization? Let's begin."

With a wave of her hand, the room and ceiling darkened and the Runes of Power gleamed like molten silver on the softly glowing Crystal Table. It was all Kiril could do to suppress an undignified expression of awe. "I believe you know the rules; the runes call on and seat the speakers."

As though in demonstration, the Fire Rune in front of Anthya blazed up in light and burned in non-consumptive flame above the center of the table.

"The runes had chosen the first speaker. Councilor Anthya...." The High Council nodded in Anthya's direction and sat down. No one else would speak as long as the fire rune occupied the center of the table.

Anthya stood slowly, the glow of the fiery rune reflecting off her silvery council robe edged in green. Councilor Anthya's smooth ivory skin, light gold hair, and serene face gave her an appearance of softness but she exuded strength, conviction, and self-confidence. Her light gray eyes reflected back the rune's fiery light as she consolidated her thoughts.

"I have been to the Devastated Continent," she began slowly. "I understand how Rojaire and Kiril feel about it." She was the only councilor who could make that claim. The words she spoke were heavy, given weight by experience ...and grief. She gave them the pause they deserved.

"The Dark Devastation nearly destroyed our world. It practically wiped us out as a species. We failed to protect our planet from near annihilation. Tens of millions died on the Main Land; hardly anyone escaped alive from Lynnara." There was an almost audible gasp when Anthya spoke the forbidden name, but she continued on as though she hadn't noticed. "The destructive forces unleashed by Droclum's evil actions scoured the island continent clean of all life and nearly snuffed out all life on the Main Land as well. And how do we make amends for our failure as an intelligent species? We refuse to call the island continent by name, referring to it as the Devastated Continent instead."

Kiril gazed in rigid wonder and anxiety as he listened to Anthya speak. His chest felt so constricted, he was unable to breathe.

"Understandably, as a species we felt remorse. But in an effort to atone our guilty souls we stripped the continent of her name and convinced ourselves that somehow we became nobler and remorseful by doing so."

Anthya took a breath; therefore so did Kiril, stunned by the fervor of the councilor's speech. At least Anthya was on their side.

"Councilor Zayla was my closest friend. I grieve her loss as much as anyone here. The expedition she and I were on together was her second trip to the island continent. Hundreds of cycles of the seasons had passed since her first expedition and she noted many changes in the landscape. Seismic activity had diminished and erosion had soften the contours of the land, and although still sparse, plant life had spread out across the continent from the Golden Sea to the Crescent Mountains. Even the interior, which Councilor Zayla never had a chance to see, supports some plant life." Anthya paused again, but the Fire Rune remained in place.

"Councilor Zayla saw the continent was healing. I believe she would want us to heal as well. It is time we stop chastising ourselves and embrace our history; we cannot change it; we must accept it for what it is. We must honor our survival and learn from our mistakes. We can do that by freeing our natural sense of adventure and curiosity, by allowing Lynnara back into our hearts and opening the continent to exploration and colonization."

And with those words uttered, the fiery rune winked out. It happened so suddenly, Kiril feared at first it was an expression of disapproval by the power of the Runes, but when the Sun Rune immediately took its place, he realized it was just a change of speaker.

Councilor Xevin rose from his seat to address the assembly. Having replaced Brakalar as Head of the Academy, he was highly esteemed in the Community of the High Council. The brightly shinning Sun Rune burnished his orangey-brown hair with golden highlights. His tall frame, bulky with muscle, erect posture, and sharp stare took command of their attention.

"Council Anthya's sentiments and viewpoints are..." he paused searching for an appropriate word, "...interesting," he settled on. "She touches on Councilor Zayla's death, but she seems to have forgotten that an entire expedition, minus one, is still missing on the Devastated Continent and have probably met their demise by dangers yet unknown." Councilor Xevin turned his piercingly hard gaze directly at Kiril.

"I'm surprised that new person Kiril, still so young and impressionable, was allowed to travel to the continent with Rojaire and his group in the first place. You can see the damage it has done," he said pointing to him. "The journal that historian/warrior-to-be Kiril turned in to us is a farce," the head master said with scorn. "It's too clean. I have the distinct feeling there are things we aren't being told. And his mind is no longer on his studies at the Academy; instead he fills his time dreaming of colonizing a sinister, dangerous place."

Kiril's face reddened in bottled up fury. The Head Master's direct statements were a crushing blow. He almost shouted out a rebuke when he remembered he wasn't allowed to speak unless the silvery Water

Rune etched in crystal before him indicated he could. Finally, Councilor Xevin's cutting gaze turned away from him.

Councilor Xevin paced a bit, letting his words sink in before continuing. "I fear Brakalar's fall is a warning to us all. The fact that an esteemed member of the High Council can so easily succumb to evil illustrates the need for continued protective control of the people. Call the abominable continent Lynnara if you insist, but keep in mind that such back-stepping isn't good for discipline and order. I firmly believe that colonization of the Devastated Continent would not be for the greater good of anyone."

Kiril breathed a silent sigh of relief when the flaring Sun Rune finally returned to its etching on the Crystal Table. The Head Master could say no more. But the next choice of speaker was hardly an improvement. The glimmering Moon Rune rose into position brightly illuminating expectant faces as Councilor Zilka, the eldest of the group assembled, stood. Kiril knew the councilor was also Proctor of the southern communities for the High Council of the Crystal Table. Her thin silvery white hair shimmered in the glow of the rune.

"Councilor Xevin is right," she stated with force right from the start, her blue-violet eyes sparkling in the light. "The murder of one councilor by another should never have happened. Such an action was unimaginable before we started sending these expeditions to explore. Brakalar's moral descent has tainted the people's confidence in the High Council. Instead of opening the Devastated Continent to settlement, we should be shutting down access to the threatening continent all together. There is no shortage of land to settle and explore here on the main continent." After pausing for a breath, she continued.

"I fail to understand why anyone would want to live in a land where energy can't be drawn from the elemental forces. It would be a hard brutal life far from civilization. I doubt Explorer Rojaire could find twenty people on the whole planet who would be willing to take up such a venture."

Kiril glanced at Rojaire seated between him and Anthya. His finely sculpted facial features revealed no reaction to Councilor Zilka's words.

"I'm sure Explorer Rojaire's talents can be put to better use. I think I've made where I stand on this issue quite clear," she said and started to sit down. She had had her say, and apparently the Moon Rune agreed, for it left the center of the table.

Almost instantly, the Soil Rune took up the position.

Kiril feared the wrath of Defense Master Jarlon at the Academy even more than the Head Master. This was not going to be good. Refusing to appear intimidated, he bravely kept his head up, although he was shaking in his bones.

"I'm in agreement with Councilor Zilka and Councilor Xevin," Jarlon said. His dark brooding eyes and fixed scowl amply expressing his dissatisfaction with leniency and sentiment in general and his contempt for the topic under discussion in particular. "Student Kiril has undeniably been lax in his studies and training; and Explorer Rojaire has unquestionably been an unsavory influence in young Kiril's life." His words were cold and hard and he glared at Rojaire with obvious disdain.

"A colony requires human resources. Who do you think is going to volunteer to go on such a venture ...besides that female friend of yours? Who else would willingly follow you to such a place?"

Of course Rojaire wasn't permitted to answer. Kiril noticed that Rojaire continued to sit rigidly upright in the wide crystal chair, his face still expressionless. Jarlon continued to speak to Rojaire directly.

"As Councilor Zilka said, it is doubtful you could mass together twenty colonists, men and women, to go with you; anything less would hardly be viable. I suppose you harbor some progressive ideology of excessive breeding to rapidly produce an abundance of unguided offspring."

Kiril detected the venom in Jarlon's words. Apparently there was some bad blood between Rojaire and Jarlon that dated back to Rojaire's rogue explorer days. Jarlon would have continued speaking, but the Soil Rune abruptly left the center of the table, effectively bringing his stance to an end. There was only a brief moment of hesitancy before the Void Rune rose to prominence in the center of the table. When ignited, the Void Rune appeared as a glittering primordial light around a center so dark and opaque it appeared as a hole in the Crystal Table.

Councilor Renna, Aaia's Representative to the Worlds' League, stood silently for some time carefully considering her words before she spoke. An effort had been made to contain her long reddish-brown hair in jeweled ties in the style worn by High Councilor Clova, but in

Renna's case, contained did not mean controlled for several curling strands wildly escaped confinement.

"I find it surprising that two important representatives of the Academy, the very foundation of knowledge and enlightenment, would shut portals to exploration. Has the Academy fully abandoned the principles it was founded on? We explore other worlds; should we not explore our own?" She turned toward Councilor Jarlon. "I sense fear. Shouldn't the Master of Defense be fearless?"

Kiril wanted to applaud Renna's jab at Jarlon. Finally someone appeared to be on their side. He eagerly waited for more, but Renna's say was brief as the Void Rune returned to its etching before her. Then the vacancy was quickly filled by the Air Rune and Councilor Kreeze, Proctor of the northern communities for the High Council of the Crystal Table, took his stance.

Kiril held his breath in worried expectation. Kreeze lived in Kiril's home village. As one of Kiril's community fathers who helped raise him from birth, Kreeze knew him quite well. Studious and judicious, his graying brown hair shimmering in the soft airy light of the rune, it was uncertain what position he would take.

"Well ...where do I begin?"

Kiril groaned inwardly. *I'm in for a lecture now. And if the Air Rune doesn't cut him off, everyone is in for a long speech.*

"I'm not normally one to break away from tradition; and if asked, I would have to admit I'm somewhat resistant to change, but..." the councilor paused for effect, "Lynnara was Lynnara long before the name was banished from maps and the land branded as the Devastated Continent. To this day I'm not quite sure I understand the initial reasoning behind that action. I suppose it helped appease the emotional trauma running so high at the time, but there are other ways to recognize our history without stripping a continent of its name."

Kiril allowed himself one tiny silent sigh of relief, and then he heard his name.

"Regarding Kiril, son of my own community; the reports from his masters are dire, and he and I will have a private discussion later and another with our community. Suffice it to say, he should be severely disciplined for his lack of diligence in his studies."

Kiril guiltily dropped his head down, but he could still feel Kreeze staring him down, with his eyes and his mind. It was going to be an uncomfortable home visit during the Academy session break about to start.

"Then there is the matter of colonization of Lynnara," Kreeze said after a brief pause. "I have to say I'm as surprised as Councilor Renna at the Academy's lack of interest in further exploration of Lynnara. Making the unknown known is acquisition of knowledge, and knowledge is potential." Proctor Kreeze paced around the table as he lectured. "Right or wrong, I can sympathize with one view of colonizing the lost continent or the other. But the true underlying debate here is, 'How much freedom of choice should the people be allowed?" or perhaps another way to word it might be, "How much control over the people should the High Council exert?"

Kiril was sure he gasped audibly, but the startled expressions around the table were not directed at him. Expecting the High Councilor to intercede, he glanced her way, but Clova had not moved and showed no outward reaction to Kreeze's bold statements.

Then almost as an afterthought, Kreeze made a suggestion nearly as startling as his previous comments. "If everyone here is so certain that Rojaire couldn't put together a group to follow him, why not let him take on Councilor Zilka's challenge. If Rojaire can find twenty people who want to form a colony in Lynnara, perhaps we should give the colonists a chance?"

It was obvious to Kiril that Kreeze had more to say, but he never had the chance. The Air Rune disintegrated in the center of the table and to Kiril's amazement, the crystal dome ceiling above them brightened. The silver etchings of the eight Runes of Power glowed softly in their places as they did before and the center of the table was remarkably empty. The session was obviously over. Neither Kiril nor Rojaire had been called to speak, which was probably a good thing. Speaking might have made things even worse. All that remained was High Councilor Clova's final decision, a decision guided by the Power of the Runes of the Crystal Table.

High Councilor Clova rose to speak.

"Our work here today is now concluded. A decision has been made. From here on the Devastated Continent will once more be known as

Lynnara, and the diminutive island off her west coast is once again Alaia Island. As for the colonization of Lynnara, Accepted One Rojaire will have three rotations to promote his cause. If he can sign on twenty colonists in that time the High Council will grant a charter for a colony on Lynnara."

High Councilor Clova did not wait for a response. There was no need to. Guided by the wisdom of the Runes of the Crystal Table, the councilor's decree would not be challenged. Immediately, she stepped off the dais, and with barely a nod of acknowledgment marched out the chamber.

☆☆☆☆

Kaylya paced nervously up and down the stone balcony outside the living quarters she shared with Rojaire. Like the room behind her, the small amphitheater balcony had been carved out of the mountain itself by artisans. The view from this height was spectacular overlooking fruit orchards, the Academy and the distant Golden Sea, but Kaylya's mind was too occupied to see it. As Kaylya reached the southwest corner of the balcony, a ray of the lowering sun lit her golden brown hair and smooth chestnut skin.

Traevus watched her pace, his own fist clenched against his thin lithe body in tense impatience. What could be taking them so long? He had just as much to lose as Rojaire and Kiril. He had been on the mapping mission, and he had conspired with them to keep secrets. What was keeping them; soon the sun would be dropping behind the western mountains, and still they anxiously awaited Rojaire and Kiril's return from the council chamber.

Kaylya had invited Traevus to wait it out with her for moral support. Once Rojaire and Kiril return, assuming the High Council even lets them return, the four of them will either celebrate or commiserate over the High Council's decision. She and Rojaire had hoped to embark on further exploration of Lynnara with a support team after returning to Aaia from Earth. But a whole season had passed and no expedition had been granted. Kaylya was hoping without much hope that Rojaire would return from the summons to the High Council with good news, despite some of the overlying issues.

Few seemed to understand why she and Rojaire would want to leave the Main Continent at all. It wasn't like they were unhappy. As promised, upon returning from Earth, she had received Accepted One status in the community, and they had been appointed exceedingly comfortable living quarters in the palatial caverns of the Community of the High Council. And of course there was still the joy of her and Rojaire being together again after so many seasons of separation, seven years as measured on Earth. Her contribution to the community so far has been the scribing of volumes of her experiences.

Kaylya yearned to return to the Lynnaran continent ...the seasons spent there with Rojaire had been the happiest seasons of her life. But it didn't stop there; since their return Rojaire had told her fabulous, wondrous tales of a passage through the Crescent Mountains and about a strange and beautiful valley secretly hidden from the rest of the world. A valley that not only supported exotic plant life, but even several species of never before seen animal life. Even more exciting was the fact that five colonists already inhabited the valley; colonists that the High Council knew nothing about. Well the council had been informed that Theon had remained behind on Lynnara and Tassyn and Edty had elected to stay with him. What the council did not know was that two more members of the lost expedition had also been found and also remained behind.

Kaylya's golden eyes reflected light from the setting sun as she turned toward Traevus. She twitched with a spasm of cold fear. *What if the High Council discovered that Rojaire and Kiril were harboring secrets? What consequences would they face?* Another cold chill ran down her spine at the thought.

"What is it? Have you heard anything?" Traevus asked in response to her twitch.

"No...," she shook her head, barely above a whisper. Then she asked the question she feared asking the most. "What will happen if the council learns there are secrets?" She knew Traevus could hear the tremor in her voice.

"I don't know; let's hope we don't find out."

The pacing and fist clenching continued as the sun set lower painting the sky in a kaleidoscope of colors. Kaylya didn't look forward to the long Aaian night, three Earth rotations in length. Fortunately during the winter season Seaa, the nearest star, provided its subdued light during the long darkness. She was spoiled by Earth's rapid rotation and frequent alternations between day and night. She exhaled deeply for stress relief. Just when she was sure she couldn't bear the tension any longer, Kaylya froze in her tracks.

"They're coming," she gasped.

"Who...?" Traevus stammered his delicately masculine facial features strained with uncertainty.

"Rojaire and Kiril."

No sooner said, the two long awaited companions appeared beside them.

"Rojaire..." Kaylya rushed to him holding him out at arm's length as though examining him carefully for possible damage.

"We're all right," he assured her. "At least we haven't been taken into custody," he added somewhat disparately.

"What happened?" Traevus confronted Kiril, no longer willing to wait for the information to be volunteered. "What did the High Council say?"

"Well, I was severely reprimanded, with likely more to come. But Lynnara and Alaia Island have been given back their true names and Rojaire will be granted a charter to establish a colony if he can sign up twenty colonists in the next seven rotations."

"Twenty colonists, that's not so many...we can do that, can't we?" Kaylya asked gazing into his gold-flecked blue-green eyes, eyes that usually gleamed roguishly, but now glared with anger.

"I don't know; I doubt it," he said breaking from her hold.

"Rojaire, what's wrong?"

"The High Council is mocking us." It was Rojaire's turn to pace. "They're certain we won't be able to find the following we need, and they are probably right, so that will be the end of it."

"Do they know about Ollen and Caleeza?"

"No, but they suspect there is something we aren't telling them."

"Who said that?" Traevus asked.

"Councilor Xevin. He and Councilor Zilka not only opposed the idea of a colony; they think people will suffer morally by returning the continent's name. Jarlon accused me of wanting a colony to excessively breed unguided offspring."

"Did you have a chance to speak?" Kaylya asked.

"No, and that's probably fortunate."

"Someone must have been on our side?" Traevus questioned.

"Yes, Councilor Anthya, and surprisingly, Councilor Renna. Proctor Kreeze presented the council with a long diatribe on logical application toward the issues and ended up offering the challenge of finding colonists as a solution."

"What if we don't find twenty colonists?" Traevus asked.

"We will be prevented from returning to Alaia Island, effectively cutting us off from Lynnara," Rojaire informed him.

"Won't Captain Setas secretly help us as she has before?" Kaylya asked.

"Maybe. But things have changed. The High Council is on to us. If Captain Setas defies the High Council's orders she could be arrested for treason. If she were to help us we would have to take her with us for her own protection. I don't know if she would be willing to leave Alaia Island."

"She might, to join Theon. I'll follow you," Kaylya said embracing Rojaire gently.

"Sign me up," Traevus said.

"Me too," Kiril added quickly.

Rojaire stared hard at Kiril. "You will do no such thing. You heard the headmaster; you will focus on your studies."

"I'm going," Kiril stomped his foot emphatically. "I'm going to Lynnara with you and you can't stop me." Kiril hated the quaver in his voice, but Lynnara was more important to him than life itself. Theon was there, the map, and his journal. It was his valley too. *There is no power on Aaia that can stop me from returning*...or so he told himself.

The five habitants of the vast fruitful valley hidden deeply in Lynnara's Crescent Mountains were gathered around a small bonfire under the star-studded Aaian sky, their bellies full after a good meal. The fire was built on a stone ledge that extended out in front of their multi-chambered cave dwelling overlooking the valley. It would be a while yet before Seaa, the closest star after Aaia's own sun, rose above the eastern ridge to bathe their world in soft iridescent light.

"How long will you be gone?" Theon asked. Although crinkled and grizzled with incredible age, Theon sat regally straight with the helpful support of his hefty staff. He hated departures, however simplistic, for they were all starting to feel final. He would never see his cherished Earth-born daughter again, that was certain. Nor was it likely he would see the eventual return of Rojaire, Traevus, and Kiril.

"I don't know," Caleeza said gently, "it depends on what we find at the other end of the valley." The glow of the fire highlighted her red-orange hair and violet eyes. She felt unease over leaving the First in Longevity in the care of only Tassyn and Edty for an extended length of time even though she knew they would do their best to follow her instructions.

"We will return as soon as we can," Ollen said. "All we plan on doing is hiking the length of the valley and back to get a better idea of what it has to offer." He spoke softly with confidence, his shoulder-length charcoal black hair glimmered in the firelight. He had survived cycles of seasons alone in the Cremyn Valley and did not fear the empty continent's secrets.

Ollen and Caleeza, both members of the lost expedition, were found by Rojaire's mapping team. Ollen was found on the coastal side of the Crescent Mountains, amazing Rojaire's group with the shelter and kiln he had built and the ingenuity he had applied to establishing a comfortable existence. They had no trouble talking him into joining them.

They found Caleeza on the interior side of the Crescent Mountains. She had been to Earth and back through an energy field in the Crystalline Landscape and told a bizarre story of Sarus, the leader of the lost expedition, becoming part of the Crystalline Landscape. Caleeza had also been eager to join their group.

"What about wild animals?" Edty asked trembling at the thought of an animal encounter even though, in the season they have lived here, no one has been attacked. His short gaunt frame, huddled fearfully by the fire, made him look childlike in the light of the dying embers, despite his weathered stubble-covered face and shortly cropped gray hair.

"I'm sure we will be all right," Ollen gently reassured his easily frightened friend. "We will take one star stone with us for protection."

"And when do you plan on leaving?" Tassyn asked. With Ollen and Caleeza gone he would be left with Theon, delicate from advanced age, and Edty, just simple-minded. That meant most of the responsibility for the duration would fall to him.

"We will leave after we rise from sleep and Seaa is high in the sky," Caleeza said.

"Shouldn't you wait for the next period of light?" Theon asked.

"We decided to travel across already familiar terrain by Seaa's light, thereby reaching new territory by sun rise. At least that's our goal," Ollen explained.

A contemplative pause ensued. Ollen stood, and in silence their eyes followed his loose-jointed gait, visible in tannish white pants as he went for more wood to replenish the fire. His black hair and weathered dark brown skin blended in with the darkness. By the time he returned with an arm load of wood, Tassyn had stirred the coals in preparation for the added fuel and Theon had lowered his staff and eased back into his chair.

"I wish I had the energy to go exploring with you, but these old joints wouldn't appreciate it one bit," Theon lamented. "Still, I do not wish to deny Tassyn and Edty the chance to go adventuring. I do not need staying with," he said with grumpy indignation.

"Edty and I wish to stay here," Tassyn said. For the most part it was true; Edty definitely didn't want to go and he definitely couldn't leave Edty with Theon. "Another time," he added.

Tassyn's quietness belied an active mind kept hidden behind dark bushy eyebrows, straggly orange-brown hair, and a mild disposition. He had always been at odds with the dictates of the High Council and had always taken care of Edty who had suffered much of the same. Tassyn's first taste of real freedom came when he, Edty, and Stram had illicitly followed Rojaire to the Devastated Continent. Then Stram had ruined everything. But now he and Edty were part of a group in which they could feel they belonged.

The atmosphere around the fire was subdued. With Ollen and Caleeza leaving, however brief the separation, the feeling of security the five of them shared when they were all together would be compromised. They all felt it.

Little else was said as the group of friends watched the fire burn down to embers. There was no need to express feelings they all shared. Eventually, one by one they sought their beds.

CHAPTER 3

Earth

Maggie knew Vince would take Melinda's departure hard. She had become a daughter to him.

"You want to just drop her off in the woods and leave her there?" Vince asked incredulously. "When I suggested a similar plan to return her to her home years ago you practically bit off my head."

"She was a frightened orphaned child back then who wanted to withdraw from the world. Now she is a capable young adult who wants to re-enter society," Maggie explained.

"Rahlys will be watching over her with the help of the crystal till Melinda makes safe contact with others," Ilene added to relieve some of Vince's anxiety. Melinda listened quietly as Maggie, Ilene, and Rahlys shared all they had discussed during their retreat to Rahlys' guest cabin.

"Melinda needs to reclaim her true identity as a natural American citizen," Rahlys explained. "To assume a false identity would only complicate her life. Now that she is an adult she will be more in control of what she chooses to reveal about her past."

The five of them sat around Vince and Maggie's family room table, the women having a late breakfast after finally catching a couple of hours of sleep before returning to Vince and the children. Leaf, Rock, and Crystal were playing quietly in the boys' room, but Melinda could sense Leaf listening in.

Melinda knew Leaf would take her leaving the hardest. When she was seventeen she had promised him she wouldn't leave until she was an adult. She had kept her promise. Still she worried about leaving him to deal with all the trouble his abilities got him into without her help.

"When is this going to happen?" Vince asked with resignation in his voice.

I would like to leave tomorrow morning.

Melinda's telepathed message reverberated in stunned silence. It was her first contribution since the discussion became heated.

I love all of you. I will always love you. And I will see you again, but it is time for me to put my life together. I don't see any reason to wait; I've waited long enough.

"Oh sweetie, I'm going to miss you so much," Maggie cried reaching for Melinda in a sobbing embrace. Melinda gently returned the hug and tried to soothe the loving soul that had been a mother to her in every way but birth.

I'll miss you too.

She fought back tears of her own.

Not crying became even harder later that night when the house slept and Leaf crept to her bed.

"Melinda, you awake?" Leaf whispered, a pale wraith in the moonlit night.

Of course she was awake; how could she sleep with tomorrow's plans looming in her head. *Here, get in the covers.* She knew Leaf could easily draw energy from the elemental forces to warm the air around him, but she moved to a cold spot and flipped back the covers to let him crawl in beside her. His little body was warm.

Why do you have to leave? Leaf asked.

It was a question Melinda knew he would eventually ask and she had been striving in her mind for a way to explain it to him.

I love you and Mom and Dad, and Rock and Crystal...

And Keiluk?

And Keiluk. What I am trying to say is, there is a whole world out there...

There's more than one world out there... Leaf said with certainty. After all, Quaylyn came from Aaia, a world far, far away.

I meant Earth. The point is this. When you grow up you must seek your destiny.

What's destiny?

Well, it's sort of like deciding what you want to be, but instead of things working out like you plan, life steers you in a different direction. That's your destiny.

Why? Leaf asked.

Melinda decided to try a different tactic.

What do you want to be when you grow up?

Leaf didn't even hesitate to consider options. *I'm going to be a warrior like Quaylyn and travel the galaxy.*

Well, becoming a warrior like Quaylyn and travelling the galaxy may be your destiny, but if it's not, things may happen along the way that cause you to become something entirely different.

But that's what I want to be.

And maybe you will ...if that is your destiny...

Oh...

The telepathed message was so faint Melinda barely discerned it. The sound of his soft regular breathing close to her ear indicated he had fallen asleep.

☆☆☆☆

"We're almost there," Seth said pushing ahead of Alice as they thrust their way through the tangle of trees and vines. It was another unusually hot spring day, the heat stifling without a breeze. Alice could feel her thin cotton blouse sticking to her back.

There could be no doubting Seth and Alice's relationship as brother and sister; with the same shade and length of wavy sandy hair and nearly identical freckles they were male and female versions of the same prototype. Justin was certain that, if counted, they would have the exact same number of freckles on their faces.

"There it is," Justin announced nonchalantly coming to a stop. He gave Alice a leering smile that sent chills through her body despite the exceedingly warm day.

Alice peered through the dense brush and slowly her eyes picked out the contours of a large weathered structure through the camouflage.

She had thought Seth loony when he came home after skipping school (and she knew about that, too) babbling about him and Justin finding an old, old dilapidated house deep in the woods. But here it was ...for real. She followed Seth and Justin with open-mouthed wonder to the bramble-choked front yard.

Instead of risking the rotting front porch, the boys led Alice around the house to a back door. A huge live oak dominated the overgrown yard, its massive trunk as big as a small house. The tree's dense crown of smooth dark evergreen leaves provided a sanctuary of shade, claiming a large area for itself. Long thick gray moss draped its equally massive branches reaching out in all directions like giant tentacles. As they neared the back door, Alice saw the crumbling brick and mortar remains of what must have once been an old cistern for catching rain water. The disintegrating cistern sat on an arched brick and mortar foundation that had also seen better days. It was now a little brick cave littered with crumbling masonry.

The boys led Alice to the back door which no longer closed completely in the tweaked doorframe. A laser-cutting machine nearly filled the back room just as Seth had described. But even forewarned, it was a shock to see. Having just traversed the thick jungle growth to get here, the presence of the laser cutter seemed surreal.

The old Cajun house was a wonder to see, built of long-enduring oak beams and cypress planks that had survived a century of hurricanes. After making their way around the laser machine they entered what Alice was certain had been the kitchen. Most of the massive oak plank shelving was still intact and the huge double fireplace separating the kitchen from the rest of the house was something she had only read about in books. As she made her tour of the rooms, she imagined a family living here long ago, a mother and father ...and maybe a grandparent or two... with a passel of children and little else, living happily off the land. Only the computer and several pieces of modern furniture scattered about the rooms, and looking decidedly out of place, ruined the effect.

"I wonder who was staying here," she said out loud.

"I doubt it was a nature worshiper, not with a laser cutter and computers," Seth said.

"I bet it was someone sinister," Justin said dramatically and walked around like a zombie. Suddenly the bright sunlight seeping in through the pane-less windows went dim.

"This had to have been a secret hideout, but where is the guy now?" Alice asked looking at the chewed up bedding in disgust.

"Maybe he got caught by the law away from his hideout," Seth said. The light was getting noticeably dimmer.

"It's getting dark out, must be rain coming," Alice said walking to a window to take a look. Seth noted Justin's eyes on her.

"Do you think there's treasure hidden here?" Seth asked to distract Justin from watching Alice.

"If this was a secret hideout there must be treasure hidden here somewhere," Justin agreed, "a stash of money or maybe even gold." The boys began to hunt for the secret stash, Justin's lustful stare turning to greed. To Alice's amusement, they started tapping floorboards and walls listening for a change in sound that would indicate a hidden space filled with treasure. When nothing was found, they searched for loose bricks around the fireplace that might conceal a hidden storage space.

"It looks like it's going to downpour," Alice predicted as lightning flashed brightly followed by a boom of thunder.

Seth and Justin didn't seem to hear her or they weren't paying attention, for their minds had turned to treasure.

I wonder what has been stored on these computers, Alice pondered. "I'm going to look for a generator," she said after a while. "There must be one here somewhere," she said glancing at the electronics.

Alice made her way around the laser-cutting machine to the backdoor and stepped outside into the heightening breeze. Dark clouds churned overhead blotting out the sun. The shower was coming on fast. Looking around through the young trees that had taken over what yard remained unclaimed by the giant oak, she found no outbuilding to house a generator.

Since there was no generator in sight on this side of the house, she walked around the back, circling the old cistern, forcing her way through young trees and vines as she searched for anything that could pass for a generator shed, but found nothing. How strange!

A sudden gust of wind rattled the trees and the sky darkened even further. Before she had circled back to where she had started, heavy drops of rain were pelting her and the ground. She thought about visiting the old oak tree, letting its umbrella shelter her from the rain, but then lightning flashed and thunder rolled and she feared it might act as a lightning rod, being taller than everything around it. Of course it had survived many thunderstorms before, but the storm seemed to have a sinister quality to it that warned her away. By the time she re-entered the house the storm had hit in all its fury.

The ferocity of the storm even distracted Justin and Seth from their unrewarded search for gold. Wind stirred the trees, lightning flashed, thunder rumbled, and then hail pounded overhead, the noise deafening on the old tin roof. They watched the storm together in fascination.

Then suddenly there was a flash of lightning so close, Alice thought she could hear it sizzle. The immediate boom of the thunder shook the house in rage. All three teenagers dropped to the floor cowering in terror, covering their ears.

"Who was struck by lightning?" Seth asked several seconds later as he recovered from the blast, his voice fearful. But both Alice and Justin sat up unharmed. Alice glanced out at the old oak tree; it was still intact.

Then just as quickly as it had approached, the violent storm died away.

☆☆☆☆

Gray mist dampened the smell of the sea. Rahlys and Melinda looked out over the coastal rainforest sloping toward the ocean. Southeast Alaska was so different from the northern Susitna Valley. It was warmer and more humid here in Ketchikan, Alaska's southernmost city at the lower end of the panhandle, but the high humidity made it feel chillier. It would never get as warm here as inland in the summer, but milder winters also meant little snow except at higher elevations.

"Are you sure you will be all right," Rahlys asked gently pushing back a strand of dark hair from Melinda's face. She could see that all the tearful goodbyes had been a strain on the girl. Rahlys longed to take her into another embrace, but didn't want to stress her further. She had rescued Melinda from Droclum's clutches; now it was time to let her go.

I will be all right.

Rahlys nodded, detecting Melinda's strength and resolve. Then to her surprise, Melinda grabbed her and held her tight.

I love you.

I love you, too.

After quietly shedding a few more tears, the two women pulled apart and Rahlys teleported away.

Melinda looked around her; she was alone. Of course Rahlys would track her progress through the power of the crystal until she was safely settled, but for all practical intent and purpose she was alone. She breathed in deeply the intoxicating smell of the sea riding on the breeze, the salty air flavoring the green aroma of the forest. She had been land-locked for so long. Thick dense forest of hemlock and lush Sitka spruce blocked her view of the ocean from where she stood, but she could feel the moisture in the air. The maritime climate felt inherently familiar to her; she was home. According to Rahlys, the crystal had placed them in a wooded area close to the North Highway. As she stepped out with purposeful resolve heading for the highway she knew ran along the coast, a misty rain began to fall.

There was no mistaking what direction to take, despite the lack of sun. All terrain in Southeast sloped steeply to the sea. Thankfully the slope of the rocky forested terrain where she stood wasn't quite as steep as in most places. The Oracle of Light had thought of everything.

There had been much discussion over whether or not Melinda should carry a pack, but in the end she had decided the less she had on her, the less she would have to explain. All she carried with her besides the clothes she wore was the mysterious key hidden in a pocket. Melinda had been concerned that Rahlys may detect the key's presence when they "travelled," but she remembered the ominous warning of the evil essence taunting her, "Rahlys cannot hear you."

After waking from the nightmare that gave her possession of the key, Melinda had feared that she and Rahlys could no longer communicate telepathically, but that did not prove to be the case. Now she understood that it was the key that was shielded from Rahlys' detection.

Slowly she emerged from the forest onto a rocky outcrop. A vista of land and sea spread before her. Islands of deep green forested mountains capped in snow sheltered protectively the narrow inlet of deep dark blue water. As though in greeting, the misty veil of fog lifted momentarily and a faint gleam of sunlight shimmered on the water. Below her ran the ribbon of highway not too far away. The mountain slope steepened here; she searched for the easiest way down, found it, and soon reached the highway.

There had also been much discussion over whether Melinda should show up at her aunt's house or go to the police as a missing person. She had created numerous dramatizations of both possibilities in her head, and based on what she could remember of her Aunt Adele, she leaned more toward going to the authorities.

Aunt Adele was her mother's sister and after her mother passed away she had made a brief effort to be a surrogate mother to her, but the demands of a husband and four sons at home and the remoteness of Melinda and her father's home had quickly put an end to that. Aunt Adele was a constant talker, chattering endlessly, often to no one in particular, or even to an empty room for that matter. Papa used to say that raising a houseful of boys had driven her batty. Her cousins had been older than her, so of course they were all grown men now.

The clouds thickened again and heavier rain began to fall. Melinda pulled the hood of her jacket up over her head and walked along the highway as far away from its edge as sea and mountain permitted for reasons she couldn't really explain. It was highly unlikely that anyone would recognize her since she was no longer a little girl and she and Papa had only occasionally come into town on their fishing boat the *Taku*. The fishing shack they had lived in was far from town and only accessible by boat.

Following the road she soon came to a State Trooper office on the north side of town. Melinda came to a stop, then hesitated, staring at the State Trooper emblem on the door. *Follow your plan* she reminded herself and nervously went over the guidelines she had set, renewing her resolve before going in.

The plump blond female officer working at the desk closest to the door looked up when Melinda entered and watched her intently. A second officer across the room who looked like he was of native descent only gave her a fleeting glance before going back to his work. Melinda froze in place, momentarily losing her resolve to go on.

"Hello, there; are you all right?" the female officer asked, concern growing over Melinda's mute daze.

The officer sounded kind; Melinda managed to nod.

"Well, good; I'm Officer Lilly," she said rising. "Can I get you something to drink ...water...coffee, tea?" The young woman continued to stand mute before her. Lilly pulled a chair up closer to her desk. "Why don't you have a seat over here and tell me what's on your mind." When her hand brushed against the girl's jacket it was damp to the touch. She must have been walking in the rain. "Hey, Frank, you want to get this young woman a hot cup of cocoa for me?" she called out to the other officer. Lilly didn't want to leave the young woman to get the hot cocoa herself. The girl may be a victim in distress and if left alone, she may possibly bolt.

"Certainly, my pleasure," the male officer said quickly assessing Lilly's situation.

"What's your name?" Officer Lilly asked after Melinda was seated.

Feeling a bit safer, Melinda took a deep breath. She didn't dare communicate telepathically, so she made a writing motion with her right hand while holding her left hand flat like a writing tablet. Officer Lilly quickly handed her a pen and tablet. Melinda smiled feebly in response. Then taking the tablet, she wrote down her name and handed it back to the officer.

"Melinda Poponof," she read off the tablet and typed it into her computer. "And what can I do for you Miss Poponof?" she asked handing back the tablet. Then she stared with shock, which she quickly erased from her face, at the police report that had popped up on her computer screen. Melinda Poponof and her father had gone missing nearly seven years ago and were presumed drowned at sea.

Officer Lilly's shocked reaction had been expected. The look on her face gave her away, but Melinda would have been able to pick up her response to the discovery from the officer's unguarded thoughts even if she had managed to keep her face composed. She sat quietly waiting for something to develop.

Officer Frank brought over a steaming mug of hot cocoa overflowing onto a saucer he had fortunately included. "Here you go." Melinda nodded her thanks and he set it on the edge of Officer Lilly's desk. She pretended not to notice him glancing at the computer screen as she reached for the cup. Officer Lilly gave him a questioning look. Was this some kind of scam?

The young woman sitting before them looked to be the about the age Melinda Poponof would be today and appeared to be of native descent, but if this was the real Melinda Poponof, where has she been all this time? Officer Lilly was relatively new to the area having moved to Ketchikan only a few years ago, but Officer Frank's father had been friends with Pete Poponof, this girl's father ...if indeed she was who she claimed to be.... He vaguely remembered a little girl with him, but he didn't think she was mute. He did know of a family connection though living here in town.

"I'll make some phone calls," Frank whispered under his breath.

"So Miss Poponof, what can I do for you?" Officer Lilly asked again with as little urgency as she could muster.

Melinda took a sip of the hot cocoa she had been blowing on. It was deliciously sweet and warm; she hadn't realized how chilled she had become.

"It says here you have been missing for quite a while. Can you tell us where you have been all this time?"

Melinda hunched her shoulders slightly. Here was the unanswerable question.

Lilly watched as the girl quickly took another sip letting it warm her from inside. The girl was dressed in decent clothing that fitted her and she looked healthy and clean. How had she taken care of herself?

"Where's your father?" Officer Lilly asked.

Still hiding behind the mug, Melinda hunched her shoulders again. It wasn't a lie. After she had been forced to watch him die, unable to help him or save him, his lifeless body had vanished from her arms. Where Droclum had taken her father's body she didn't know.

"Do you have any relatives? Someone who we could contact and let know you are here?" *And maybe confirm your identity*, she added silently. To Lilly's surprise Melinda nodded.

"You do? What's the person's name?" she asked eagerly.

Melinda placed the mug back on the saucer and reached for the tablet once again. She didn't want to make it too easy for them. "Aunt Adele," she wrote on the page and handed it to Officer Lilly. By this time Officer Frank had rejoined them.

"She's coming," he nodded seeing the name on the paper. He pulled up a chair and sat down. "How was the hot cocoa?" he asked Melinda with a smile. She nodded and smiled in return. "We seem to have a little difficulty communicating. Can you speak?" Officer Frank asked her gently.

'No,' she mouthed and shook her head.

But she could write, the names written on the tablet were proof of that. "Tell us, where did you sleep last night?" Officer Frank asked to begin the task of tracing back her steps. Lilly handed her the tablet.

"In the woods," Melinda wrote. They didn't need to know which woods; Rahlys and the Order of Oracle had to be protected. Of course they would assume she had slept under a tree nearby.

"And what did you have for breakfast?" Officer Frank asked.

Melinda was not inclined to answer; it was best to let them deduce she hadn't had breakfast at all. Soon the officers were offering her their own lunches. She was happily munching on a ham sandwich when Aunt Adele rushed in through the door.

"Where is she? My only sister's only child. I always said she was alive somewhere." Officer Frank intercepted her at the door.

"Mrs. Swanson, do you think you can conclusively identify your niece even though she is now grown?" he asked her.

"Why, I should say I most definitely can, my own sister's flesh and blood. Take me to her."

By now Melinda had risen to her feet and Adele found herself face to face with a ghost from the past. Adele gazed deeply into Melinda's dark eyes and gasped.

Hello, Aunt Adele, Melinda telepathed in greeting.

Adele Swanson swooned, hitting the floor.

CHAPTER 4

Aaia

During the long star-lit nights, the people of the Community of the High Council came out of their homes deep in the mountains to enjoy the coolness of evening in the extensive gardens. Glow globes lit fountains, arbors, pathways, and pavilions offering food and drink for refreshment. It was in this arena that Rojaire campaigned for his cause with Kaylya, Traevus, and Kiril at his side. Quaylyn, Kaydra, and a Twakan warrior named Thayla came to hear them. Although Rojaire and Kaylya have been calling heartily for colonists, so far no one has stepped up.

"So tell me, Quaylyn, don't you wish to join our group and be a founding citizen of Lynnara?" Rojaire asked, hopeful of a positive response. Rojaire's question came after a long discourse in favor of their proposed adventure and Quaylyn had been a member of their group looking for the lost expedition. It was hard for Rojaire to imagine anyone who has been to the continent not wanting to return.

"I cannot," Quaylyn said trying to let his friend down gently. The idea of colonizing would have been far more appealing if he and Rahlys were together, but he had new responsibilities now.

Quaylyn smiled modestly bringing out his dimples and the twinkle in his deeply blue eyes before announcing, "I have some news to share with you."

The gathering of friends waited with quiet expectation.

"I have been chosen as the new councilor for the High Council."

The news was greeted with surprise gasps that were quickly followed by cheers and congratulations. "Councilor Quaylyn," they hailed him repeatedly unable to restrain their delight. The empty council seat had remained vacant since Councilor Zayla's death. Only Brakalar's position had been filled when Xevin became the new Head of the Academy.

"Oh, Quaylyn... I mean Councilor... that is such wonderful news! The Runes of the Crystal Table are truly wise in guiding the High Council in choosing you!" Kaydra cheered, her dark animated eyes reflecting her excitement.

"There could be no better choice," Rojaire added in earnest.

Three cycles of seasons ago Quaylyn, Kaydra, and Sarus were nearly inseparable friends attending the Academy. Upon completing their training at the Academy, they were assigned their First Mission, a test of their mettle before becoming Accepted Ones. As a talented sensitive, Kaydra had been sent by the High Council to the planet Twaka as a mentor, her presence on Twaka a condition for the planet's acceptance into the Worlds' League. Her initial assignment as mentor had led to a position on the Worlds' League Council.

Sarus had been assigned to lead an exploratory expedition to the Devastated Continent, only the second expedition of its kind since the Dark Devastation. The Devastated Continent had now been renamed Lynnara, but Sarus' fate remained unknown. And as far as Kaydra knew, Traevus was the only member of that expedition to be found.

Quaylyn had been given the most challenging mission of all. He had been sent to Earth to aid Sorceress Rahlys in defeating Droclum after Rahlys acquired Sorceress Anthya's powers through the Oracle of Light. The emotional bond between Quaylyn and Rahlys had been strong. They had been together for a time on both worlds, but neither could give up their own world for the other. And now Quaylyn had been selected to serve on the High Council; it was the highest of honors.

"I can understand why you wish to remain, Councilor Quaylyn," Kaylya said with a cheerful wink. "But how about you Kaydra? Would you like to be part of Lynnara's first colony? We could really use your skills."

"Sorry, Kaylya, but Thayla and I will be returning to Twaka soon."

Thayla, dressed in her native warrior attire, stood rigidly beside Kaydra, listening but not contributing to the conversation. Vermillion eyes carefully surveyed everything said and done. Like most Twakans, Thayla stood a head higher than the average Aaian. Her firm muscular body was loosely draped with shimmering fabrics woven from silky plant fibers and tied in place with brightly colored cords. She wore her hair, more green in color than gold, in a thick braid down her back. A permanent scar on her left cheek marred her otherwise smooth bronze complexion.

"I'll join your colony," Thayla said, her husky voice unexpectedly breaking the silence. Kaydra looked at her friend in shock. She had talked Thayla into visiting her world while promising her family a safe trip.

"But you can't," Kaydra gasped. "Your family is expecting your return."

Thayla stared at her friend with a glare that spoke epics about who would make decisions for her. "I would like to see this empty continent."

Before anyone could respond, Councilor Xevin entered the pavilion with Councilor Zilka. Kiril stepped behind the large Twakan warrior, hoping to remain unseen. He had been forced to report to Head Master Xevin after the council meeting and had been restricted from campaigning with Rojaire and Kaylya for colonists. He had also been given extra duties and assignments that should have kept him too busy to be socializing in the gardens. And the Head Master had made it perfectly clear once again that Kiril would not be going with the colony.

"Greetings, Councilor Quaylyn, friends," Head Master Xevin greeted with steeled politeness in passing. If he noticed Kiril he didn't acknowledge it. Councilor Zilka nodded her head in greeting, but didn't speak. To Kiril's relief, the councilors partook of some refreshments and quickly moved on. Once they had left the pavilion Thayla turned around, grasped Kiril in strong hands, and easily lifted him to her eye level.

"Hide behind me again you insignificant little clod of matter and I will pulverize you and cast your dust to the wind," she enunciated slowly in her deep drawl. Traevus, who had been quietly observing was taken by Thayla's power and beauty, scarred cheek and all.

"I'm sorry," Kiril said, nodding in understood agreement, totally forgetting his own warrior training. Thayla released him, letting him drop. Kiril barely managed to land on his feet.

Kaydra wanted to admonish her friend for her somewhat brutish behavior, but thought better of it. She was fairly certain Thayla wouldn't actually do anyone any harm, at least she didn't think so. The two women had been on several adventures together during her tenure on Twaka and although Thayla was a formidable opponent when defense was called for, Kaydra had not seen her actually kill anyone.

"We would welcome you heartily to the colony if you wish to join us," Kaylya said. She didn't know if the High Council would approve a Twakan for a colonist, but they had failed so dismally thus far at increasing their numbers, she didn't want to consider possible obstacles.

"I choose to go with you to Lynnara," Thayla announced with certainty then gave Kaydra a challenging look.

"You can't go traipsing off to Lynnara. These people aren't planning on coming back. I promised to look after you."

"You take care of me! Don't be ludicrous; I can take care of myself."

Traevus was certain that was true. Thayla looked like she could squash little Kaydra by stepping on her.

Kaydra was stunned by the turn of events. The consequences for not returning Thayla to her home could be dire. "What do you want me to tell your family?" Kaydra asked.

Thayla pondered over the question for a moment. "Tell them, I seek my destiny."

"I will not be accompanying you," Kaydra told her after brief consideration. "You will be on your own."

Thayla hunched her shoulders unconcerned. "I can handle these people," she said giving Kiril a meaningful, but not unfriendly, look. Traevus thought Thayla almost smiled.

"Welcome to the team, Thayla," Rojaire said seizing the opportunity to acquire another colonist. *That's three,* he counted dejectedly to himself. *Kaylya, Traevus, and Thayla ...I just need to find seventeen more.*

Kaylya joined in. "Kiril has invited us to visit Galeza, his home village, during the Academy session break. Perhaps you would like to join us?"

"This Kiril?" she asked pointing to the young male who had hidden behind her. She stared at him. "I haven't yet received an invitation."

Kiril met Thayla's hard stare. "W...would you like to visit my village?" he stammered.

"I would love to." There was no question about it; that was actually a rough rendition of a smile that broke across Thayla's hard features.

"Good, then it's settled," Kiril answered with audible misgivings.

When an opportunity arose, Kaylya spoke to Quaylyn quietly, off to the side. "May I speak with you Councilor Quaylyn away from the others?"

Noting the formality, Quaylyn drifted with her away from the group. "How may I serve?" he asked breathing in the fragrant scents wafting from the garden's night blossoms.

"I would like to petition the council," she told Quaylyn without preamble. Her statement caught him by surprise, but a right to petition the council is granted to all Accepted Ones.

"What is your request?" Quaylyn asked gently.

"I would like the High Council to invite Ilene to join the colony. You know how much she wishes to see her father again." When Quaylyn, Rojaire, and Kaylya returned from Earth, Ilene had very much wanted to go with them, but her mother couldn't bear to see her leave again so soon. Quaylyn sighed softly.

"I understand what you are trying to do here, but I don't believe your petition as stated would succeed with the High Council. I will petition the council to invite Ilene back to continue her studies as a healer at the Academy. What happens after that will be out of my hands."

"Thank you," Kaylya said heartily, using the Earth expression they both knew so well.

"It is my pleasure to serve," Quaylyn said with a smile, then gave her a little bow before leaving to seek a period of sleep.

☆☆☆☆

Seaa rose above the eastern mountains, the near star softly illuminating the valley. Ollen and Caleeza left the home cave quietly. Only Theon saw them go. Caleeza felt certain he was awake because of joint pain rather than a wish to say good-bye. Therefore, before they left, she brewed him a strong herbal tea to help him go back to sleep.

Guided by Seaa's light, they set out, pushing themselves hard to cross as much familiar territory as they could during the long night, stopping only briefly to rest. Then by the light of the setting star they climbed a small east facing hill, taking turns getting some sleep while waiting for daylight. The darkness gradually lightened, features became recognizable, and color returned to the landscape. Soon dark purple mountains defined the valley's edges under an azure sky. Just as they had hoped, unexplored valley lay before them bathed in the light of the rising sun.

"It's beautiful," Caleeza whispered in awe. She had seen few places that could compare ...the Crystalline Landscape, Alaska on planet Earth, and this wondrous valley. Ollen unfolded the crystal floss map he carried, laying it out on the ground before them. From their vantage point, they could see the eastern mountains, more distant than ever before, the valley broader than they had imagined. The southern end of the valley, from which they came, was veiled in early morning fog to their right. The western mountains rose solidly behind them. In the hazy distance to the north the two mountain ranges, east and west, started curving toward each other. The hill they were on rose out of an immense field of the blue-green grassy grain that supported herds of kurper. The colonists gathered the seed heads and ground them into a coarse flour to make an unleavened bread.

Beyond the meadow land, to the north and east they could see the distant edge of the forest. The river they knew cut through the valley wasn't visible from here. "Shall we continue following the western mountains north or head east toward the river?" Ollen asked contemplating options.

"Where's the next cave symbol on the map?"

"More than a day's journey from here, if I'm pinpointing our position correctly based on our new perspective of how large the valley really is." The map was obviously not very accurate in regards to scale. "The southern plateau is here," Ollen said pointing to it on the map. Looking to the south they could barely see the northern tip of the prominent plateau in the distance as the fog began to lift. "We will have to construct our own shelter if we need one whichever direction we choose." For now the sky above them was clear.

"What is that?" Caleeza asked staring hard into the distance toward the center of the vista before them where the woods seemed to take on a different texture.

Ollen followed her gaze. "I don't know," he said and studied the map again locating an area of little overlapping squares and rectangles that corresponded with the approximate location of the different texture in the distance. The strange map boasted many markings, each standing for a certain feature, but provided no key to their meanings. "I guess we will have to go there to find out."

The long trek across the meadow lands was uneventful except for the startling moments when small unseen herds of the little silver-furred creatures they called kurpers dashed away in panic at their approach. Despite the season, the winter sun soon blazed hotly with barely a breeze disturbing the chest-high ripening wild grain. When they sat down to rest for a while, the grasses closed in around them, shutting off their view, a condition neither Ollen nor Caleeza could abide for long.

The sun was high in the sky by the time their targeted destination came more sharply into focus. As they approached the edge of the forest of overlapping squares, the grasses grew shorter and the ground became soggier under their feet. Tall reedy trees that grew in sharp angles gradually replaced the grasslands.

Caleeza assumed the plant life towering before them would be classified as trees, but their growth pattern was unlike anything she had seen before. The smooth blue, green, and white streaked trunks branched out at true right angles. When a lateral branch came close to another tree trunk or branch it changed direction growing out at another forty-five degree angle, the result looking very much like the pattern of overlapping squares depicted on the map. Each growing tip, and they were numerous, sported a thick crown of silvery leaves which gave the forest the appearance of being an army of silver-haired stick figures on the march.

"Jungle gym," Caleeza said out loud.

"What?"

"A structure made for climbing; I saw a picture of one in a children's book on Earth. It looked much like this, only smaller."

The growth became thicker as they wove their way deeper among the trees. The ground beneath the jungle gym trees became increasingly soggy with water seeping into the depressions their feet left behind.

"Well, do you want to climb through the trees or backtrack and find a way around this? It looks like it's going to be too marshy to walk through."

Caleeza gave it a moment's thought before answering. "Let's climb. I want to see what this leads to."

Climbing was easy with the growth of trees and branches so thick there were always numerous branches in easy reach for grasping and stepping on. And they could go high too, but not high enough to get a view beyond the forest before the branches became too flimsy to support their weight. As they climbed their way through the trees, the water deepened beneath them. Eventually they could hear what sounded like a stream. As the water deepened, the jungle gym growth thinned noticeably, indicating a limit to the amount of water the trees could tolerate. This slowed them down considerably, making it necessary to find suitable footing and hand holds to achieve continued forward progress. Although there were no longer tree trunks growing up from the flooded marsh, the branches continued to grow out across the rushing water, reaching for the trees on the other side.

"The water is flowing in the wrong direction," Ollen said, staring down at it in puzzlement. The only river they knew of flowed from north to south where it disappeared underground at the southern end of the valley. A smaller stream fed by a waterfall coming out of the western mountains, not far from their home cave, flowed from west to east into it. This water was flowing from east to west toward the western mountains.

"Do you think we can make it across?" Caleeza asked with some concern. She didn't relish the thought of climbing down into the water.

"I don't know; we can try." They moved cautiously at a distance twice their own height above the water with Ollen leading the way.

"Why are there little holes in these branches?" Caleeza asked following him.

Ollen had also noticed the little holes that had started appearing on the trunks and branches as they approached the stream. The holes were too small to stick a finger in, so Ollen reached into his pack and pulled out a stylus. He poked the writing implement into the hole and wriggled it around. "It's hollow," he announced with surprise, but the bigger surprise came when he pulled the stylus back out and a multilegged creature as long as his thumb crawled rapidly up the stylus to Ollen's hand. Startled by the appearance of the unexpected lifeform, Ollen yelped and flicked his hand to dislodge the creature, his jerky involuntary movements causing him to lose his footing in the process. Instantly he was in the water.

"Ollen!" Caleeza screamed in alarm as she watched him tumble into the rushing stream, disappearing for a moment and then bobbing back up as the swift current carried him away. He quickly vanished from her sight, the large shaggy silver foliage of the jungle gym trees screening him from view.

☆☆☆☆

Aaia's sun arched high in the planet's white gold sky even during what was referred to as the winter season; for Aaia's seasons aren't determined by the planet's tilt, which is nearly imperceptible, but rather the planet's distance from the sun. As the planet's path around the sun passes between the sun and the nearest star Seaa, Aaia's orbit bulges away from the sun in answer to Seaa's call, bringing welcoming cooler temperatures to an excessively warm planet.

Deep in the interior of the island continent of Lynnara lay the Crystalline Landscape. The sun beamed down the monolithic crystals charging them with energy. The mental remains of Sarus' crystal-generated brain could see the larger picture. No longer in possession of a corporeal form, his firing synapses were one with the massive landscape of jumbled towering crystals stretching beyond horizons and sparking softly with color in the brilliant sunlight. The sun-charged crystals crackled like the soft whisper of snowfall through tree branches or the faint tinkle of very distant bells. Even ears made merely of flesh may perceive the crystals charging with the sun's energy, storing the excess in invisible fields.

Accessing this energy, Sarus delved deeply into the structure of matter itself, isolating a single quartz molecule, exploring the bond between silicon and oxygen with each oxygen atom sharing a part of itself to form another molecule. Delving even deeper, he entered a single silicon atom. He flew among the speeding electrons, marveling at their performance, and then spiraled down toward the atom's center to float among the protons and neutrons. He was about to dive into the nearest proton to explore the world of quarks when a rare random thought broke into his concentration.

Caleeza.

Where that thought came from he wasn't quite sure, but he "felt" it held some significance, although he had forgotten the meaning.

He concentrated hard and for a moment an image almost came to him ...before fading out of reach.

He would have to give it some more thought...

...later

...after he explored the quarks.

CHAPTER 5

Earth

Melinda let the officers take command of the situation; she didn't really know what to do and she feared any action on her part may make things worse. Her aunt quickly came out of her swoon. After Adele was helped to a chair and given a glass of water she called her son Tony, a supervisor at the cannery, who promised to come as soon as he could get away. And the questions kept coming. Adele couldn't claim with certainty the young woman was Melinda, her dead sister's daughter, but she gasped and murmured repeatedly, "She looks just like her," clasping her pudgy hands to her face, yet avoiding physical contact with Melinda in fear of what may be her niece's unearthly spirit. DNA testing was ordered as well as a medical checkup.

More officers were called in and many more questions were asked. Melinda willingly wrote down answers to all their questions up to the time of her and her father's disappearance as truthfully as she could remember, but revealed nothing about their encounter with Droclum or her life up in the Susitna Valley. Adele answered all questions directed her way, but had little imagination to apply to speculating on where Melinda may have been for the past six and a half years. Melinda didn't help them out, which resulted in a mental exam as well.

When the onslaught of interrogation finally subsided, Adele realized, with some dismay, she was expected to take the strangely quiet spirit girl home with her.

The relationship between Melinda and her aunt started out strained at best. Melinda avoided any further use of telepathy for fear of causing her aunt to go into another swoon. She tried smiling instead and answered questions she was willing to answer with pen and paper. Aunt Adele's home was located along one of the few roads that ventured inland away from the coast. It was a modest clapboard house in a modest neighborhood. Used to hard work, Melinda helped around the house as much as she could ...washing dishes, sweeping the floor, and taking out the trash. Slowly Aunt Adele relaxed a little and opened up, becoming talkative once again and letting Melinda help with the cooking.

Melinda learned a great deal about her aunt's life during the intervening years. Aunt Adele was now a widow; her Uncle Howard had died just a few years ago in a logging accident. As for her cousins, most of them were still here if not exactly still living at home, although their rooms were always ready for them. Jim, the eldest of the four brothers, was a logger following in his father's footsteps. "He's now foreman of his own crew," Adele said with pride. Melinda could barely remember her cousin Jim or her Uncle Howard; most of the time they had been off somewhere working.

Adele's second son, Tony, had a private bunkroom at the cannery and spent most nights there. This was a busy time at the cannery with fishing gearing up. He was usually the most accessible when she needed something, but he never made it to the State Troopers' office when his mother called. Still, he had rushed home as soon as he could. Of course Aunt Adele made a big issue, as she saw it, over his neglect. Tony patiently, and as good-naturedly as possible, pleaded his case. Melinda recalled her Cousin Tony's friendly playful nature and could remember him teasing her as a little girl.

The third brother, Greg, was a fisherman with his own boat, which also served as his living quarters except when he needed to wash clothes and take a shower. Adele gladly did his laundry for him; it was a small price to pay for her son's visit. Sometimes he even let her cook him a big dinner and then spent the night. This is the cousin she remembered the best for he had often accompanied her and her father on their fishing boat to help them out, especially right after her mother died, until Melinda was able to help her father herself. When he showed up for the first time, she recognized him immediately. Apparently his recognition of her was just as definitive, for he grabbed her up into his powerful arms and swung her around with joy.

Joey, the youngest of the brothers, was the closest to her own age, but the one she liked the least. She remembered him as a bully always wanting to pick a fight. As Aunt Adele's baby he was the most spoiled and tended to get his way. She was not disappointed to learn that he left the area all together a couple of years ago, seeking something different. Aunt Adele heard from him occasionally ...always from a different location. Not one of her four sons had married or fathered any grandchildren she knew of, a fact she lamented grievously.

News of Melinda's reappearance spread rapidly through the greater Ketchikan area. Many longtime residents had known Pete Poponof and even more remembered the incident of the disappearance of the *Taku,* and the subsequent search for the missing vessel with Pete Poponof and his daughter Melinda onboard. Nothing was ever found. That is until Melinda turned up at a State Trooper's office.

The local TV filming crew showed up at their front door wanting an interview. Aunt Adele, excited over the grand attention, invited them in. Melinda wanted to flee, but her aunt kept her firmly planted beside her in front of the camera ...and gladly did all the talking. The actual broadcast that evening on the local TV station was too painful for Melinda to watch. Out of sheer embarrassment, she hoped her friends and true family in the northern Susitna Valley wouldn't be exposed to the broadcast. Overnight Melinda and Aunt Adele were neighborhood celebrities.

The very next day a news crew arrived from Anchorage. Again Melinda was subjected to the horror of being filmed and the humiliation of her aunt's vociferous joy in the broadening attention. There were pictures and articles about Melinda in the paper every day. Then Aunt Adele received a phone call; a nationally syndicated news crew was expected to arrive in Ketchikan in the morning.

That night, Greg came ashore for a meal and shower, giving Melinda an idea for an escape plan. When Aunt Adele wasn't looking, she secretly handed Greg a note. *Please,* she telepathed after he had a chance to read it. Greg could hear her plea, or thought he did, and gave her a reassuring nod and wink. He would do what he could to help her. That night, Greg and Melinda snuck out the house and onto his fishing vessel *The Bounty.*

The Bounty left the docks before daylight, before Adele woke to greet the morning, and before any more reporters and camera crews could accost her. This time Melinda would manage to escape and Aunt Adele would have the spotlight all to herself.

It was a rare beautifully sunny day, the water of the sound flowed smoothly, silky in texture and radiance, reflecting mid-night blue and silver in the light. The salty fishy aura of the sea and air, the steady rumble of the boat's engine, and the subtle vibration of the deck under her feet thrilled her soul. She was back in her element; finally she was truly home.

There was little in the way of conversation. Writing paper notes was an impractical method of communication while working alongside Greg and his hired deckhand cleaning fish and icing them down. Throughout the day Melinda worked on the deck of *The Bounty,* her muscles recalling skills she learned long ago, while her mind considered options for her future.

This worked out well for Melinda since she wasn't interested in chatter and she certainly didn't want to be asked any more questions. She wished only to communicate with the sea and her surroundings. When the deckhand attempted a few questions to appease his own curiosity, Greg quickly made it clear that Melinda was not to be bothered. This gave Melinda plenty of time to think, and she had plenty to think about.

How long had it been since Rahlys brought her back to southeast ... four days? It seemed incredulous that so little time had actually passed. She did not want to stay at her Aunt's home forever ...not for a year, not even for a month. She did have some resources of her own. With her newly issued state ID and the deckhand license she now possessed, she could claim the money she and her father had stashed for her future, in an account under her name, during the years she fished with him. And then there was still the barely perceptible but persistent tug of the mysterious key she carried in her pocket.

There was no longer any doubt about the general direction the key wanted her to go; it wanted her to go south. Its directional tug seemed enhanced by the nine hundred miles south she had already covered by moving from the northern Susitna Valley to Ketchikan. Perhaps she should continue heading south.

The north wind howled over the still frozen muskeg and iced-over rivers along Alaska's west coast, blowing whatever snow it could unhinge into deep snowdrifts against solidly-built buildings and dry-docked Bristol Bay fishing boats unmoved by the wind's rage. Jack Faulkner paced his little house of memories aimlessly to the rhythm of the wind buffeting the outside walls, his head full of the newsy letter from Vince and Maggie lying open on the table. The twins were talking and Leaf was coming into true boyhood, a master egg-gatherer now that the Bradley family had a flock of chickens. Rahlys still resided a mile away through the woods, filling her time without Quaylyn painting one masterpiece after another. Jack glanced at the painting by Rahlys of Leaf and Raven playing wizard that hung on his own wall. He had purchased it last year from the gift shop and it never failed to illicit a smile from him. The biggest news was Melinda's return to Southeast Alaska. Jack wished her well. He couldn't imagine the Bradley household without her. According to the letter, nothing had changed with Ilene and her mother. Ilene made the trip up the tracks to visit fairly regularly and Elaine was still as ornery as ever.

Jack smiled at the thought of Elaine. He knew her gruffness covered up a soft side.

There was no news from across the galaxy. He wondered what Kaylya was doing on her own world; it was hard to imagine. Kaylya had been like family; he missed her, but he knew she was happy now that she and Rojaire were reunited.

The letter also invited Jack to visit, the mere thought of which lifted his spirits. Jack's last visit to the Susitna Valley had been nearly a year ago when Kaylya left for Aaia with Rojaire and Quaylyn. Travel from the west coast to the Susitna Valley had been much easier back then, with Kaylya's help.

Jack looked around the house cluttered with cheap travel memorabilia and longed for his wife Betsy, dead for more than three years. The only thing new in the house, the only thing that had changed since Betsy's death, was the painting of Raven and Leaf, Leaf in a red wizard's cape, playing in the woods. Then for the first time, Jack truly felt the emptiness of his wife's travel memorabilia and made a radical decision. Reaching for the trashcan from under the sink, Jack walked around the house brushing the cheap dusty statues of landmarks and monuments that lined shelves and filled cubbyholes into the trash. Only the photos he let remain. These souvenirs were not Betsy he finally realized ...they were just clutter.

Jack hadn't heard Mike's truck drive up because of the wind. He was just finishing up the task of throwing things away when his son Mike entered the house, slamming the door shut against the swirling snow and wind.

"What are you doing?" Mike asked, a bit stunned by the change the absence of his mother's memorabilia actually made.

Mike had inherited his father's bulbous nose, though not quite as bad, his receding hairline, though he still had an abundance of thick brown hair over most of his head, as well as his short frame although Mike did top him by an inch or two. Fortunately for Mike, he still had enough youth left on his side to counter these appearance shortcomings. Jack was certain he would never be as ugly an old man as himself and probably had his mother to thank for it. More importantly, Mike had proved himself a competitive, capable fisherman in just two fishing seasons.

"I thought I would clean up a bit," Jack answered as nonchalantly as he could muster and placed the trashcan back under the sink. "I'm glad you're here; I would like you to do something for me. It won't be difficult," he quickly added when Mike showed signs of concern.

"Ah, sure ...what do you need?"

"I received a letter from Vince and Maggie and they invited me to come visit." Jack chuckled over Mike's hopeful anticipation. "All I need is for you to help me with the travel arrangements ...using your smart phone."

"Of course, I'd be glad to," Mike said breaking into a delighted smile. Jack knew he relished having the house to himself. His girlfriend would take up residence with Mike as soon as Jack was out the door.

"You two should get married," Jack said unexpectedly voicing his thoughts.

Mike walked through his father's likely presumptions to reach his line of reasoning. Of course he knew Brenda would be staying here.

"We're thinking about it," Mike admitted after a pause.

"You couldn't find a better girl," Jack said to his son's relief.

"Thanks, Dad."

"Now, how about those travel arrangements?"

"When do you want to leave?" An especially strong gust of wind slammed against the house, drawing their attention.

"As soon as this blow is over and planes can fly again. I'll take the first seat available."

☆☆☆☆

The big weathered old house hidden deep in the Louisiana woods had become a regular secret hideout for Seth, Alice, and Justin. Every weekend they packed in enough water, sodas, and food to last them all day. The property must be owned by somebody, but no one ever surprised them by showing up.

Alice loved the mysterious house and surrounding woods, but didn't particularly like Justin's company. She thought it would be fun to bring in other friends, but when she broached the topic with Justin and Seth they both adamantly opposed and neither seemed able to explain why.

It was a hot spring day making the shade of the sprawling giant oak especially inviting. They had made some improvements on the property, clearing away brush to open up the yard between the house and the big oak tree. They used brick and concrete rubble from the crumbling cistern to outline a fire pit, and burned the cleared brush along with rotting boards from the dangerously weathered front porch to build a fire and make hotdogs and s'mores. Today Justin brought a .22 rifle to do some target shooting.

"Let's put the target on the oak tree." Justin suggested. He walked to the broad trunk of the massive old tree and tacked the shooting target in place, placing it at about eye level. Finding tools to work with was no problem. There were all kinds of tools available; most of them looked like they had never seen work.

An unease deep in her stomach told Alice that using the tree as a target probably wasn't a good idea, but said nothing. She was certain the guys would read any concern she voiced as a silly girl notion.

"You can go first," Justin said returning to the group. Seth was already lining up the sights on the barrel with the target. His first shot hit just one ring from the bull's eye. His second shot, with adjustment, hit its mark, as did the third. Alice smiled over her brother's performance with obvious pride. Seth always got his deer in the fall. She doubted Justin would do as well.

But before Justin could take up the rifle, the crystalline blue sky above them suddenly took on an eerie dramatic turn. What had been a clear blue sky now boiled with roiling dark clouds, seemingly originating directly above the towering massive oak.

"What the heck?" Seth asked.

"Looks like a storm's coming," Justin rationalized.

"You think that's a rain shower?" Alice asked incredulously. Did he and Seth not feel the lurking evil that permeated the place?

The storm quickly raged. Incredibly, wind whipped around with hurricane force and rain slashed at their faces. The giant oak tree shook and groaned, and its branches and leaves swayed violently. Lightning lit the now darkened woods and thunder rumbled mockingly as the three teenagers dashed to the house seeking shelter. Upon reaching the large inner rooms, they all dropped to the floor panting, hearts beating out of their chests. For the longest no one spoke as they tried to reason out what might have happened.

"It didn't like you shooting at the tree," Alice said matter-of-factly as they sat in a circle waiting out the storm.

"What do you mean ...*it*... didn't ...*like*... us shooting at the tree?" Justin asked.

"I'm not exactly sure," Alice said giving it some thought. "Call it a spirit, or a force, or ...an essence; ...whatever; ...there's something here ...I can feel it ...and it's very evil."

"That's ridiculous! What a bunch of bullshit!" Justin said scornfully. Seth neither backed her up nor refuted it.

"Oh, yah, well I bet you wouldn't want to spend a night here all alone," she said, daring him to take her up on it.

"Sure I would. Are you telling me that you and Seth would be too chicken-livered to spend a night in this old house because you think it's haunted?" Justin asked scornfully.

"I'm not afraid," Seth said boosting his manhood. The storm was starting to subside giving him courage.

"Then what do you say we plan on an overnighter here next weekend?" Justin suggested.

"Mom and Dad have a family trip planned for next weekend," Seth said glad that he and Alice had an excuse to back out of it.

"Then the weekend after that; we can bring lots of food, some beer, and our sleeping bags, or are you too scared?"

"I'm not scared," Seth said with more courage than he actually felt. "Count me in."

"How about you, Alice?" Justin asked. "Are you going to join us or is the idea too scary for a girl?" He edged closer to her, "Don't you want to see if we can coax out the ghost ... boo ...!" he teased daringly.

Alice didn't want anything to do with it. "I have no intention spending a night in this old house. Who knows what may lurk here."

"Aw come on," Seth said, thinking *safety in numbers.* "You don't really believe there's an evil spirit lurking around, do you?"

Alice hesitated before answering. She didn't want to leave her brother unprotected, but she didn't relish an entire night in Justin's company, even with Seth as a chaperon. Nor was she too keen on spending the night in the company of whatever claimed the area around the old house. But she also didn't want to be accused of being a superstitious coward.

"I'll come," she said finally in a low voice, unhappy with her own decision.

CHAPTER 6

Aaia

The water was deeper and the current stronger than Ollen had thought possible while suspended in the jungle gym trees above it. By the time he surfaced again, Caleeza was already out of sight, screened by the trees' thick shaggy foliage. He heard Caleeza cry out his name as he struggled to keep his head above water, but the swirling current repeatedly sucked him back under before he could call back to her. He sought to reach something he could grab on to. The south shore was no longer an option since the bank now rose into a sheer rocky cliff undercut by swiftly moving water. Gym trees rising out the water on the north shore were closer and more accessible, so he doubled his efforts in that direction. But before he could actually reach his goal, a familiar roar announced he soon faced quite a different threat ...dropping off the edge of the world.

And drop he did, the powerful tug of the waterfall taking him along for the plunge. Fortunately the drop proved not to be too great ...or too perilous ...for he quickly bobbed back up in a large pool. The landscape had changed to his advantage. Instead of jungle gym trees, open mixed forest, brush, and grasses lined a broad stream contained within rocky shores. Ollen's feet touched gravel bottom as he pushed his way to a shallow shoal. Once out of the main current, he paused, holding on to a rock to catch his breath. Then giving up the water's buoyancy, he crawled to shore, taking on the full weight of Aaia's gravity.

Ollen's first thought after regaining his feet was finding Caleeza. There was no frantic urgency; after all, Caleeza could take care of herself, and she carried the star stone which offered her better odds against adversity. But the unease he felt over the separation was compelling. He glanced repeatedly at the stream, as he tried to get his bearings, half expecting her to float in at any moment. From where he stood, the waterfall he rode down was still visible in the near distance. To his right, the stream curved out of view behind a wall of boulders.

What should I do? Should I wait for her here since she knows the direction to take? Would she find me? Or should I back track to find her and risk possibly missing each other along the way? I would need to take a different route to reach her.

Ollen decided to build a fire and dry things out, giving Caleeza a chance to reach him. He emptied his pack, which he had managed to hold on to, and spread out its contents on heated rocks in the hot moisture-thirsty sun. For further input into planning a course of action in the event Caleeza didn't make an appearance in a reasonable amount of time, he unfolded the wet crystal floss map and studied it carefully, comparing the map to his surroundings. It didn't take long for him to realize they didn't match up.

He was standing in a rocky chasm, the opposite bank rising high above the stream. The map, despite its errors in size and proportion, had ...so far... faithfully rendered basic features of the valley, but there was no indication of the presence of a stream. There were some markings however that may have indicated the presence of a marsh around the overlapping squares and rectangles that represented the jungle gym forest. Nor was there any indication of a drop in the terrain. In fact the bank on which he stood didn't look anything like the more familiar terrain and growth he could see growing uniformly on the cliff across the water.

Something catastrophic had taken place here since the map was woven. Some great force had churned the terrain topsy-turvy where he stood, leaving the far bank undisturbed; which made sense considering the map was woven before the Dark Devastation. But Ollen wasn't convinced the disturbance occurred that long ago. Further reflection on the landscape suggested the disturbance that took place here occurred more recently than the seeding of the forest on the opposite bank. Still the event, whatever it was, happened a long time ago, as new growth, including some trees, had taken root in the jumbled rocky terrain with spotty success.

☆☆☆☆

Caleeza could only watch in horror and near panic as the current swept Ollen away. *Calm down. Stop and think.* Ollen would eventually come ashore somewhere. All she had to do was find a way to reach him.

She could make out what looked like a low ridge and dry ground to the north through the trees. It was the direction she wanted to go, but an open gap in the reach of the jungle gym tree branches made crossing over the main current of the stream impossible. Then she remembered she had the star stone in her possession. With it she could draw upon enough elemental energy to teleport herself, within a limited range, across the rushing water ...the distance across was within that range she hoped.

Calming her rapidly beating heart and forcing her mind to focus, Caleeza's fingers caressed the small smooth golden stone stashed in a secure pocket inside her tunic and willed herself to a cluster of branches beyond the deep rushing current. A breath later, to her relief, she was clinging to her new perch on the north side of the stream.

"Ollen!" she called out again, searching for Ollen in the water and in the trees. She teleported several short jumps to the shore. As the ridge of dry land drew closer, the jungle gym trees thinned and ground became exposed. Caleeza climbed down to stand on soil once again.

Drawing energy from the elemental forces took its toll. Caleeza paused briefly, breathing hard, and replaced the star stone to its pouch. She could hear the distant rush of water, a sound quite different from the softer murmur of the stream. With rising panic, she hurried downstream calling out his name, then listened for a response, but no voice returned her call.

Following the bank of the stream she eventually came to a drop off into oblivion through high rocky cliffs that barred her progress. She would have to take a circuitous route over rocky terrain to the lower level.

Leaving the waterfall, she hadn't gone far when she came upon a new crisis. Ice cold terror coursed through her veins.

"Growl...l...l...!" The horrendous roar paralyzed her with fear.

Caleeza's heart pounded hard in her chest, her limbs shaking, her blood throbbing past her ears. It was Theon's meat-eater, the species he claimed kept the plant eaters in check. The colonists had seen the enormous tracks, but never before had any of them actually encountered one ...until now. The scaled beast, twice her height and ten times her weight, reared up on its massive hind legs.

Theon had predicted bear like creatures kept the valley's plant eaters in balance. Caleeza had actually seen Earth bears during her long sojourn in Alaska, but the beast that threatened her now, despite its long sharp claws and teeth, looked more like the pictures she had seen of Earth dragons. It didn't breathe fire, but Caleeza could smell its foul breath as it roared at her again. Trembling uncontrollably, she slowly stumbled backward, away from the beast, away from the stream, away from the direction she needed to go. The beast approached slowly studying its unfamiliar prey. Not daring to take her eyes away from the predator to look behind her, she stepped on something thick and soft that squished under her feet. Then losing her footing, she began to fall. Almost instantly the sky disappeared.

The fall down a rocky hole turned into a long bouncing, sliding ride down a narrow slippery tunnel that glowed with a phosphorous green light. Frantically, she tried to stop her momentum, but the angle of the tunnel was too steep. She grabbed at the iridescent green growth, but it had no strength to hold her. Nor did it slow her down. The thick glowing succulent growth cushioned much of the course except for the occasional bruising from protruding underlying rock. Finally Caleeza landed with a jolt, her head hitting hard against a rock upon landing ... and she lost consciousness.

The long awaited holiday break from the Academy finally arrived. The long *dreaded* holiday break would be a more apt description in Kiril's opinion, but there was little he could do except take the punches. Rojaire, Kaylya, Traevus, Kiril, and Thayla teleported from the academy gardens to Galeza, Kiril's home village and the home of Councilor Kreeze,

Proctor of the Northern Provinces. Councilor Kreeze would have his chance to further reprimand and mete out punishment; and his chosen mother and chosen father, as well as his entire village, would have a chance to refuse to allow him to join the colony. The only one he was looking forward to seeing was Drak; Drak at least would understand.

But it would be a long time before Kiril would have Drak to himself. Everyone in the village wanted to meet the visitors, and as host it was Kiril's responsibility to make sure everyone did. And of course his chosen mother Zaloka and his chosen father Wessid wanted to spend as much time with Kiril and his friends as possible.

A grand feast had been prepared in anticipation of their arrival and was being served in the village park pavilion. All two hundred and eighty-three permanent residents of Galeza were in attendance at the grand pavilion and the surrounding park. Built over a babbling brook that helped to keep it cool, the pavilion and the surrounding park were shaded all around by the thick dark canopies of mature *cantanut* trees. The smooth creamy-white trunks of these beautiful shade trees stood out elegantly against the dark reddish-purple leafy foliage. Stone pathways and footbridges built of lavender, rose, and cream colored stones wove through trees, shade-loving gardens, and trellised alcoves.

News of Rojaire's mission to recruit colonists for what was now Lynnara had reached the village ahead of the visitors. Everyone wanted to hear more, even if no one showed interest in becoming a colonist. So after appetites were sated and fermented drinks began to flow, Rojaire and his group were encouraged to speak.

Rojaire gladly accommodated them. He described the vast island continent with the love of a father that failed to see his child's talent deficiencies, telling them of recovering coastal hills and valleys with flowing streams of fresh water and an abundance of edible foods available. Then he described the impregnable, formidable Crescent Mountains that spiraled through the center of the continent isolating the coast from the drier, more barren interior. And he totally won their awe with his vivid detailed descriptions of the Crystalline Landscape, and what they may have learned about its possible dangers, that surrounded Mt. Vatre for many leagues in the center of the continent.

The villagers listened spellbound, asking questions to encourage him to tell more, but the villagers were more practical than adventurous, and although they greatly enjoyed Rojaire's tales, no one spoke up in favor of joining the colonists.

"How many people have signed up so far?" one villager asked.

"A few..." Rojaire answered cautiously, unwilling to disclose just how few.

"Building a colony without the ability to draw energy from the elemental forces sounds like a lot of hard labor," said another. "We are already comfortable here; what incentive is there for us to move to Lynnara?"

"Freedom..." Rojaire said giving the word deep meaning. "Freedom to move about as you want and plan your own life agenda. Freedom to pursue your own dreams and interests instead of those of the High Council and the Academy. Freedom to raise a family as people did long ago. Look about you."

Not sure what Rojaire expected them to see the villagers glance about.

"Where are the children? Do you see any new persons? There should be babies, and toddlers, and young ones playing and running about."

A woman spoke up. "We have applied to the High Council to choose a mother and father to produce another new person for the village," she said.

The woman's words sounded peculiar, even a bit insane, to Kaylya after living in western Alaska. *How would a woman from Earth respond to a statement like that? I do not want the High Council to decide if Rojaire and I can have a child together. Their answer would most certainly be no.*

"Listen to what you just said," Rojaire voiced loudly, apparently experiencing a similar reaction. "You applied to the High Council to choose a mother and father to produce another new person for the village." Rojaire repeated, pacing in excited agitation. "A man and a woman should be allowed to make that choice for themselves."

"Your words speak treason," an elderly woman hissed. "Lack of control breeds chaos."

"The freedoms I speak of are rights that are our due as intelligent dignified individuals."

Drak listened quietly to the discussion, which was contrary to his usual outspoken nature, shaking his head at the small-mindedness of some of his neighbors. A quick glance at Kreeze made Drak chuckle. The philosophic councilor appeared to be in a quandary over the appeal of Rojaire's ideals and his loyalty to the High Council. No doubt the councilor would be lecturing Kiril on his duties while he was here. Drak studied Kiril watching Rojaire with envious pride. Poor boy! He looks miserable. I can easily guess why; the High Council will forbid Kiril to leave the Academy, a right they hold in reserve until Kiril becomes an Accepted One.

Kiril had shared with Drak a complete verbal chronicle of the mapping expedition through the Crescent Mountains and the discovery of the wondrous hidden valley that fit the descriptions on the ancient map Drak had given him. In fact, Drak was looking forward to meeting with Rojaire and his team in private. There was much he wanted to discuss with them. He had every intention seeing the valley his great grandfather discovered before the Dark Devastation, but he wasn't going to announce it to the entire community for they would surely find merry sport with his decision.

It wasn't until long after the great feast, followed by a period of sleep and more unplanned visiting, before Rojaire, Kaylya, Traevus, and Kiril hailed Drak at his cottage door. By then the sun blazed hot on the long Aaian day.

To Rojaire's relief, Thayla had accepted an invitation earlier to go on a food gathering trip in the hills for the next feast. So far, Thayla knew nothing of the map and the secret valley they wished to discuss with Drak, and until Rojaire was certain she could be trusted, he preferred it to stay that way.

"Greetings, my friends!" Drak exclaimed upon opening the hand-crafted wooden door to his quaint cottage made of stone. Drak's long silvery hair glistened in the sunlight and matched the radiance in his eyes which expressed with ease his delight in seeing them.

"Greetings, Drak. We are grateful for your invitation," Rojaire said, gazing with fascination at the man who had provided Kiril with such a prophetic map. Rojaire quickly introduced Kaylya and Traevus. "Kiril I believe you already know."

Drak ushered them in. "Welcome, welcome, please come in and be seated.

"It is such a pleasure to finally meet you," Kaylya said. "Kiril has told us so much about you." They chose sturdy handcrafted wooden chairs softened with cushions and sat around a highly polished dark wood table.

"Where is the other woman in your party? I hope she hasn't taken ill."

"She has gone on a food gathering party," Kaylya filled in.

Drak immediately began pouring drinks. "It is my pleasure to serve ...some of my choice elixir," he said, adding his special twist to the standard expression.

Milky blue porcelain decanters and tumblers as well as several small pouches made of crystal floss, a rare nearly indestructible material no longer found, were spread out on the table. Kiril resisted the urge to reach out and touch the pouches. "Drak brews an excellent beverage," he said instead with contrived sophistication while vowing silently that he would sip with caution ...this time.

"Well, in that case, I'm looking forward to trying it," Rojaire said as Drak filled his cup.

"I see you collect relics," Traevus said eyeing Drak's extensive collection overburdening shelves and cubbyholes built into the stone walls.

"Yes, I've always had a great interest in history. In my younger days, I spent most of my time, when not performing my assigned duties, exploring and digging for relics." Drak's sparkling dark gray eyes reflected experience and aged wisdom; his weathered skin bespoke of a man who spent much time outdoors.

"You found all these things," Kaylya gasped with surprise. "Where?"

"Mostly deep in the interior of the continent, far from the ravaged coastlines."

Kaylya stared at him, her mouth agape. She and Rojaire had done much the same thing. They had also ventured deep into the continent and found relics which Rojaire sold to Councilor Brakalar, Head of the Academy at the time, to obtain secret illicit transport to the Devastated Continent after the Academy and the High Council refused their petition to explore it.

"Of course, feel free to dig and browse all you wish, but I have a few items here that come from a very special valley in the Crescent Mountains that you might find even more interesting and stories to go with them. Stories handed down from my great grandfather to my father and eventually down to me. But first let's drink to the establishment of the first settlement in the new Lynnara."

Kaylya certainly couldn't argue with that. So with their curiosity piqued they all sipped at the golden brew, except for Drak who took a hearty swallow. Kaylya only touched it to her lips and she could taste its fiery strength.

"So tell us about your great grandfather," Traevus said to get Drak talking. "What was his name?"

"His name was Vestan. All I can tell you about him are the stories my father related to me. He was an explorer, an adventurer, who would go missing in the Crescent Mountains for cycles of seasons, then unexpectedly show up again. He was a weaver by trade, at least when he actually worked, and as rare as crystal floss is, he supposedly found enough of it to weave the map I gave Kiril as well as the pouches and a second map I have here on the table."

"Kiril didn't bring back the map you gave him, but I can vouch it is safe," Rojaire assured him. "We felt it was needed in the valley it depicts."

"I do not doubt your word and I agree," Drak said. "When Kiril returned with tales of a valley that fit the map I was elated. Of course there was a time when I was skeptical. During his longevity, my Great Grandfather Vestan was considered a fool. It felt good to have him finally vindicated." Drak took another gulp from his tumbler before continuing his tale.

"Back in his day, gemstones were of great value and the maps marked the locations of his many finds, but he never revealed the location of the valleys. Perhaps he thought there was time for that; he didn't anticipate the Dark Devastation. My grandmother escaped Lynnara with my father, who was a small child at the time, and with what you see here." Drak waved his hand over the table.

Reaching from his chair he grabbed one of the pouches and emptied its contents into his hand. Brilliant thumbnail-sized blood-red gemstones gleamed in the light of a small glow overhead. "My grandmother probably assumed the gemstones would support them in the aftermath of the calamity, but the destruction of our world was more devastating than anyone could have imagined, and the gemstones became worthless." One by one Drak revealed the contents of the pouches ...diamonds, sapphires, emeralds, and purple amethyst. They admired the beautiful large perfect stones taking turns handling them and holding them up to the light.

But it was the map they were more interested in. Kiril could hardly keep his fingers in check, the urge to reach out for the map was so strong. The existence of a second mysterious map sharpened his fervor to reunite with the map he had to leave behind.

"Is the map of another special hidden valley full of gemstones?" Kiril asked.

Drak didn't miss Kiril's eagerness to get to the map. *I'm surprised it took him this long to bring it up.* "There's more to it than that. It is my understanding that somehow the two valleys are connected. By what means I couldn't tell you." Drak unfolded the crystal floss map revealing a woven representation of a place that no one living has ever seen.

"What are these?" Kaylya asked studying something woven into the margin. There were line drawing of some kind of creature in the lower left hand corner of the cloth. To Kaylya they looked like a child's drawing of teddy bears.

"I have no name for them, but they are the strangest tale of all. My grandmother believed Vestan encountered these small feathery creatures, or so he claimed, living isolated from the rest of the world. He considered them to be quite intelligent. According to the story I grew up with, they stood waist-high to my great grandfather and had padded hands with opposing thumbs which allowed them to use simple tools and craft a few useful items. They supposedly could walk upright, but moved much quicker on all fours. Great Grandfather Vestan wasn't much of an artist, but this supposedly is his rendition of what they looked like."

"Well, we haven't encountered anything that looks like this," Traevus said. "But we have discovered a few other amazing living species." Traevus delighted them with descriptions of silver kurpers and delicate twirling callelas. In a world void of animal life, these life forms were more precious than all the gemstones together.

"Yes, Kiril has described them to me. It's a wonder they survived all the devastation!"

"We've also encountered tracks indicating the presence of a large predator, but no one has seen it yet," Rojaire added.

"So I've heard. I would love to see these wonders with my own eyes."

"I can't wait to see them for myself," Kaylya said. There was a long contemplative pause. Then the group turned their attention to the map. Drak topped off their cups and took another gulp of the fiery brew.

Rojaire looked up from his study of the map. "What are these swirling markings? They seem to indicate movement. There's nothing like that on the map you gave Kiril."

"I have to admit, I don't know. My grandmother claimed Westan's explanation never made much sense to her."

"I know it is a lot to ask," Rojaire said after a while. "But would you consider letting us take this map with us to Lynnara?"

Drak held them in suspense for a moment before answering Rojaire's question with another question. "How much time do you have left to round up enough colonists?" Drak asked.

"Not long ...another rotation."

"And how many colonists do you actually have lined up at this point to join your colony?"

"A few," Rojaire answered with some hesitation.

"How many?" Drak asked emphatically.

"Three," Rojaire admitted dismally.

"Four!" Kiril shouted in defiance. The group turned to look his way, but no one had the heart to contradict him.

"Then make that five," Drak said. "For I intend joining you."

"Oh, that's wonderful," Kaylya gasped.

"I assume you have an alternative plan if you don't find twenty colonists to sign up," Drak said.

"I might," Rojaire admitted not wanting to give anything away. "We'll see."

Drak raised his cup. "Then I won't pry. Just give me the word when the time comes, and I'll be ready. Till then, let's drink to Lynnara."

"To Lynnara...!" they joined in chorus raising their cups.

Kiril took a larger sip to celebrate. Drak had counted himself as the fifth colonists to join Rojaire. That made Kiril the fourth. There was a ray of hope after all. For the first time no one said he wasn't going.

CHAPTER 7

Earth

The last winter storm finally left western Alaska bringing in pleasant spring sunshine. Breakup in Alaska is not a very pretty sight. Brown ground writhes mushily in the throes of thawing between decaying mounds of dirty snow. There had been a promise of spring in the air when Jack flew out, after waiting two days for the storm to break permitting flights out of King Salmon again and another day to let the backlog of cancelled flights clear. Spring may be coming to Bristol Bay, but not fast enough for Jack.

Jack's disposition improved greatly as soon as he reached Anchorage and warmer weather. The city was already turning green with grass growing and trees leafing. He generally enjoyed himself the few days he spent in Anchorage waiting for the next passenger train north to the Susitna Valley. He walked around downtown during the day, sampling eateries and visiting the museums, even taking in a movie. At night he ordered in and watched the city from his hotel window.

It was a warm early May morning and Jack's spirits were running high as he finally boarded the northbound train. The last time he visited the Bradley Family and other members of the Order of the Oracle, he had to painfully say goodbye to Kaylya. On a happy note, he hoped to spend some time with Ilene and her mother Elaine. The train ride was long, and to pass the time Jack chatted with brave early season tourists, regaling them with tales of commercial fishing in Bristol Bay and life on the rugged frontier.

Hours later the slow moving train pulled up to the little passenger platform in the tiny end-of-the-road town where Elaine and her daughter Ilene had their gift shop. To his surprise he spotted the two women on the platform. *Were they boarding the train?* In answer to Jack's question, they picked up small carry-on packs and approached the steps. Jack rose to greet them as they entered the passenger carriage waving them over. Spotting him, Ilene ushered her mother over.

"Jack Faulkner!" Ilene exclaimed with delight. "It's so good to see you. We were hoping you would make it up this weekend."

"I'm delighted to see you, too," he said with a warm hug. Ilene quickly stepped aside into a seat giving him clear access to Elaine. "Elaine, my lady," he said taking her hand. "You are the highlight of my day, the sweet dreams of my night. What a pleasure it is to be in your company once again!"

"I doubt all that, but greetings to you too," Elaine said gruffly, easing into the seat beside Ilene. It was obvious Jack had hoped she would choose to sit with him instead. Ilene stared out the window so her mother wouldn't see the grin on her face. It was funny beyond belief. Jack was wooing her mother and her mother was sweet on him ...she just had a strange way of showing it. The remainder of the trip went quickly as the three of them attempted to catch up on news over the click-clacking of the train. Then the train slowed as it approached the Bradley trail head and eased to a stop.

"Jack!" Leaf exclaimed when he saw Jack following Ilene and Elaine down the steps off the train. The sun glared harshly off of what remained of the snow.

Jack spared a glance at the boy before navigating the loose gravel of the rail bed to the clearing beside the tracks that denoted the start of the narrow trail leading into the woods to Vince and Maggie's house. Rahlys, who had joined the Bradley family welcoming party gave Elaine a hand down the gravel bed while Vince collected their baggage. When they were clear, the train pulled away. As soon as it was safe, Leaf released Keiluk's collar and rushed up to Jack before anyone else could reach him.

"Hi, Jack! Guess what I have?"

"My man Leaf, good to see you," Jack greeted him jovially. The boy had sprouted a couple of inches since Jack saw him last. And the white dog beside him had filled out in proportion to the size of his paws.

"I have chickens," Leaf announced proudly since Jack didn't take a guess.

"Chickens and a dog; you are coming up in the world. Do your chickens lay eggs?"

"Lots of eggs."

"Bear bait, the whole lot," Elaine muttered.

Soon they were all gathered together. "We are so glad you could come," Vince said reaching over Leaf's head to shake Jack's hand.

"I am indeed glad to be here; thank you so much for inviting me. And look at the lovely female escorts I found along the way." Vince looked to where Rahlys, Elaine, and Ilene were exchanging hugs.

"I always knew you were a ladies' man," Vince said giving his friend a wink.

"Where's Maggie?"

"To make the trek to the cabin easier, Maggie stayed at the cabin with the twins."

"Jack!" Rahlys cried coming to greet him.

"How's my favorite sorceress?" Jack asked squeezing her hard.

"I'm doing great. It's wonderful seeing you again."

"We might as well get a head start, Elaine, since we are the slowest," Jack said gallantly offering her his arm for support.

"I reckon you are right, if you think it's safe," Elaine agreed.

"I'll protect you," Leaf offered, Keiluk running circles around them.

"I'm sure you will," Jack said as the four of them headed off together.

Everyone knew the routine. Packs and boxes were stashed on the four wheel ATV for Vince to take up to the cabin. That didn't leave room for passengers. Vince took off on the packed four-wheeler and the rest of the group headed up the trail on foot. It wasn't long before Jack, Elaine, Leaf, and Keiluk were forced to step off the trail to let Vince pass.

The trail itself was bare of snow, but some large patches of winter's revenge still remained. Jack inhaled the warm spring air and the earthy scent of newly exposed forest floor with pleasure.

"Ah...spring...my favorite time of year!" he said.

"They're all your favorite time of year," Elaine jabbed, but she understood what he meant. There was something invigorating about spring beyond just a reprieve from winter.

For the most part, Elaine and Jack were able to stay up with the youthful Leaf and Keiluk since boy and dog required frequent stops to sniff and investigate the intoxicating sights, sounds, and smells of the awakening forest long the way. Still the trail's long inclines quickly took a toll on both Jack and Elaine. Ilene and Rahlys saw them pause again up ahead.

"Elaine probably never realized before how much Quaylyn had helped her along the trail in the past," Rahlys said in tender remembrance of the kind attention Quaylyn always gave Elaine. The two women easily caught up with the couple. They looked like they had had enough exercise for the day and still had half the distance to go.

"Well," Rahlys said stepping up to them, "I think instead of juggling you two along, I better teleport you the rest of the way...if that's alright with you."

"Oh... ah...," Elaine stammered always reluctant to go from here to there without all the spaces in between, but before she could offer up a solid protest, Jack jumped in.

"That would be wonderful, Rahlys, thank you; I miss Kaylya in more ways than one." Rahlys smiled at his mention of Kaylya.

"Go ahead," Ilene urged, "Leaf, Keiluk, and I will be there shortly."

So Rahlys gently encompassed the elderly couple in a draw of power and teleported to Vince and Maggie's yard. Almost instantly Maggie and the twins rushed out the cabin to embrace them.

"You get more gorgeous every day," Jack said taking Maggie's hand.

"You tease; good to see you," she said kissing him on the cheek.

When they were all reunited with Keiluk barking excitedly, their numbers seemed greatly diminished. The absence of Quaylyn by Rahlys' side was quite noticeable and Rojaire had come for Kaylya, returning with her to their own world. But even though she was still on Earth, it was the absence of Melinda that left the greatest void. The quiet girl without speech had always made her presence known.

"You're just in time to rototill the garden," Vince said indicting a rototiller under a tarp, primed and ready to go.

"Sure," Jack said.

"No!" Maggie admonished. "He's only joking. You can help us plant."

Of course, it was the twins who had changed the most, transforming from stumbling toddlers to a little girl and a little boy. Crystal and Rock held back, too young to clearly remember Jack's previous visits.

"Who are you?" Crystal asked coyly.

Jack smiled; he could tell she had her mother's spunk.

"I'm Jack, and if I'm not mistaken, you're Crystal."

Crystal nodded tilting her head, "How do you know that?" she asked.

"I'm good friends with your mom and dad. And this must be Rock. Nice to meet you again, Rock," Jack said giving him five. Rock slapped his hand with more force than Jack would have credited him.

"Why is your nose so big?" asked the diminutive replica of Vince with Maggie highlights.

"My proboscis?" he asked pointing to the center of his face. "Why it is something I am very proud of. A large nose denotes great strength and incredible intelligence."

"Oh," said Rock touching his own little button nose with some concern.

A merry party ensued. It was far too nice a spring day to spend indoors, so everything needed as far as food, cooking utensils, toys, and drinks was brought outside.

Everyone participated in a dodge ball game, even Jack and Elaine who were easy targets and the first ones out. Taking their turn tossing, Jack surprised everyone by taking out Vince. Far less ambitious, Elaine focused her ball on Crystal. Opting out of returning to the game, Jack and Elaine gratefully sat down and watched. There was much taunting and squealing as the players ran up and down the yard avoiding Crystal's throws from one end and Vince's from the other.

Then unexpectedly, as always, the message came.

ANTHYA APPROACHES.

Rahlys froze. A year has passed since Rahlys has received a message through the Oracle of Light; a year since Quaylyn's departure ripped her apart. Startled and distracted she felt the ball tap her in the back to the cheers of the others. Crystal was more than pleased with herself.

"You're out," she laughed just feet away. Rahlys graciously conceded defeat.

"Anthya's coming," she announced to everyone's surprise. The dodge ball game collapsed and within moments the image of Councilor Anthya wearing a sapphire gown shimmered in the spring sunshine.

"Greetings, Sorceress Rahlys, Guardian of the Light, Warrior Vince, Warrior Maggie, Healer Ilene, Warrior Elaine, Warrior Jack, Sorcerer Leaf, new person Crystal, and new person Rock," she said naming them all. To Anthya, all of Rahlys' friends/followers were warriors except for the very young. She made an exception for Leaf, acknowledging his mental strength.

"Greetings, Councilor Anthya. It's been a long time," Rahlys said. "How may we serve?" She wanted to ask about Quaylyn and Kaylya, but felt it best to listen to the councilor's message first.

"The High Council wishes to extend an invitation to Healer Ilene to return to the Academy to study. It has been determined it is her right to do so since she is as much a part of our world as she is of Earth."

Rahlys heard Elaine gasp in response to the announcement, then saw Jack step up to offer Elaine moral support. Jack understood Elaine's anxiety. If Ilene accepted the High Council's invitation to return to Aaia she may never see her daughter again. Yet they all knew Ilene wished to return to the Academy to study healing.

Ilene seemed too stunned to react at first, then uttered a heartfelt, "Oh, I would love to." For Ilene it was a dream come true; Kaylya must have spoken up for her after all.

Anthya smiled warmly and nodded toward Ilene. "You have made a wise choice. I am looking forward to instructing you once again. You must be ready to depart in three Earth-days."

"No...," Elaine cried softly. *I will be all alone,* she added silently. But Rahlys heard her and so did Anthya.

"Warrior Elaine, I ask that you be strong. The opportunity Healer Ilene is being offered is a great honor. She has done well, but has much left to learn. Once her training is complete, she will be returned safely to Earth."

Then Councilor Anthya was gone...her image vanished...and Rahlys hadn't even had a chance to inquire after their friends. This is not how it was supposed to happen. Anthya had made contact with them and there had been no message from Quaylyn.

The sudden appearance and disappearance of the messenger from across the galaxy had completely changed the dynamics of the day. The children finding the adults too engrossed in the new developments went off to play by themselves. Ilene, jittery with excitement, fought to calm her own elation before trying to console her mother.

"My daughter agreed to return to Aaia; it's my greatest nightmare come true," Elaine cried.

Jack put comforting arms around her. "Now, now, Elaine, you can't keep treating Ilene like a little girl. She's twenty-five; she has a right to live her own life. She's a smart woman in need of challenges; just like my son. Our jobs are done; it is time to let them go."

"It's not her I'm worried about; it's me. I don't know how I can live without her."

"I will show you how, my lady," Jack said gallantly.

"Who will help me at the gift shop? I can't run it on my own; it is too much work for just one person."

"I will help you and you don't even have to pay me," Jack offered. "I will find a little place to stay in town and you can train me. How hard can it be?"

"Plus you already have Angela working full-time now," Ilene added seeing an opening to plead her case. Her gratitude toward Jack for being there brought tears to her eyes.

"We have a place in town within easy walking distance from the gift shop," Vince said stepping in to help. "It used to be my bachelor pad." He grinned suggestively. "You are welcomed to stay there rent free ... as long as we can continue to park our truck in the yard and spend the night once in a great while when we need to."

Ilene could hardly believe it; things were falling into place so smoothly.

"Oh, Ilene, I'm going to really miss you," Maggie said giving her a tearful hug. With you gone, it's going to get even lonelier up here."

Rahlys sensed the truth of Maggie's words and felt a tightness in her stomach. "I have something for you, Ilene," she said collecting herself.

"What is it?" Ilene asked. Rahlys conjured a little purple velveteen drawstring pouch to her hand and offered it to her.

Intrigued, Ilene opened the drawstring and emptied the contents of the little pouch into her hand. It was a star stone, the same star stone

Melinda had found in the creek and given to Rahlys as a good luck charm before they left for Aaia to join the mission to find the lost expedition on the Devastated Continent ...was it only three years ago?

"You better take it with you, for luck," Rahlys said. *Just in case,* she added telepathically. She didn't say in case of "what," but Ilene understood. If she were to return to the Devastated Continent, the star stone would make it possible for her to draw limited energy from the elemental forces.

"Oh, Rahlys, thank you. I will give it back to you when I return."

No rush, Rahlys telepathed to her so Elaine wouldn't hear. If Ilene returned to the Devastated Continent, she could be gone a long time.

"It wasn't easy convincing their parents to let them go on an overnight camp-out with friends, but in the end they relented. Seth promised to watch over Alice and Alice played down any possible threats by promising never to be out of Seth's sight. They met up with Justin mid-afternoon with convincing packs that included tents (which they wouldn't be using) and sleeping bags as well as a small ice chest of food ...to contribute to the party. Justin had volunteered to bring the beer. How he planned to get ahold of it, the twins didn't ask.

It was a hot day in south Louisiana with the start of summer just a few short weeks away. The air in the woods didn't stir; as a result the captured humid heat was stifling. It was a relief to finally arrive at the old weathered house that had become a secret hangout over the past month. They immediately sought the dark dense shade under the sprawling old oak tree and dropping their gear, stretched out on the cool shaded ground. With hours left before dark the teenagers decided food, drink, and possibly a nap while waiting for the evening to cool was in order.

The beer was ice cold. Alice rubbed the cold can against her body, especially her hot neck and forehead. The coldness of it was delightful. Then she opened the can and took the biggest gulp of beer she had ever taken in her life in an attempt to quench her thirst. The guys were doing pretty much the same.

By the time the first cool breeze of evening brought relief from the stifling heat, a pile of empty beer cans had begun to pile up. Already feeling a bit woozy, Alice reached for a bag of potato chips to absorb some of the alcohol in her system. "Do you want a sandwich?" she asked the guys reaching into the ice chest for a sandwich and a soda pop this time instead of beer.

"Sure, I'll have one," the boys said in near unison and she tossed out pre-made ham and cheese sandwiches.

"So what do you think will happen after it gets dark?" Justin asked around a mouth full of sandwich, reminding Seth and Alice they were here on a dare.

"Probably nothing," Seth had to admit getting another beer. "Spending the night was a good idea. It'll be fun and we can put this evil presence thing to rest."

"Hey, toss me another one, too," Justin piped up. The tossing action caused the beer to spew foam when he pulled the tab and Justin made a dramatic effort to suck it all up.

After eating, Alice left the boys to more beer consumption and carried her pack and sleeping bag into the house. There was no evidence of anyone having visited the site; everything was just as they left it. Nothing had changed since they were here last. As the only female in the group, she claimed the empty front room as her own, for a modicum of privacy from the boys if they should decide to actually sleep at some point tonight.

She was headed outside again to join them when Justin startled her. He deftly blocked her way to the exit, crowding her into a corner between the laser-cutting machine and the wall. *Oh, crap,* she moaned to herself. She hated being caught alone with Justin; she had already turned him down twice for the prom, but he just wouldn't give it up.

"So how about it, Alice, you and me, stealing the show at the prom next week-end?" He reached up and touched her hair. "I really like red hair," he said breathing on her. His breath smelled like beer.

"I said no; get it into your thick skull," Alice said angrily slapping his hand away.

"You know you want me," Justin sneered. Alice pushed him hard against the laser cutting machine and slipped around him toward the door.

It was then that Seth walked in. “Has anything changed in here?” he asked letting Alice pass before walking into the house, to check it out. To Alice’s great relief Justin followed Seth through the house as though nothing had happened.

The sky remained clear, and as night drew closer they built a fire in the outdoor fire pit to roast sausages on sticks under the stars. The sky quickly darkened and more stars spangled the cosmic dome above them. As the sausages cooked, fat dripped onto hot embers in the fire pit, setting off little flares that competed with the lightening bugs for attention. Alice quickly put the incident with Justin behind her and drifted into a feeling of complacency staring into the fire, the boys’ intoxicated blabber merely background noise. It turned out to be a beautiful night, putting to shame her concerns of something evil lurking around. The cooking sausages’ fatty spicy aroma whetted their appetites. When the sausages were done, they wrapped them in bread and loaded them with mustard.

Washing down dinner with more beer, Justin and Seth sprawled out beside the fire using their packs, which had been retrieved from under the oak tree, to lean their back against. They quickly got into a heated debate about cars which lead to a debate about pick-up trucks. Since neither topic held Alice’s interest, she turned her attention to stargazing.

At first Alice didn’t note anything out of the ordinary; she located the few constellations she could identify, watched the light of a satellite cross the backdrop of stars, and gazed at the faint thumbprint of a distant galaxy. Then she noticed stars starting to disappear. Bats or birds flying overhead was her first logical explanation, but even more stars vanished and the starless blackness continued to strangely expand. Alice’s senses bolted alert.

“Hey, guys,” she said in alarm, “I think something is happening.”

Seth and Justin were reluctant to drop their horse-power conversation, but slowly they relented and followed her gaze upward. They almost turned their gaze away again when the phenomenon of disappearing stars finally registered in their sauced brains. Then unseen tendrils of icy chill brushed against their skin, turning the warm night frosty cold.

"What's happening? What's doing that?" Seth asked in mounting panic.

"I don't know," Alice said her voice shaking. For once she couldn't supply her brother with an answer. "Whatever it is..."

"I have a gun for protection," Justin announced and quickly pulled a loaded pistol from his pack. Alice caught a glint of reflected light off metal from the dying glow of the campfire. The light from the stars had been snuffed out.

"What do you think you're going to do with that, shoot shadows?" Alice asked astounded. "Let's get out of here!" By now they were all on their feet.

"I'm not afraid of any ghost!" Justin snarled.

A low, faintly perceptible moan of horrific pain and inconsolable sorrow infused the thickening darkness around them. They could no longer see; another wave of bone-chilling cold brushed against them in the impenetrable blackness.

Justin shot wildly at the dark; one shot after another.

Alice felt something drop to the ground beside her.

A gust of chilled wind stoked the fire into sparks and flame. In its light, her brother lay motionless at her feet, a bullet hole in his forehead.

"Seth...!" she screamed. Her shrill cry brought an end to Justin's shooting. Alice dropped down to her brother's side, groping for him with her hands. He wasn't breathing, his pallid freckled skin already chilling in the moaning cold wind that engulfed them.

"No...! Look what you're done! You're mad! You're evil!" she screamed at Justin over the roar in her ears. This couldn't be happening for real; it wasn't possible; she would wake soon from this terrible nightmare; she had to.

"Come on; wake up!" she shouted as much to her dead brother as to herself. Seth didn't wake up; nor did she. The grief that washed over her was unbearable.

"How could you do this?" she screamed at Justin. "My, brother!"

Justin didn't respond; he just looked at her coldly.

Suddenly Alice realized that she was in grave danger, not from the evil essence that permeated the air around them, but from the cold emotionless soul staring down at her. *Run,* an inner voice told her. One final quick glance at her beloved brother and Alice took off running through the shrouding darkness. Shots were fired behind her, one shot hitting a tree nearby as she fled. She couldn't tell if Justin had taken up pursuit; it would have been impossible to hear him over her own pounding heart, her crashing retreat, and the moaning of the cloaking darkness.

Alice ran on, guided only by blind terror and gasping for breath. How long did she run ...for minutes...hours...days? She didn't know. All she knew was that she couldn't stop. By the time terror loosened its grip on her mind, she had reached the edge of a road. The last thing she noticed before collapsing in front of a screeching car were the stars shining brightly overhead.

CHAPTER 8

Aaia

Caleeza flowed slowly back toward consciousness ...but there was no need to hurry. She didn't want to leave; she was happy. She frolicked through the fragrant Academy gardens with Sarus by her side full of new hopes and dreams. What fun it was to be together again! Arm in arm, they twirled through the gardens, the orchards, and then they followed the river before gliding out to sea. It was a long spirit journey across the Golden Sea, but finally they landed in a landscape of crystals.

Caleeza became increasingly aware of several points of physical pain throughout her body as Sarus was pulled away from her, never to be her heart mate again. Suddenly she was overwhelmed with lost love, but then physical pain demanded her attention. It was her head that hurt the most. *Where am I?* The last thing she remembered was falling down a long glowing tunnel. She tried to open an eyelid, but the effort was just too great. Giving up, she drifted away again.

When pain drew her back to total awareness she sensed much time had passed. Not quite ready yet to expend the energy necessary to open her eyes, she focused on other senses for clues to her surroundings. For one thing, she was lying flat on her back and she could feel some sort of bedding beneath her. So Ollen found her after all and was taking care of her. Did he encounter the dragon-like beast? As she came closer to the surface of consciousness, the areas of her injuries became more defined. She tried to move to shift position, but the effort just made things worse.

Caleeza opened her eyes ...slowly. The living ceiling and walls that surrounded her glowed luminously green, the dull throbbing pain in her head grateful for the subdued lighting. Then turning her head, she saw it and gasped. The life form seated beside her was not Ollen or like any creature she had ever seen before.

Upon noticing Caleeza's eyes were open, the little creature jumped up and moved away, then sat on its haunches watching her. *Was it seeking a safe distance from her?* She watched it from where she lay, studying it carefully. At a glance its movements and many of its physical features almost looked human ...a very small humanoid ...covered in ... were those brownish orange feathers? It wore something across one shoulder, cinched at the waist ...was it worn as clothing, or did the article have a more utilitarian purpose?

Caleeza tried to sit up, but her body's painful response arrested all further movement. Although reluctant to take her eyes off her companion, she lay back down and closed her eyes briefly. When she opened her lids again her feathered benefactor was crouching by her pallet offering her a gourd cup filled with water.

Tiny feathers outlined the exposed brown flesh of its forehead and cheeks. Round dark violet eyes stared down at her with ...did she detect compassionate concern? A little crinkled nose and a bit of a snout for a mouth detracted some from the humanoid appearance of its face.

Caleeza lifted her head enough to drink with the creature assisting by holding the cup. Its hands had the dexterity of a human's, but the fingers were short ending in little claws and the palms were padded. The water was cool and refreshing.

"I am grateful," Caleeza said expressing her thanks.

Caleeza received a string of incomprehensive chittering in response. She had difficulty distinguishing variety in the syllables. Did it have a language? Did the strange repetitive sounds have meaning? She attempted to introduce herself.

"Caleeza," she said pointing to herself. "My name is Caleeza. What's yours?"

More chittering sounds.

"How about I call you Chitter?"

More chittering.

"Ok, then."

Placing the water cup within Caleeza's reach, Chitter dropped down on all fours and loped off, vanishing around a curve of rock that must lead into another chamber. Caleeza laid back to ease her head. *Where am I?* Although the rock ceiling and walls were covered with the same luminous green plant growth she had fallen through, she could see no evidence of the tunnel chute that brought her here.

Then she recalled the star stone in her possession and reached for it, digging in the pocket of her tunic. With the stone she may be able to draw at least a little helpful healing energy for her tortured body. But the star stone was not there. *Did I have the stone in my hand when I encountered the big beast?*

Chitter returned standing upright and carrying a small crudely carved bowl of sorts filled with an aromatic broth that set her stomach growling. Upon reaching the pallet, Chitter squatted down on her haunches and placed the bowl of broth beside the water cup. For some reason Caleeza felt certain Chitter was female.

Once again Caleeza made the effort to sit up. She felt every scrape and bruise as she gingerly pushed herself up into a sitting position, unable to suppress a few moans. Taking her time, she eventually managed it, which changed her perspective notably. For the first time she could look down at Chitter, and when Chitter picked up the bowl and stood up to offer it to her, they were eye to eye level.

Caleeza took the offered nourishment graciously. It was only half full to prevent spillage and since no eating utensil was provided, she cautiously brought it to her lips and sipped. The savory broth was warm and tasty. She hungrily emptied the bowl in a few gulps and almost immediately felt very sleepy. It was then she realized the broth must have been spiked with a sleeping potion. She didn't want to lose consciousness again, but there was nothing she could do; her eyelids became too heavy to keep open. Chitter gently took the bowl from Caleeza's hands as she painlessly lay down to sleep.

After floating for what seemed like days through a kaleidoscopic vision of light and color, Ilene felt the warmth of a sun and inhaled the intoxicating perfume of an extraordinary flower garden. She had been here before. Recognizing the cloying fragrance of the Academy gardens, Ilene opened her eyes.

Standing with her in a trellised alcove covered in flowering vines with stunningly large blossoms of rose, violet, and white were Councilor Anthya, Kaylya, Rojaire, and another male who looked about her age, or so he appeared. Ilene was aware that life expectancy for Aaians was vastly different from that on Earth. She wouldn't be surprised to learn the "young man" was more than a hundred Earth-years old.

"Greetings, Healer Ilene. Welcome back to Aaia," Councilor Anthya greeted her with serene formality.

"Thank you," Ilene said, quickly orienting to the interstellar change in scenery. It had been a hard good-bye for her mother to take. The stress of departure had been eased only by Jack's attentive care. Jack was her hero for stepping up and offering to watch over Elaine while she was gone. Ilene knew her mother could be a handful.

"You already know Kaylya and Rojaire," Anthya said. Trying to put her worries on Earth aside, Ilene focused her attention on the friends she long missed.

"It's so good to see you again, Ilene," Kaylya said giving her a healthy Earthly hug.

"Oh, Kaylya, thank you so much."

"Welcome to Aaia," Rojaire said getting a bit of hug of his own.

"Crystal shards!" Kiril breathed, his gaze transfixed on Ilene ... Theon's daughter ...Theon's daughter of Earth! She was beautiful, astoundingly bouncy, and overflowing with emotional energy.

"It's wonderful seeing the two of you together," Ilene said. Then she wondered about Quaylyn. She had imagined he would be here to greet her and inquire after Rahlys, but Quaylyn was nowhere in sight.

"And this is Kiril, also a student here at the Academy," Anthya said drawing Ilene's attention to the stranger. "He is studying your language and will be your guide when Kaylya and Rojaire aren't available." The High Council had decided that mentoring Ilene would be a suitable distraction to take Kiril's mind off the colonization of Lynnara.

"I will leave you with your friends for now so you can visit," Anthya said with undue formality. "They will show you to your quarters. I will summon you to lessons after you have settled in." Without waiting for a response, Anthya teleported away.

"Hi, Kiril, I'm Ilene." She offered him her hand.

Speechless, he took her hand and nodded in response.

"What's wrong with you?" Rojaire asked, giving him a soft slap on his side.

The tap helped steady him. "Welcome to Aaia. It is my pleasure to serve," Kiril said finding his voice.

"Have you seen Jack lately?" Kaylya asked right away.

"Yes, just before I left. He's courting my mom."

"Oh really; I thought I detected an attraction between them before Rojaire and I left Earth."

Ilene sighed deeply. "I wouldn't have been able to come if it weren't for Jack easing my mother's pain over my departure."

"How's Quaylyn?" Ilene asked.

"He's fine," Kaylya said. Ilene waited for more, but Kaylya moved on. "Let's take you to your lodging; I believe refreshments are waiting for us there."

The living area assigned to Ilene was much like the one she had been assigned to a few years ago when she, Rahlys, Theon, and Raven came to the Community of the High Council to join the team searching for the lost expedition. The rooms and even the furnishings were carved out of the lavender, rose, and creamy white stone of the mountain itself. The rooms were open to a stone balcony overlooking the extensive gardens, orchards, fields, and athletic arenas that surrounded the Academy Buildings and the Council Hall of the High Council.

The greater view from the balcony was stunning. A cascading river cut through the coastal mountains embracing a wide river valley opened to the Golden Sea.

"So tell me about Quaylyn," Ilene said when the group finally settled on finely woven cushions that softened the carved stone seats encircling a highly polished stone table laden with nuts, bread, fish, and fruit.

"Quaylyn is now Councilor Quaylyn of the High Council of the Crystal Table," Kaylya informed her with a smirk.

"Get out of here!" Ilene exclaimed.

Not understanding the meaning of Ilene's outburst, Kiril was shocked. *Did she ask us to leave?* Kiril telepathed Rojaire.

I don't think so, Rojaire telepathed having experienced similar confusion over the expression before. *I think she is just expressing surprise over the news.*

"Yes, he filled Zayla's vacant seat," Kaylya informed her. "And the High Council agreed to give the Devastated Continent back its real name."

"What is the Devastated Continent's real name?" Ilene asked.

"Lynnara," Kiril said, responding unexpectedly to the topic he was so passionate about.

"Lynnara, that's pretty. So how did you get chosen for the job to be my mentor, Kiril?" Ilene asked with enthused interest.

"Your father and I are close friends," he said pulling himself together. Kiril could hardly believe he was seated here with Theon's daughter. Theon had often spoke of Ilene and how much he missed her. If only Theon could see her now.

"Kiril was with Theon and I on the mapping expedition through the Crescent Mountains," Rojaire explained.

Ilene knew Theon was on the Devastated Continent...Lynnara. "What can you tell me about my father?" she asked, fear of the worst gripping her heart. "When was the last time you were with him?"

"A season ago in a grand valley deep in the Crescent Mountains. We are going to build a colony there," Kiril blurted out with no regard to secrecy.

"That's something we need to discuss," Rojaire said in all seriousness.

Ilene could feel the time/space lag taking its toll. "But my father is alright, isn't he?" she asked suppressing a yawn.

"Yes, and you may yet have a chance to see him," Rojaire assured her.

"We have much to tell you about," Kaylya broke in. "But first you need to get some rest."

"Kaylya is right," Rojaire said. "It is time for us to leave." Heavy weariness prevented Ilene from protesting as they rose to leave. "Get some rest."

☆☆☆☆

Captain Setas couldn't help smiling to herself in her little sheltered garden grotto woven out of living trees and fruiting vines. She set out refreshments on a small table carved from a block of reddish wood. Rojaire had contacted her and wished to talk. Setas was certain this was not an official visit. *Rojaire is up to something; probably something the High Council doesn't approve.*

Of course, not everything she did met with the High Council's approval either. In the eyes of the Community of the High Council, Setas was a trusted ferryboat captain in their service. To Rojaire, she was an ally for a greater cause. Alaia Island was also called Limitation Island because it marked the closest point to the once devastated mainland that energy can be drawn from the elemental forces. Access to the mainland is granted by permission of the High Council only. It was she who ferried those across wishing to span the considerable distance from her island to Lynnara, the Devastated Continent. There was no other way to reach its shores.

It has been quite some time since there has been any contact by the High Council or anyone from the Academy. She still makes occasional trips from her own Alaia Island to Lavender Beach, the gateway to the continent of Lynnara. Several missing persons remain unaccounted for on the continent. She always imagines Theon standing on the beach waiting for her as the ferry approaches, but Theon is never there. No one is ever waiting for her.

Of course, Setas doesn't expect to ever see Theon again, but thinking about him brought her back to Rojaire's impending arrival. She smiled again in anticipation and sat down to wait.

Captain Setas lives alone on the island. In truth, she is more a botanist than a ferryboat captain. Alaia Island is a garden island. Over centuries Setas has cultivated every inch of it, from mountain slope to water's edge, collecting seeds and starts from all over the planet and even a few other worlds in the galaxy in exchange for the service she provides. Because of the overflow she has slowly been introducing hardy species of food producing plants to Lynnara, close to Lavender Beach. She even had Rojaire's mapping expedition plant tree seeds across the continent's coastal region from Lavender Beach all the way to the Crescent Mountains. The little tree seedlings should be emerging about now.

"Greetings, Captain Setas," Rojaire said suddenly standing before her. "Seek heart, not soul."

The ancient woman stared at him studying him intently without speaking. Even seated she looked formidable.

"It is my pleasure to serve," Rojaire added formally bowing to her.

"Greetings, Rogue Rojaire," she crooned hoarsely. In Captain Setas' eyes Rojaire would always be a rogue. This visit was proof of that. "If you are so eager to serve, serve me a drink and be seated. Pour a drink for yourself, too."

Obeying orders Rojaire did so, settling into the only other chair available with a drink in hand.

"So tell me, how have you crossed the High Council this time?" Setas croaked.

"I haven't crossed them yet." Rojaire paused. "For that I will need your help."

"I'm listening."

That was getting to the point fast. Taking a few deep breaths before starting, Rojaire told his tale. He described the meeting with the High Council and the Councilors' decision to return to using Lynnara's original name. Even Stoic Setas proved unable to hide her expression of surprise at this unexpected turn of events.

"Alaia Island, too?" Her frail-looking body almost jumped up out the seat.

"Yes. I petitioned the Council for a charter to start a colony on Lynnara."

Setas gave him a questioning look and motioned for him to continue.

"As you can imagine, my proposal was met with a lot of opposition, but in the end I was offered a challenge. I had three rotations to sell my project to the people. If I could find twenty colonists to go with me by the deadline, I would be granted my charter."

"Ah...," she could see where this was going. "I take it you were unable to find twenty colonists," she rasped, "are you wouldn't be here."

Rojaire hung his head in abject failure. "Five, six at the most, and my time is almost up."

"I see. Tell me about your last mission."

Rojaire told her all, including the secret valley hidden in the Crescent Mountains where Theon, Tassyn, Edty, and two members of the lost expedition, Ollen and Caleeza were currently living. The passage of time was lost to them as they talked, drank, and nibbled on exotic delicacies grown in Setas' gardens. Then Rojaire reached into a pocket of his tunic and pulled out four paper seed packets with colorful depictions of their potential on the fronts and printed instructions on the backs.

"These are seeds from Earth: tomatoes, peppers, watermelon, and corn," Rojaire said handing them to her. "I had a chance to enjoy all these foods on Earth. I don't know if they can adapt to our long days and long nights." Maggie had been planning her Alaska garden shortly before he, Quaylyn, and Kaylya left Earth, and he had asked her to help him acquire seeds of some heat-loving vegetables.

Setas was greatly pleased. She held the seed packets like treasures. For a while they both sat quietly enjoying the beauty that surrounded them. A refreshing breeze beat off the heat.

"Seek heart, not soul," Setas said after a time. "I will help you cross the High Council and the Golden Sea to Lynnara. Let me know when you are ready and how many are going with you when the time comes.

Rojaire could hardly express his gratitude it was so great. His next concern was for Setas. "You should consider coming with us, Captain. The High Council will not be pleased when they discover you have betrayed them."

"Let me worry about that, but I will take your words into consideration. Get your group ready before it's too late." Setas paused. "Be careful, Rojaire. Do not underestimate the power of the High Council."

"I would say the same to you. Seek heart, not soul, my lady." And with that Rojaire was gone.

CHAPTER 9

Earth

Retired Officer Gerald LeBlanc, retired for less than a year, worked tirelessly at establishing a new routine he could live by. He rose at seven, put on the coffee and walked out onto his backyard patio, rain or shine, a small sheltering roof over the door left no room for excuses, to greet the morning before having his first cup. Today he breathed in the promise of another hot Louisiana day.

Then the phone rang.

The unexpected phone call jarred his senses. Gerald had no children to check up on him. The few friends he had contact with had a regular agreed upon schedule for calling and knew their time slots. No one should be calling at this time of day. The phone rang again demanding his attention. With irritation Gerald stepped back in the house, before the coffee even finished brewing, to answer the phone.

"Morning, Gerald!" he heard in his ear before he could say "hello."

"Boss...?" Gerald responded in surprise.

"I called to tell you we found the laser-cutting machine."

It had been months since Gerald heard the Boss's voice and he had to think a moment before figuring out what he was talking about. Slowly the whole episode of disappearing people and a vanished laser-cutting machine among other things came back to the forefront of his mind.

"You found it...where?

"Yeah, well, that's part of the mystery.

"Are you sure it's the same one?" The surveillance recording of a laser-cutting machine vanishing from the science research center in

Baton Rouge played through his head. Gerald recalled his encounter with the bogus Dr. Jeff Robertson, Director of Paranormal Phenomena at the bogus Paranormal Phenomena Research Center in New York City, his Assistant Director Ms. Lucy Sutton who could move objects with her mind; and Brak Alar, the man they were looking for who could vanish in a breath.

"Beyond a doubt; serial numbers match. We found the laser-cutting machine and a lot more ...including a murder scene."

"Murder...."

"You'll want to see this. I'll be by to pick you up in twenty minutes. We can talk on the way there."

The Boss hung up before Gerald could protest he hadn't had breakfast yet. But Gerald had to admit he was intrigued by the news. *Am I about to find out where the laser-cutting machine made its reappearance?* But what about Brak Alar; where did he disappear to?

Despite the inconvenience, Gerald managed to be ready when the Boss pulled up in his driveway. During lulls in the chatter on the police radio, the Boss filled him in.

"Seth Blanchard, age sixteen, was shot in the head by seventeen year old Justin Landry. The only witness to the shooting is the victim's twin sister, Alice Blanchard. She was picked up late last night collapsed along the side of the road and is currently in the hospital recovering from trauma. She tells a bazaar story. According to Alice Blanchard, Justin Landry pulled out a gun when a freezing cold darkness covered the sky and descended upon then while they were having a cookout. Allegedly, Justin Landry started shooting wildly at the dark, hitting her brother and then turning the gun on her, forcing her to run for her life. Justin Landry is already in protected custody. He claims Seth's death was an accident."

Teens playing with guns, Gerald thought to himself, shaking his head sadly. He didn't personally know the kids involved, but he felt sorry for the families. They drove pass the high school, and then the Boss surprised him by turning off the road onto the headland of a sugarcane field.

"The titanium laser-cutting machine was found in a sugarcane field?" Gerald asked incredulously. He could see several vehicles including a swamp buggy parked up ahead.

"No, the incident occurred deep in the woods at the site of an old Cajun house nearly swallowed up by the woods," the Boss said. "I'm telling you, this house must be a hundred and fifty years old ...at least."

"Does either of the families involved own the property?" Gerald asked, his interest piqued.

"No, according to the girl, the boys discovered the place after running off skipping afternoon classes at school. Once found, it became a week-end hideout for the three teens."

They were slowing approaching the gathering of people and vehicles up ahead. A homicide always created a lot of interest.

"The owner of the property, including these cane fields, is ninety-two years old and in assistant living. His name is Charles Broussard. It was *his* grandfather who built the house. Charles Broussard's son, Mark Broussard, now looks after his assets and leases out the farmland. He says he hasn't been to the site of the original family home in years."

When they pulled up, there were more people buzzing around than Gerald originally thought. Several officers guarded the perimeter against curious onlookers gathered with news reporters who could only speculate. Two officers were waiting for them by the swamp buggy. "We're ready to go, Boss," one of them announced and dropped a two-stepper down for easier access into the oversized vehicle.

Gerald had never ridden in a swamp buggy before and became engaged in the experience, but as they progressed deeper into the woods, the idea that the vanishing laser-cutting machine had been found in here seemed increasingly absurd. The woods were dense and in some places trees and brush had been cleared for easier access. Finally they arrived at the house, which looked every bit as old as the Boss had claimed. Gerald couldn't help but reflect on what it must have been like living in the swamplands of South Louisiana back then. The area was cordoned off with police tape and he was not surprised to find as many people milling around here, mostly forensic gathering, as there had been back on the headland. Near the cold remains of a campfire, a stark outline of the victim marked the exact spot where the body once rested. A sprawling, towering, majestic live oak benignly overlooked the crime scene.

"The laser-cutting machine is in here," the Boss said guiding Gerald toward the backdoor. Before entering, Gerald stopped momentarily to gaze at the crumbling masonry of an old cistern by the back of the house that once collected rain for fresh water. It was probably a snake den now he thought as he followed the Boss into the dilapidated back room of the house.

The incongruent presence of the laser-cutting machine would have been laughable were it not for the aura of tragic death that surrounded the place. There was barely space to walk around the massive chunk of steel; the worn plank floor sagged under the weight.

"So how do you think it got here?" the Boss asked Gerald.

It certainly was a good question. Gerald couldn't even speculate; there was no logical explanation that he could come up with. He tried to connect in his mind the video he had seen of the laser cutter disappearing from the science lab workshop and its reappearance here.

"I guess it got here the same way it left the science research center," Gerald said after some thought. Of course, the Boss didn't know anything about Brak Alar, the man the fake paranormal research team had been looking for, and Gerald suspected there was a connection, but it would further defy logic to try and explain how they were connected.

Gerald and the Boss worked their way around the laser-cutting machine and into the central rooms of the house where even more people milled around. A middle-aged man with a slight paunch and a full head of wavy dark-brown hair approached them immediately.

"Mr. Mark Broussard," the Boss said, introducing him to Gerald. "His family owns the property. Mark, this is retired Officer Gerald LeBlanc. He worked the case of the missing merchandise found here."

"Glad to meet you," Mark Broussard said shaking Gerald's hand. "I'm really sorry about what happened here." Gerald felt his sorrow was sincere. "I know the families," he added sadly. "I can't imagine how all his stuff was brought in ...or why? Anyway, when you fellows are done with the investigation, I have a crew ready to dismantle the house. There is quite a bit of valuable old wood in here; it will help pay for Dad's long term care."

Gerald thought it was a shame to tear down such a monument to the past, but he understood the financial burden long term care placed on families.

☆☆☆☆

Despite his promise to help Vince and Maggie with planting the garden, Jack wasted no time settling into Vince's old bachelor pad in the little end-of-the-road town and offering Elaine his assistance at the gift shop. He knew it didn't matter about the gardening. Gardening requires a lot of stooping and bending and Jack didn't have a lot of stooping and bending left in him. He gently swept the plank floors of the crowded little shop, leaning on his broom for a moment to glance up at Elaine closing the till. His heart longed to ease the stark sadness that perpetually sculpted her thin face. It's hard to let a grown child loose to pursue their own life; but ultimately, doing so eventually offers its own rewards. It is harder still to let an adult child leave for another world innumerous light-years away. Jack put the broom away in its closet. *I need to show her that life isn't over...not yet.*

"I'll see you tomorrow," Angela called out as she headed for the door to depart. Angela, now an indispensable full time employee, was the life of the shop; her cheerful industry covering for Elaine's despondency.

"Thanks, Angela. See you tomorrow," Jack said for Elaine, silently lost in her own thoughts.

Before walking out, Angela's eyes met Jack's in mutual unspoken concern for Elaine. *Is she going to be all right?* Jack gave her a reassuring nod and locked the door behind her.

"What do you say I cook dinner for us tonight and we can pass some time playing cards? I make a mean pot of chili and I'm terrible at cards, a win/win situation for you."

While his suggestion didn't raise a smile, she didn't readily refuse.

"I could do the cooking at your place, your kitchen is better equipped than mine, and you could put your feet up while you watch me work. I happen to have a fairly decent bottle of wine to share, too."

Was that a glimmer of a smile? No, false alarm.

"If you want," was all she said dispiritedly and prepared to leave the shop.

An hour later Jack arrived at Elaine's apartment door above the gift shop with a bag of groceries and a bottle of wine, gasping for breath after the long climb up the stairs. "Perhaps my place would have been a better idea after all," he wheezed when Elaine opened the door. "I forgot about the stairs."

"Are you doing all right? You're as white as a ghost," Elaine snapped with a bit of her old bluster to cover genuine concern. "Come in and sit down before you pass out," she ordered, her nurturing instinct taking charge.

Soon Jack had quite recovered and they were browning meat and chopping vegetables. Elaine quickly mixed up a batch of cornbread and put it in the oven. Then with filled wine glasses in hand they headed to the living room to give the chili time to simmer and the cornbread time to bake.

In passing, a painting by the door caught Jack's attention. He had been too winded to notice it before.

"A Rahlys original I see," Jack said pausing in front of the painting to examine it more closely. "It's the crystal, the Oracle of Light; what a beautiful rendition of it."

"It was a gift to Ilene from a former suiter."

"Oh, who was that? I don't recall Ilene ever having a boyfriend in the couple of years I've known her."

"He's dead now; mauled by a bear." Elaine took a seat on the sofa, put her feet up on a strategically placed pillow on the coffee table, and took a sip of wine. "The crystal may have been responsible."

"What...?" Jack came to join her. "What do you mean?"

So Elaine told Jack the story as she knew it, leaving out Theon as much as she could. "It is believed by some that the Oracle somehow purposely led Aaron astray and into the marauding claws of a grizzly because he had evil intent against Rahlys and the crystal."

"That's horrible!"

"He wasn't a very nice guy," Elaine assured him, taking another sip of wine.

Jack could hardly believe what he had heard. When he got up to stir the chili, he stopped momentarily and stared in horror at the portrait of the crystal. Did the crystal have a malignant streak? Was the Oracle judge, jury, and executioner? Despite his skepticism, he felt a cold chill trickle down his spine. As he stared, he thought he saw the crystal float out the picture and even stepped back in panic. Then the timer on the stove clanged loudly drawing his attention. When he looked back, the image of the crystal was firmly embedded in the painting. It must have been his imagination playing tricks on him.

It was almost midnight in the northern Susitna Valley, but still light outside; such was life in the land of long late spring days and marginal nights. "Are you coming to bed?" Maggie asked rising from the sofa, the quilted afghan that had been keeping her feet warm falling to the floor. "You have been at it for hours." Picking the quilt up off the floor and throwing it back on the sofa, she yawned deeply, strolled to Vince and looked over his shoulder at the computer screen that remained a blur without her reading glasses.

"How's it coming?" she asked massaging her husband's shoulders when he failed to respond.

"Fine; that feels good." Vince flexed his back and shoulders enhancing the benefit from her massaging hands. His absorption in his writing had reached a peak that wouldn't subside now until the manuscript was completed.

"You know we have a busy day tomorrow planting the garden," Maggie said kissing him behind the ear. Rahlys will be here early."

Rahlys' participation had been a great help in the overall project and had worked wonders improving her mental state. Over the past few weeks they had teamed up every day preparing the soil, making the rows, and planting peas, potatoes, carrots, lettuce, kale, beets, and turnip seeds. In addition, Maggie had dozens of garden starts, started indoors and hardened off ready to go into the ground: broccoli, cauliflower, cabbage, green onions, kale, zucchini, and yellow squash. To Rahlys' delight Maggie had also started an array of flowers, some already blooming.

Vince had also constructed a small greenhouse of milled lumber and clear plastic for tomatoes, peppers, and cucumbers. The greenhouse conveniently sheltered the garden starts overnight while waiting to be planted.

Tomorrow was June 1st, the so called "first guaranteed frost-free day" for gardeners. There have been years when this rule of thumb didn't pan out. But spring had come on strong this year with little fear of a late killing frost.

"You go ahead and get some rest. I'll be there shortly," Vince assured her.

"Okay," she said giving him a kiss. "Try not to stay up too late."

But when Maggie woke the next morning, she still had the bed to herself. The brilliance of a sunny day seeped through a sliver of a gap between the curtains. From the sounds of chatter and the rattling of dishes, the rest of the family was already up. The smell of bacon, eggs, and blueberry pancakes, Vince's specialty, wafted in from the family room.

I definitely won the lottery when it comes to husbands, Maggie smiled as she tied on a robe.

"Look, Mommy, Daddy made me a heart pancake!" Crystal pointed out excitedly when Maggie walked into the room.

"Mine is an airplane," Rock informed her.

"Good morning, sweetheart," Vince said giving her a kiss and placing a plate with another airplane pancake in front of Leaf. "And what shape pancake would you like this morning?"

"Round will be just fine, thank you. Did you get any sleep last night?"

"I slept a couple of hours on the sofa."

"Why didn't you come to bed?"

"I didn't want to disturb your sleep. We have a busy day of planting ahead of us. And you are a busy mother; you needed to get some rest."

"What about you? You need rest too."

"I'm fine. The manuscript is moving along well and the garden is almost in. I'll have plenty of time later to rest."

After a long leisurely breakfast, the Bradley family poured out of the house into the invitingly warm sunshine. The sunshine was subject to change as some dark scattered clouds were already moving in. "Perfect weather for planting," Vince said.

Vince and Maggie carried trays of plants from the greenhouse where they had spent their last night protected from the elements. "You want to help Mommy and Daddy plant the garden?" Maggie asked the children. The children responded with youthful enthusiasm. "And Leaf, you have to make sure Keiluk doesn't tramp on the rows," she reminded him. Training Keiluk how to behave in a garden was another ongoing project.

"Don't worry, Mom, Keiluk won't step on the rows anymore, huh girl?" Keiluk gave a quick bark of reassurance and Leaf petted her behind the ears.

"I'll get a bucket of water to water the plants," Vince said putting the tray down close to the plant's new home.

"We also need a trowel," Maggie said guiding the young ones to help her carry out more trays and pots of plants from the greenhouse. Then once they were all set, Vince and Maggie showed the children how to trowel out a nest in the row for the plant's new home. They carefully removed a little cabbage plant from its starter container and placed it in the garden soil enriched with composted chicken manure and kitchen scrapes. With colorful plastic cups the little ones watered the cabbage plant in and watched in fascination as the water seeped down into the dirt. Then Leaf pushed dirt over the roots and patted the soil down. One down and many more to go. It was still mostly sunny, although the sun had darted behind a cloud momentarily.

Before they had completed a row, the children started to lose interest and drifted off to play. Maggie and Vince let them off the job; planting would go faster without them anyway. They wanted to finish before it started to rain. "Stay in the yard where we can see you," Vince reminded them.

To Rock and Crystal's delight, Leaf picked up a Frisbee from where it lay on the lawn, right where he had stored it last, and tossed it for Keiluk to chase and catch. Keiluk ran, jumped, and caught the Frisbee, snatching it out of the air. The children cackled with glee.

Vince and Maggie quickly got back to work, the sound of the children's playful shouts reassuring in the background.

"Do it again, Leaf!" Rock sang out.

"Throw it higher," Crystal begged.

Leaf threw the Frisbee higher and further than before. Once again Keiluk performed a flawlessly spectacular catch. The game continued on with the kids joyfully running and shrieking after Keiluk. With each toss Leaf made, the children gradually moved away from the garden site. Maggie and Vince were aware of the sounds of the children playing, but were so engrossed in their work they failed to register over time the increasing distance between them.

"Throw it again, Leaf," Rock cried.

Leaf glanced quickly toward the garden to make sure their parents weren't watching and found them bent over their work with their backs toward them. "Okay; watch this," he said. To impress Crystal and Rock, Leaf drew a little elemental energy from the natural abundance that surrounded them and sent the Frisbee sailing harder, higher, and further than ever before. It flew far and wide, curving in a wide arc downhill, finally landing on the edge of the creek. Keiluk made an astonishing dash for it, arriving at the landing spot in time to catch it. Leaf, Rock, and Crystal quickly ran down to join her.

"She caught it," Rock shouted with excited admiration.

"Of course she did," Leaf said, never doubting Keiluk's magnificence.

"Good, girl," Crystal praised Keiluk, reaching for her to give her a hug. But before Crystal could put her little arms around Keiluk's neck, her foot snagged on an exposed tree root causing her to lose her balance. Instantly Crystal went airborne, arms and legs flailing, as she splashed head first into the rushing creek, swollen from the spring melt.

The cold water instantly took her breath away, paralyzing her as the rushing current carried her away.

"Crystal...!" Rock cried out in a gasp ready to go in after her. Keiluk barked in alarm and jumped in. Leaf's reaction was swift and immediate. In an instant he drew heavily on the elemental forces that surrounded them, teleported Crystal from the frigid waters and gently placed her limp body down on the bank of the creek.

Leaf and Rock quickly dropped down beside her. Keiluk jumped out of the creek and shook off the water before joining them. Something was terribly wrong. Leaf had often heard stories told by Grumpy George and his buddy Jack Faulkner about how quick a man could die of hypothermia in Alaska's frigid waters. Crystal was just a little girl.

"Crystal," Rock moaned unable to comprehend her lack of response. "Why isn't she moving, Leaf?"

Leaf reached out to his little sister; Crystal's arm was cold to the touch, like touching an icicle. He probed deeper and all he could read was cold.

"She's cold; I'll warm her up." Leaf drew deeply on his energy reserves, first warming Crystal's skin, then drying out her wet clothes and hair, and finally sending warmth deep into her core.

"Crystal, wake up," Rock pleaded.

Keiluk barked again; this time with more urgent concern. Keiluk's bark, far more distant than it should have been, drew Maggie and Vince's attention. How did the kids get so far from the garden without them noticing? Moving in the direction of the sound, they quickly spotted the group down by the creek...exactly where they didn't belong.

"Leaf, Crystal, Rock...get back up here," Maggie shouted down to them. "You know you don't belong down there by yourselves."

At that moment Crystal began to move. Leaf continued to stream healing warmth into her body.

"Now!" Vince shouted down for more emphasis when the children failed to get a quick move on.

"We're coming!" Rock shouted back just as Crystal opened her eyes. Keiluk barked again for good measure.

It was then that Rahlys finally arrived for their daily gardening session. Her sudden appearance in the yard distracted Vince and Maggie's attention momentarily, giving the children time to collect themselves.

"Are you alright?" Leaf asked as Crystal sat up. Keiluk circled around them with exuberant relief.

"I fell in the creek," she said matter-of-factly. Leaf and Rock helped her to her feet.

"Leaf had to warm you up," Rock said his voice still trembling some.

"And my clothes are dry," she added, her young mind amazingly acute.

"It's best we don't say anything to Mom and Dad," Leaf conspired as they started back up the hill toward the garden. "They will just get upset."

That made sense.

"Okay," Rock and Crystal readily agreed.

CHAPTER 10

Aaia

"Thank you for showing me around, Kiril. You are a wonderful guide," Ilene said graciously.

"It is my pleasure to serve. I am grateful I had this opportunity to be of service." They had taken a detour through the orchards on the way back to her lodging. He handed her a succulent piece of red-violet fruit freshly plucked from the tree under which they stood.

"Thank you," Ilene said taking the fruit.

"You use those words frequently," Kiril noted.

"Don't you have a simple way to say 'thank you?'" Ilene asked Kiril puzzled.

Kiril struggled to find English words to explain. He was the one who was grateful ... to serve. Expressing gratitude could never be rightfully achieved with the utterance of a single word, or even two ... but the language escaped him.

Ilene didn't hear whatever elaboration Kiril struggled to add. Out of the corner of her eye she spotted Quaylyn walking toward them a short distance away.

Kiril followed her line of sight and understood immediately he had lost Ilene's attention for now. Seeing Councilor Quaylyn reminded him that the councilor may be on Rojaire's side, but Kiril was still not approved. Guiding Ilene around the Academy and surrounding community had proven to be a delightful distraction, but nothing would detour his adamant decision to join the colonists, not even Theon's bewitching daughter.

Ilene took a step toward Quaylyn extending her hands which he cupped in his own, greeting her with a warm smile. "Ilene, it's such a pleasure to see you again. Welcome back to my world."

"Oh, Quaylyn, it's so good to see you," Ilene said exuberantly. Then, "sorry," she added contritely, "Councilor Quaylyn, I should say."

Quaylyn's glacier blue eyes twinkled warmly. "I will always be Quaylyn to you. I'm sorry I haven't met with you sooner."

"I know you have been busy."

"If you would grace me with your company, I would hear news of the friends we share; Vince, Maggie, the children, your mother ... and Rahlys." Ilene noticed his voice softened when he spoke her name.

Kiril fought against an unreasonable surge of jealousy ... or was it envy? Ilene and Quaylyn's friendship had been forged over years of acquaintance. Quaylyn had been to Earth twice, and Ilene and Quaylyn had both been on the mission to Lynnara to search for the expedition led by Sarus. Word had it that Quaylyn lost his heart to Sorceress Rahlys, but still Kiril couldn't help being a little envious of the ease with which the new councilor and Ilene greeted one another.

"I am free right now and would love to chat," Ilene declared, ignoring Kiril.

Then he realized Ilene and Quaylyn were staring at him. Kiril didn't know what to say.

Quaylyn solved the problem for him. "Greetings, Kiril, I'll relieve you of your charge for a while. I promise to see her safely back to her lodging."

He had been dismissed.

"Thank you," Kiril said unexpectedly when no other response came to mind. Shocked by his own utterance, he ported away quickly in embarrassment.

"You are having an impact on him already," Quaylyn said after a moment of stunned silence, then made a suggestion where they could go to talk.

"I would like to take you to a special place where we can be alone. Do you like beaches?"

"I love beaches; especially warm ones."

"Hold on, and I'll take us there." No sooner than he touched her arm they were standing in a sparkling oasis.

Ilene withheld a gasp of awe as her senses absorbed the new surroundings. Several misty waterfalls cascaded down rose, aqua, and creamy white stone into a tropical lagoon embraced by protective cliffs draped in the low colorful foliage. The waters of the lagoon gently licked the sand-painted beach, changing the patterns of swirling color.

"Where are we?" Ilene asked.

"Well, as you would say in Alaska, we are in the middle of nowhere," Quaylyn said with a dimpled smile. They walked the beach to the soothing whispers of the waterfalls. "So how have you been?"

"Great, but what you really want to ask is 'How has Rahlys been?'"

"Am I that easy to read?" Quaylyn asked bowing his head.

"It's your sweet outer demeanor," Ilene laughed. Quaylyn cringed over her comment. Then Ilene spoke to him quietly.

"Rahlys missed you terribly at first. For weeks she was despondent, then she buried herself in her painting. For the longest, she couldn't bear to mention or hear your name. She has slowly returned to us. I spent some weekends with her over the winter, drawing her out. Here lately she has been visiting Vince and Maggie, helping with the garden and sketching scenes with the children."

Ilene paused to let him absorb her words at his own pace. For the longest they strolled silently side by side, each lost for a moment in his and her own thoughts.

"Rahlys will always be the love of my heart," Quaylyn said in heavy sadness long after Ilene expected a response. "Tell me about my good friends Vince and Maggie. I miss them greatly."

"They miss you, too," Ilene reassured him. "Maggie has been gardening hardy and Vince is writing another action/adventure novel. Otherwise, the children keep them busy; you wouldn't believe how big they have grown. Maggie and Vince have their hands full; especially now since Melinda left." The news about Melinda startled him.

"Melinda left her home with Maggie and Vince?" he asked with more concern than she expected. Quaylyn had sensed an inexplicable connection between Melinda and the essence of Droclum... a connection that could still spell trouble for the future, but spared Ilene his concerns.

"Yes, she has returned to Southeast, Alaska, and is staying with her aunt in Ketchikan."

"And Jack Faulkner and your mother?" he asked changing the subject.

Ilene sighed deeply. "Mother is probably brooding over my departure. She is so overly possessive of me," Ilene sighed. "Fortunately, Jack is watching over her. He's staying in Vince's old bachelor pad in town and helping out at the gift shop. He seems to have a real crush on Mother, which is both cute and pathetic."

"Oh? Who is being overly possessive now?"

"I didn't mean it that way at all. Actually, I'm quite grateful that he is there. It's just, really, at their age." They had reached the foot of the nearest waterfall and paused to admire it.

"There is something else I would like to discuss with you," Quaylyn said. Ilene sensed an uneasiness and could easily guess what he was alluding to.

"Does this have anything to do with Rojaire and Kaylya's goal to colonize Lynnara?"

"It does."

Ilene knew Rojaire and Kaylya were having a difficult time finding the minimum number of colonists required. What loomed largest in her heart and mind was the knowledge that Theon was somewhere on that island continent. More than anything she longed to see him. She could only hope that her father was still alive despite his prolonged longevity.

Quaylyn gently turned Ilene to face him and held her hand in his, gazing earnestly into her eyes.

"I want you to know the risk you take if you flee to Lynnara without the High Council's consent."

Ilene stared at Quaylyn in return. Rojaire said Quaylyn had supported his petition at the council meeting. "What do you mean?" she asked cautiously.

"I'm not trying to influence your actions," Quaylyn explained quickly, "Only stating facts. If you cross the wishes of the majority of the council members, you will become a rogue in their eyes and may never see Earth and your mother again."

Ilene gasped at the dire warning.

"So, you think Rojaire could manage transport to Lynnara without the High Council's intervention?"

"He's managed it before."

"But Brakalar is dead," she said, remembering his involvement. *Captain Setas with her ferry was the only access. Could Captain Setas be bribed? Perhaps she sided with Rojaire and Kaylya philosophically.* Ilene couldn't help but wonder.

Then Ilene was struck with an awful fear. "Will you inform the other councilors?"

"I am not a threat to Rojaire," Quaylyn reassured her. "What I really wanted to say is that if you ever need to call on me, I will do all I can to help you ... in any situation."

☆☆☆☆

After Ilene and Quaylyn departed company, she went straight to Kaylya to ask her a few questions. Ilene realized she had been so caught up in the excitement of being back on Aaia, she hadn't paid much attention to the details of the colonization project other than to say she wanted to go. The visit with Quaylyn had opened concerns.

"I had an interesting meeting with Councilor Quaylyn," Ilene said.

"So, that's where you were; I tried to find you to call you to our meeting."

"How much time does Rojaire have left to find twenty colonists?" Ilene asked her friend.

"None," Kaylya say solemnly shaking her head.

"None?" Ilene whispered back startled. Her heart raced. *Will I have to make a decision so soon?*

"Quaylyn said if...." But before Ilene could share her frightening concerns with Kaylya; Rojaire, Traevus, Thayla, and Kiril walked in carrying packs; a tense bunch to be sure. Ilene noticed Thayla wore a blade at her side and carried what looked like another weapon strapped onto the back of her pack. They gathered around Rojaire without saying a word. *Are these all the colonists?*

"Drak is on his way," Rojaire said.

People here have an uncanny knack for answering unspoken questions, Ilene mused quietly to herself.

Rojaire drew energy, enclosing them in what he hoped was a tight dome of concealment. "We have much to discuss," he stated bluntly to those seated around the elegantly carved, gold-flecked stone table that graced Kaylya and Rojaire's living quarters.

"The time granted us by the High Council to find enough colonists for a charter has passed." Rojaire's voice was stern, but to Ilene's surprise there was no sign of bitterness. "If you do not want to go against the wishes of the High Council, you should leave now."

Everyone looked at everyone else, but no one stood to leave. Ilene didn't think her legs would support her if she were even to try. *Will I ever see my mother again? Why is it always a case of having one parent at the expense of the other?*

Rojaire gave Kiril a hard stare, but did not order him to go.

"When do we leave?" Traevus asked to break the silence.

"As soon as Drak arrives."

"I don't have my pack with me," Ilene realized suddenly speaking up; she hadn't known about the meeting ahead of time. It was obvious from Rojaire's reaction that he didn't want her to risk detection by going to get it.

"I have an extra pack and some clothing more suitable for our climate than your own that will fit you," Kaylya readily offered, solving the problem. "I think I can supply everything you will need."

Ilene thought of her flute, which Kaylya would not be able to replace, but said nothing. With a sense of relief she secretly touched Rahlys' star stone stashed in her pocket. It was fortunate she always carried it with her.

There was a commotion at the entrance, and then Drak entered, probably after a silent invitation from Rojaire.

"I brought you some more colonists," he boasted boisterously, burdened with a large pack. He was followed by Zaloka, Kiril's chosen mother, and Wessid, his chosen father, also carrying packs. Kiril jumped out of his seat with alarm, the gasp from his throat masked by Kaylya's startled reaction to the unexpected arrival of Kiril's parents. Had they come to stop Kiril?

"Greetings, Provider Wessid and Ceramist Zaloka. How may I serve?" she asked wondering how to handle the new situation. Kiril may not have a chance to go with them after all.

"Relax, Kaylya; we are here to join you, not betray you," Zaloka huffed. "I'm not letting my boneheaded son slip away without me in his life."

"Greetings, Rojaire and Kaylya. It is my pleasure to serve," Wessid said in the more traditional phrasing. "We have indeed decided to go rogue and join you, if you will have us."

"Are you sure you have thought this through?" Rojaire asked gently.

"Don't look so condescending, Rojaire," Zaloka snapped at him. "We know you plan on sneaking out of here and we're going with you. After all, you wouldn't want us to reveal your plot."

"Calm down, Zaloka," Wessid said. "I don't think threats are needed."

"Welcome," Rojaire beamed. Zaloka and Wessid would be great assets to the colony. "Of course we will have you join us," he said placing a hand on Wessid's shoulder. "You won't regret your decision."

Kiril couldn't believe what he was witnessing. Did his parents really decide to walk out of their comfortable established lives to become rogues ...sacrifice their status as Accepted Ones ...for him? Suddenly he was overcome with love and gratitude and rushed to greet them in a warm embrace.

"Someone else is approaching," Kaylya said before Zaloka and Wessid could even settle into the last two available carved dark wood seats.

What now? Probing gently with his mind Rojaire found Inventor Sulyan at their portal.

"Greetings, Inventor Sulyan," Rojaire addressed him, puzzled by his presence, but inviting him to enter.

"Ah, yes, greetings," the disheveled old inventor muttered, his back slightly hunched under the weight of a pack. Inventor Sulyan was seldom seen among the people and only Rojaire recognized him. The last encounter he had with Sulyan was when he and Theon visited his workshop and were given a compass and a star stone.

Sulyan's thinning spiky red hair gave him a look of confusion as he gazed about at the gathering. Those gathered around the table gawked back. "So why are you gracing us with your presence, Inventor Sulyan? Is there something we can do for you?" Rojaire asked graciously.

"Oh, yes ...," he said as though trying to remember, "there is." Another pause. Then he spoke with certainty. "I want to be a colonist."

After Rojaire's visit to Alaia Island, Captain Setas stayed busy. Her disdain for the High Council compelled her to give her support to Rojaire's dream. She had her own plan of resistance. Without the support of the council, the colonists would be in need of provisions; provisions that she could easily supply. There would be risk to her if caught. Rojaire's warning rang true, but she didn't fear for herself.

In preparation, Setas filled every available vessel, sack, basket, and improvised container she could conceive of with dried fish, grains, fresh and dried fruit, nuts, roots both for consumption and planting, seeds, and even plant starts. The deck was also loaded with tools, household items, even some building materials that could be used to construct a crude shelter. All the provisions sat ready, neatly stacked and tightly secured on the deck of the ferry boat that would take them across the Golden Sea to Lavender Beach on the southwest coast of Lynnara.

Only small narrow catacombs of space remained for Rojaire's few followers. Having done all she can to prepare, all that was left to do was wait.

Setas walked her island kingdom with an understandable sadness. Through centuries of Aaia's revolutions around the sun, Setas' hard work had transformed the little island into her very own paradise.

I had thought I would spend the end of my longevity here, an end long overdue, but apparently I have one adventure left. Let the High Council come after me if they wish; they will have to reach me first. We just have to make it a short distance beyond the bay to escape. Alaia Island can take care of itself.

That thought brought on a sense of urgency. Where was Rojaire? He should be here by now. As though summoned by her will, Rojaire and an amusing mismatch of characters appeared before her. Setas cackled with dry raspy laughter. "You call these colonist?"

"Greetings, Captain Setas..." Rojaire began, but he wasn't given a chance to finish.

"You're late!" Captain Setas croaked. "Get on the ferry before we have a visit by the High Council." There were a few more bodies than Rojaire had indicated, but she would squeeze them in somehow.

Unwilling to argue, the colonists climbed on board. "What is all this?" Rojaire asked as they sought room to settle.

"Our survival," Captain Setas replied, releasing the mooring, and engaging the crystal powered drive. By Seaa's light reflecting luminously off the water she eased the cumbersome vessel out of the bay, slower than she would have liked, but the heavily laden deck gave her no choice. They were too low in the water to go fast. The ferry was leaving the protection of the bay and diving into a gently rolling sea when she detected a faint message from the High Council ... which she decided to ignore. They were already beyond the range of teleportation and soon they would be beyond the range of telepathy. Alaia Island receded in the distance. Finally she took a deep tension-releasing breath.

"We made it," Captain Setas chortled when Rojaire squeezed through covered mounds of cargo, dampened by sea spray, to reach her at the control pedestal.

"Are you sure?" he asked hopefully, watching the ferry's long pointed prow pierce the rolling waves.

"Absolutely, at least until they can build a boat," she chuckled.

There could be no doubt about it; Captain Setas had abandoned her island. The extent of her sacrifice nearly overwhelmed Rojaire.

"So tell me about my fellow colonists," Captain Setas said after the pace and direction had become comfortable to maintain. "I see you've added a few since our last communication."

"There were a few surprise last moment joiners. You didn't leave much space for passengers," Rojaire admonished her mildly. He couldn't help but smile.

"You exceeded my expectations." Setas' raspy voice was barely audible above the low hum of the crystal-powered drive and the hiss of rushing water. "I thought new person Kiril was to be left behind."

"He would not be denied. Also things have changed. Two of the new-comers are Kiril's chosen parents, Zaloka and Wessid."

"A rogue family...interesting. And Theon's Earth daughter returns."

"Yes, she hopes to see her father again."

I hope to see her father again, too, Setas admitted only to herself. She lapsed into thoughtful silence, her reflections dancing with the starlight on the surface of the water. *Could Theon still be alive?*

"Who's the big muscle woman?" Captain Setas eventually asked.

"Thayla is a warrior princess from Twaka; a friend of a friend. I have to admit I don't really know much about her myself. Apparently every world produces its ratio of free spirits."

"High credentials. Do you know more about the older, confused-looking fellow?"

"That's Inventor Sulyan."

"Inventor Sulyan!" she barked in surprise. Even Setas had heard of the eccentric recluse. She would have said more except for the fact that she had also joined the group and was just as unlikely a colonist. "And the other fellow?"

"Drak is a furniture builder, hobbyist historian and cartographer, also from Kiril's community." Rojaire did not elaborate on the role one of Drak's maps had already played in the project. There would be time for that after they landed in their new world.

After repeated refusals by Setas to let Rojaire relieve her at the controls, he slipped back through the cargo to rejoin Kaylya, Traevus, Kiril, Ilene, and Thayla in a protected pocket nearly enclosed by sacks, baskets, and crates of food from which everyone had already had their fill. Zaloka and Wessid had found their own little cubicle of space he was informed, and Drak and Sulyan must have done the same.

"At least we won't go hungry right away," Rojaire said biting into a crusty roll after settling in next to Kaylya.

"So Captain Setas is joining us?" Kaylya asked with a hand wave indicating all the freight."

"Yes, for her own safety, she must." Rojaire didn't realize how exhausted he was until he allowed himself to relax.

"Do you think she can make the trip to the valley?"

"Theon made it. Captain Setas is as tough as Theon."

Kaylya didn't get a chance to ask another question. With a piece of uneaten bread in his hand, Rojaire fell asleep. Feeling tension and stress ease now they were safely out of the High Council's reach, Kaylya cuddled up next to him. Through the remainder of the period of darkness and into the dawn of a new day Rojaire and Kaylya slept a dreamless sleep.

Groggily Kaylya opened her eyes to a new period of light. Beside her Rojaire slept still. The ferry moved smoothly through the water. Were they almost there?

"Wake up," Kaylya whispered gently. Rojaire opened his eyes to bright sunlight and jumped up.

"Why didn't you wake me?" he asked struggling to get his bearing.

"I just did, love of my heart."

The others were gone. Rojaire climbed up on some crates he hoped could withstand his weight to get a view. Lynnara loomed before him. He spotted several of the colonists on perches of their own where they could watch the approach.

"What do you see?" Kaylya asked.

"We're coming into the bay now," he informed her, and offered her a hand, helping lift her up to him. Leaning over a covered bale of something, they shared a lingering kiss as they entered the calm waters of the bay. Then climbing back down, they made their way to Captain Setas. Lavender Beach stretched out before them. Off to the right the Zayla River rippled into the bay. Beyond the sandy beach an abundance of lush colorful fruit bearing bushes and edible plant life grew thickly, thinning as they moved inland. With astonishing precision, the captain pierced the lavender sand with the ferry's long pointed prow, then powered the point in and shut off the power.

They had arrived.

The group disembarked from the ferry to stretch cramped limbs with near reverence for the significance of the event. For Drak, Wessid, Zaloka, Thayla, and Inventor Sulyan it was their first encounter with their new home, but for Rojaire, Kaylya, Traevus, and Kiril it was a homecoming. Things were different for Ilene and Captain Setas who looked upon the land with mixed emotions.

Ilene had dreamed of returning to the "Devastated Continent" one day; although she had seriously doubted she would ever have the opportunity. In her dreams, her father was always there waiting for her when she arrived. In reality she didn't know if she would find him alive. Several years ago when she had joined the search for the lost expedition, she had been promised a safe return home once the mission was complete. This time she had been given a warning that she may never return. Yet, as she looked out over the quiet undisturbed vastness, the landscape tugged at her heartstrings.

Instead of facing inland, Captain Setas stared out toward the little opening that led out to sea. The urge to leave was strong. She forced herself to turn about and study the land. She had been here many times, but never with the intent to stay. The area near Lavender Beach and along the Zayla River boasted a variety of food producing growth. Many of the plant species that now flourished along the coast, she had introduced. So why didn't Theon settle near Lavender Beach where food was relatively plentiful? It didn't make sense.

After a quick look around to take it all in, the colonists were ready to get to work. Everyone turned to Rojaire for leadership, so he called a meeting. They gathered in the shade of some shrubbery near the stream. Even though they were in the winter season, it could still get hot in the sun. A rock matted with a covering of dead grass provided Captain Setas a much needed seat.

"Where is the colony?" Setas croaked. "Where are Theon and the others? I think it is time you tell us."

"Gladly; I have been longing to. I didn't want to talk about it until we were safely on Lynnara," Rojaire explained. "It's a long story with some surprising twists, so you might as well get comfortable."

"I like stories," Thayla said, which got a chuckle from the group. Positioning the satchel that held the blade into a position of readiness, she settled cross-legged on the ground. The rest followed suit. Kaylya translated for Ilene. Although Kiril and Traevus had shared the adventure, they sat back and let Rojaire tell the story.

"On our last trip, along the way in route to the Crescent Mountains, we found Ollen, a member of the lost expedition. He was living quite comfortably in a shelter he built in what we now call the Cremyn Valley."

"You may be interested to learn, Zaloka, that Ollen even built his own crude kiln to fire pottery," Traevus added.

"Interesting, so is that where we are headed?" Setas asked.

"Yes," Rojaire said, "but Ollen isn't there. He agreed to join our mission and went with us to map the passage through the mountains."

"You found another one!" Ilene exclaimed after Kaylya translated. They had found only Traevus on the journey to find them. "So you must know what happened to Cremyn and the others."

"He told us what happened to Cremyn," Rojaire answered in English. "According to Ollen, Cremyn disappeared in the ruins of the Temple of Tranquility. When she was finally found, her mind was totally blank."

"I hope we aren't going there," Sulyan whispered.

"We aren't," Rojaire assured them. "Ollen volunteered to take Cremyn back to Lavender Beach for pickup by Captain Setas, but she died along the way. Ollen buried her in the grave we found in the Zayla Valley." Kaylya translated for the others.

"Ollen's shelter in the Cremyn Valley is not our final destination, although it could be for some of you. It is quite a substantial shelter as you will see. Our actual destination is in the Crescent Mountains. The route is a long and difficult one. It was particularly hard for Theon, but he persevered." Rojaire stole a quick glance at Setas and Sulyan; once again they would be slowed down by elders.

"Drak, if I may include you in the story."

"Of course, Rojaire, proceed." Kiril had already told him of discovering his great grandfather's special valley. He assumed Rojaire was about to reveal the discovery to the others.

"Before Theon, Traevus, Kiril, Tassyn, Edty and I left on the mapping expedition through the Crescent Mountains, Drak gave Kiril a map. The map depicted a secret hidden valley." Faces turned to look at Drak and Kiril with interest.

"Deep in the mountains, we came across a rock slide that had opened up the side of a lava tunnel giving access to a small valley. The small valley lead to a grand valley, the secret hidden valley depicted in Kiril's map."

"You found a secret valley? What is it like?" Zaloka asked in amazed wonderment.

"I'm liking the story so far," Thayla said. "Who made the map you gave to Kiril?" she asked Drak.

"Great Grandfather Vestan, I guess you could say, he was a rogue explorer in his own time," Drak chuckled.

"Our valley is beautiful ... lush ... bountiful ...." Rojaire nearly danced with excitement with each word. "Waterfalls cascade down rock cliffs ...

gemstones sparkle in elaborate cave systems ... and living animals graze in open meadows."

"What? Animals!" Wessid exclaimed in surprise. There were shocked gasps all around. "What kind of animals?" His son Kiril had been part of all this. Was it because of this valley that he so wanted to return?

"Life forms never seen before," he said with awe. Rojaire could see their excitement grow. He described herds of silver kurpers, tall creatures that ate trees, and delicate flying callelas. He also told them about the large prints they'd found that Theon believes belong to a large carnivore.

"Has anyone been eaten?" Inventor Sulyan asked with concern.

"No, nothing like that."

"There is no beast I can't fight," Thayla assured Sulyan tapping her blade.

"Is my father in this valley?" Ilene asked.

"Yes, and there's more," Rojaire said in both languages, drawing back their attention. "We still had our mission to complete, and when we came to the end of the passage through the mountains we found Caleeza, another member of the lost expedition.

"Another one?" Drak couldn't contain his surprise. Kiril had told him of finding the valley, but had said nothing of Ollen and Caleeza.

"The same Caleeza who visited the Bradley family on Earth?" Ilene asked.

"The same. She told us a bizarre, but fascinating, story of how the members of her expedition vanished in the Crystalline Landscape. She also described her own trip to Earth and back, to find Sarus transformed, melded with the field of crystals."

"Where is Caleeza now?" Ilene asked. She knew Maggie and Vince would be glad to hear that Caleeza had been found. Then she remembered she would never have the opportunity to tell them.

"Theon, Tassyn, Edty, Ollen, and Caleeza are settled in the valley hidden in the Crescent Mountains ... waiting for us to join them."

CHAPTER 11

Aaia

When Caleeza opened her eyes again she was alone in the little cave dimly lit by the iridescently glowing foliage covering the ceiling and walls. *How long have I been out? I have to find my way back and find Ollen.* She could picture Ollen desperately searching for her. There was little chance he would find her here ...wherever here was.

The pain in her head had diminished down to a dull ache. Over her body's resistance, she forced herself up into a sitting position, then paused to rest. When the dizziness subsided, she swung her legs off the pallet that served as a bed so her feet rested on the floor of the cave, then rolled onto her knees. Ready to try standing, Caleeza gingerly pushed herself upright. She wobbled dizzily at first, but became more stable in time. Once she felt firm on her feet, she moved about searching the small chamber for the shaft she had fallen through, but could find no evidence of it. *That's strange; I thought it was right here.* Chitter couldn't have moved her far.

Then she remembered she couldn't find the star stone. Reaching into a pouch of her tunic she searched for it again. It wasn't there; she really must have lost it in the fall. She then began searching the rough stone floor, but found nothing.

Caleeza left the little chamber following the curvature of the cavern walls and soon found bright sunlight streaming in from the cave entrance. Her violet eyes squinting, she stepped unhindered out into the warm sunshine. What she saw before her was a jungle wilderness in flower. She sniffed the perfumed air, detecting a whiff of wood smoke among the scented blossoms. There was no movement, no sound. Where was Chitter and those like her? Looking around there seemed to be no evidence of habitation in the area.

Caleeza made her way to the nearest massive tree seeking shade. The distance was short, but the excursion drained her of energy and she dropped down on a conveniently located spongy soft mound of vegetation. Angry chittering erupted loudly above her. Looking up into the wide-spreading branches of the tree, Caleeza spotter Chitter high above her. She watched amazed as Chitter looped down an astonishing network of woven vines, finally landing gracefully on the ground beside her. She still wore the unusual sash. Seeing it in the bright light of day, Caleeza realized the sash was actually a tool belt of sorts with pouches to carry implements. It was made of crystal floss, aged from wear and use. The pouches appeared to be empty.

Chitter! Chitter! Chitter!

The creature seemed agitated about something, but she could make no sense of it. Caleeza was sure she was getting a thorough chewing out. Finally after much gesturing and chittering, there may have been some variations in the sounds, Caleeza realized that she was sitting on a table laden with harvested food. No wonder the creature was so upset. She got up from her comfortable seat as quickly as her weakened condition would let her and tried to apologize. “I’m so sorry, I didn’t know. I’m not thinking straight.”

Chitter! Chitter! Chitter!

Then the creature pulled out what looked like a sharp stone knife. So there are things in those pouches after all. Was she about to be attacked? Her senses on heightened alert, she took a step back, but Chitter diverted her attention from Caleeza and began cutting up the squashed produce.

Caleeza took a couple of calming deep breathes to ease her heart rate. *I have to find a way to communicate.*

Circling around to the other side of the work area, Caleeza sat down on the ground opposite her hostess. The table was low, more suited for Chitter’s height, especially when she sat on her haunches. When she managed to make eye contact, Chitter gave her a questioning look. Seizing the moment, Caleeza pointed to herself and said, “Caleeza.”

Chitter. Chitter.

She said her name again. "Caleeza."

"Cha-lit-ta."

Maybe she came a little closer to producing the sounds; Caleeza couldn't really tell. So she tried something else.

"I ... Caleeza," she said pointing first to herself and then to her companion "...you ...?"

"Chittere," she said softly to Caleeza's surprise. It sounded so much like "Chitter," but when she tried to reproduce it, the response from her companion was negative. After several tries Caleeza finally gave up.

"I will just have to call you Chitter and you can call me whatever you like."

That seemed to be agreeable to Chitter for she nodded her head and returned to her task of chopping vegetables. Were the vegetables to be cooked, Caleeza wondered? The sleeping broth she had been given had been heated. She glanced around looking for a fire place.

As though reading her mind, Chitter returned the knife to its pouch, gathered up the corners of the woven mat the vegetables had been chopped on, and tied it up with a piece of cord she pulled from another pouch of her sash. Then she motioned for Caleeza to follow her.

Caleeza's bruises protested as she slowly rose to do so.

Chitter led her down a shaded jungle path through trees and blossoming foliage to a small open meadow where a ring of hot coals encircled a center cooking stone in a stone pit. Placing her bundle down, she picked up a long stout stick with a blackened tip and slipped it through the tied corners of the fiber mat. Using the stick as an extension of her arms, she carefully placed the bundle of chopped vegetables onto the cooking stone, woven mat and all. A large gourd filled with water stood near the fireplace. Chitter picked up a small gourd attached to a long stick and used it as a dipper to sprinkle water over the woven mat of plant fibers, creating steam. Soon the aroma of steaming herbs and vegetables seasoned the air. Dinner was on.

Caleeza indicated the water and dipper. "May I have a drink?"

Chitter chattered what came across as an affirmative in intonation and inflection and even served up a dipper of water to her. After drinking her fill, Caleeza handed the dipper back.

"Thank you," Caleeza said, using the English vernacular for expediency ...after all, Chitter wouldn't know the difference. After months spent on Earth she had been thrilled to hear her native language again when Sarus returned her to the Crystalline Landscape and Rojaire and this team found her in the interior of the continent. More recently, she and Theon conversed in English from time to time to enjoy its vivid "color." Theon had spent most of his longevity on Earth and was a master of centuries of its many subtleties.

After steaming dinner one more time, Chitter led her into the shade of the trees where a moss covered stump invitingly served for a chair. This time Caleeza checked carefully to confirm it was what it appeared to be before sitting down. Chitter didn't require a chair, preferring to sit on her own haunches.

Having quenched her thirst, it wasn't long before Caleeza's stomach began to growl. Chitter heard it and loped off a short distance on all fours to a tall, broad-leaf purple and orange shrub and plucked off two large pieces of fruit covered with bright orange shaggy husks. Chitter walked back upright and handed Caleeza one. The outer husk dented easily in her hand indicating a soft interior. Following Chitter's example, she peeled back the husk revealing a creamy white fruit with the consistency of vanilla pudding and a citrus smell. Chitter showed her how to tear off a sliver of the harder outer husk near the stem and utilize it like a spoon. It was delicious and tasted like yogurt, a food she had experienced on Earth. The worse of her hunger was quickly abated.

"Where are the others?" Caleeza asked looking around, still confused by Chitter's seemingly solitary existence. Chitter's almost human facial expression became sadly pensive, but she didn't respond. Caleeza chalked it up to an inability to communicate, although at times Chitter seemed to telepathically understand. A long silence ensued. She had to try again.

"Where did you find *me*?" she asked next, just to dispel the quiet. Once again, Chitter reacted as though she understood the question. Beckoning for her to follow, she led Caleeza back down the jungle path to the small cavern covered in iridescent plant life. Caleeza's heart swelled with hope. She had to find her way back to the others. That hope was dashed when Chitter led her back to the small cave with the pallet bed and the iridescently glowing plants.

"You found me here?" Once again her eyes scanned the walls and ceiling. "But how did I get here?" she asked exasperated. She had already searched the place. There was no long tunnel or shaft emptying into the cave that she could see. Unless the plant growth concealed it.

Without offering any explanation, Caleeza hurried off to retrieve the long cooking pole from their picnic site and returned with heart pounding. Lifting the pole straight up overhead, Caleeza began tapping the ceiling and walls of the cave. Over and over again she pushed the end of the pole up, inadvertently breaking off clumps of the luminous growth. Over and over again the tip of the pole met with solid rock. Chitter chattered at her questioningly, apparently thinking she had lost her mind. With growing frustration and despair she tapped on until there was no place left to explore.

There was no opening to be found; no pathway back to Ollen, Theon, Tassyn and Edty. Her energy reserve now exhausted, she slumped down to the gravel floor in exhaustion.

☆☆☆☆

"Where did you plant my trees?" Captain Setas asked Rojaire after a lengthy discussion among the colonists ended in an agreed upon course of action. The plan was to transfer all the freight on the deck of the ferry to Ollen's shelter in the Cremyn Valley which would be the encampment for the first leg of the journey to the valley hidden in the mountains. It would require several trips, but the effort would be worth it. Rojaire estimated the strongest among them; Kaylya, Traevus, Wessid, Thayla, Ilene, and himself could make a couple of return trips in the time it will take for Kiril to lead Captain Setas, Inventor Sulyan, Drak, and Zaloka to the shelter. Rojaire had a lot more on his mind than trees, but he remained patient. The food and supplies Captain Setas had supplied would maintain the colonists for some time. He owed her his gratitude.

"The first planting isn't far from here," Rojaire said pointing toward the northeast. "Kiril should be able to pinpoint the area for you."

"What about my ship?"

"We will anchor it more securely and hope it is still here if we should ever need it. There is no telling how long it will be before the High Council finds a way to come looking for us. Hopefully they won't bother trying."

Rojaire moved off to join the pack team and secure the ferry as promised. The pack team would blaze the trail ahead, doubling back after a rest to bring in another load. Kiril, Drak, and Zaloka would also carry full packs even though they would be traveling with the slower group while Inventor Sulyan and Captain Setas were only required to carry their personal belongings and the food and water they would consume along the way.

The pack team loaded up on food, tools, and some useful household items. Kiril wished to be with them. How did he get stuck with the slow ones and separated from Ilene? Led by Rojaire and Traevus, the pack team headed out right away and were soon out of sight, leaving Kiril to organize the second group into forward motion.

"Are you sure you know where we're going, Kiril?" his mother asked.

"Let's hope so," Inventor Sulyan added.

Drak answered for him. "Of course he knows where we're going; he was part of the mapping expedition, remember?"

"Is everyone ready?" Kiril asked hopefully, still wishing he were part of the pack team.

"Lead on, boy," Captain Setas croaked. "We will follow you."

They had only gone a short distance ... a distance that took longer to cover than it should have in Kiril's opinion ... when Captain Setas asked again, "Where are my trees?" By now they all knew the story of the tree seeds Captain Setas had entrusted the mapping expedition to plant along the way.

"A little further ahead, we're almost there." Kiril had participated in the actual planting of the tree seeds and wondered curiously what they would find.

When they were near the site of the first planting, Kiril had them drop their packs and follow him. He led Captain Setas, already provided with a walking stick, up a low rise that quickly flattened out again overlooking the valley. Upon reaching the meadow, the colonists paused to catch their breaths and to admire the view. The Zayla River snaked through a broad valley of low gently rolling lavender hills under a gold white sky. Colorful foliage and shrubs of blue, blue-green, pinkish green, red, orange, and gold grew along the banks of the river, but this vegetation quickly became sparse on the hills and valleys further from the river and the coast. A few groves of Zaota trees could be seen in the distance.

Zaloka noticed Captain Setas scratching at the ground through the sparse low growth with her stick and walked to her. "What exactly are we looking for?" she asked.

"This," Setas said beaming as she continued to cultivate around a little blue and orange tree seedling about a hand span high. With the discovery of one, a search for more began in earnest, and soon they had found dozens of the promising little trees.

"We did it," Kiril beamed as he located more of the little saplings. But they needed to move on. Setas didn't really want to leave her little trees and would have stayed if the tree seedling could have provided her with some shade. With some effort Kiril got the group focused back to moving on their way. Finally with visions of a mature forest in Lynnara's future, they headed back down the low rise to their packs.

The sight of what may one day be a little patch of forest, inspired the group with a new surge of determination. After that, progress was steady despite frequent grazing on berries and ground nuts, but as the day progressed the vegetation grew sparser and the sun glared hotter, requiring frequent rests to cool down in the shade of the scant clumps of bushes along the way. They were scheduled to take their first prolonged rest when they reached the confluence of the Cremyn and Zayla rivers, but it was obvious to Kiril they wouldn't make it that far before they would need some sleep. So when they came to a clump of zaota trees offering natural grass hut like shelters, Kiril called a halt.

Zaloka, Sulyan, and Drak had never seen a zaota tree before. To Zaloka, zaota trees looked more like giant leafy domes than trees. But Captain Setas understood their significance and without a word to the others, parted one of the tree's long thick blue-green and gold skirts enough to pass through and disappear within. No one dared challenge the captain's privacy.

"Where did she go?" Sulyan asked a bit puzzled.

"To her private sleeping chamber," Kiril explained.

There were three trees in the small zaota grove growing several long paces apart for five people. Drak and Inventor Sulyan, having already forged an unexpected friendship on the ferry crossing, decided to share a shelter. Kiril led his mother to the other.

"We will be comfortable in here," he said, parting the long billowing growth to reveal the invitingly dark interior.

"How fascinating," Zaloka said, grateful for a retreat from the hot sun. Upon entering the cool, roomy shade under the zaota tree, she immediately dropped her pack and settled down onto a cushiony bed of dry shriveled leaves. "Yes, this is nice; I will sleep comfortably here; and I'm so tired."

"Would you like something to eat?" he asked although they had been foraging all day. "No, I'm too tired to eat. I can only imagine how Captain Setas and Inventor Sulyan must feel." Following his mother's example, Kiril also got comfortable.

For some time mother and son lay quietly, separated only by the tree's sturdy trunk. Kiril could not sleep. He tried to bring up the topic of coming to Lynnara, but he didn't know what to say. Should he apologize, ask forgiveness, plead his case, try to win her over? Her life has changed forever, and it is all his fault. He was still grappling with the fact that Zaloka and Wessid had joined the quest and assumed Zaloka was already asleep when she broke the silence.

"I understand," she said simply.

The words were heartfelt and Kiril understood he was forgiven. Salty tears burned his eyes.

"But why ... why did you come? Won't you miss all your friends, everyone you know, life in the community?" he asked.

Zaloka gave herself some time to think before answering. Was it just because of Kiril? Her life had been comfortable, if not especially adventurous. She did what she was told, made her pottery, and never lacked for anything; at least she had all the High Council felt she needed. When she and Wessid were chosen to produce a new person, she had been elated. It was an honor bestowed on few.

"I want to be free to think on my own," she said finally. "I want to feel what it is like to be totally free."

"How did you know...?" he asked, his voice gargled with emotion.

"How did I know you would defy me, your chosen father, the Academy, the High Council, and common sense?" Instead of sounding angry she almost sounded proud. There was a pause before she answered.

"Because you are my son, and you are destined for greatness."

After their period of sleep and prolonged rest, they continued to follow the Zayla River northeast, the valley narrowing as they drew nearer to the mouth of the Cremyn River. Captain Setas demanded to see every tree planting. To her delight, they found many more promising tree seedlings along the way.

Things went smoother as time progressed. It was still slower going than Kiril would have liked, but he no longer complained. He could now see the positive side of things and felt content. He was back on Lynnara and had family with him. Drak fell in that category along with his parents. He was headed back to the valley where Theon and the others waited; it was just going to take a while to get there. Furthermore, Theon's daughter was with them. And the best part, he was finally free of the Academy. He just had to learn patience.

The sun had begun its descent toward the west when Kiril's group reached the confluence of the two rivers, making it obvious they would not reach the shelter before the period of darkness as he had hoped. At the rate they were going, Kiril doubted they would even make it to the canyon. Then would come the hard part. The steep rocky canyon would force them to leave the Cremyn River and trek across high country to reach the Cremyn Valley and Ollen's shelter on the other side. They can follow the Cremyn River to the canyon, but then they will have to cross the highlands to circumvent the impassable canyon. Having traveled with his group this far, he now understood their strengths and weaknesses. Going uphill was going to be difficult. How was he going to get Captain Setas and Inventor Sulyan across?

Kiril didn't know it, but the answer was coming toward them. Soon after he called for a pause to take a short rest; Rojaire, Kaylya, Traevus, Ilene, and Thayla appeared around a curve in the riverbed. Kiril walked out to meet them.

"Greetings, Kiril, I see you made it this far without losing anyone," Rojaire said after taking a quick distant head count.

Kiril was about to point out that Rojaire was short one person when Zaloka came running up behind him.

"Where's Wessid?" she asked worriedly.

"We left him back at the shelter with a slightly sprained ankle. He's fine; he just needed to rest." He didn't tell her Ilene had drawn on healing energy while examining Wessid's ankle using her star stone.

"Hello, Kiril," Ilene said sidling up to him along the way. "Good to see you. We made it to the shelter. This Ollen fellow did a good job," she said excitedly.

"Hello..." Again Kiril searched for words, furious over his failure.

"Hello, Kiril," Thayla said coyly imitating Ilene, coming up on his other side. She gave him a teasing wink. "Good to see you."

"You speak English, too?" Kiril said surprising himself.

"We have been speaking English all the way back from the shelter," Ilene explained. "Rojaire and Kaylya already have a grasp of the language and Thayla and Traevus wanted to learn it. Thayla is really doing great!"

"I fast learn," Thayla said proudly, which made Kiril feel even worse.

"Traevus and Ilene have volunteered to relieve you, Kiril," Rojaire said when they joined the others resting on rocks along the stream bed. "They will lead your group across the hills and you can help Kaylya, Thayla, and I take in another load."

"We'll trade packs," Traevus said offering Kiril his empty one. "And I'll need the star stone."

"Ilene also has a star stone," Traevus whispered to Kiril. "We will help Captain Setas and Inventor Sulyan over the highlands."

Kiril couldn't believe his luck. He took the empty pack and handed Traevus the star stone. There was only one thing wrong with this arrangement; once again he and Ilene were in opposite groups.

☆☆☆☆

"Why haven't Ollen and Caleeza returned yet?" Edty asked Tassyn.

It was a question Tassyn had been asking in his own mind for quite some time. He had his back toward Edty as he stoked the fire in the outdoor cooking pit, a good thing since he didn't want Edty to see the concern in his face. Edty may be slow with concepts, but he read emotions well.

"Perhaps the valley is larger than we thought," Tassyn said as nonchalantly as he could. He thought of searching for them, but he couldn't leave Edty and Theon to survive on their own for such an unknown length of time.

The colony had seemed so sustainable when they had been together. Even after Rojaire, Traevus, and Kiril left, although the valley was lonelier, the remaining five continued to survive comfortably. But their survival seemed far more tenuous without Ollen and Caleeza. When Theon was gone, it would be just Edty and him, alone in a big empty valley on a big empty continent.

"But why aren't they back?" Edty whined. He wasn't willing to give up the topic that easily. "They said they would be back by now." His voice quivered and his thin shoulders slumped forward. "The bear monster might have eaten them." Ever since they found clawed prints in moist soil and Theon described the bears in a territory on Earth he called Alaska, Edty has dreadfully feared the bear monsters.

"They haven't been eaten," Tassyn said simply.

"How do you know?"

"Because one of them would have gotten away to tell us about it," Theon said in aggravation. Tassyn and Edty turned and watched Theon's slow aching progress forward to his favorite cushioned seat by the fire. Edty jumped up to offer assistance, but Theon fought him off with his walking staff.

"Out of my way!" he bellowed. With proud determination he pushed himself even harder, then eased into his seat with a suppressed sigh. Tassyn poured a cup of the tea Caleeza had instructed him to steep to ease the pain in Theon's joints and served it to him. "I don't want tea. Give me some food."

"Drink it anyway," Tassyn ordered. Then he ladled up a bowl of hearty soup made with wild grains and vegetables. "Try this," he said, taking it to him.

"Where's the meat?" Theon asked eyeing it suspiciously. Tassyn didn't bother to answer. The herds of kurpers were no longer around. Where they had gone was unknown. Theon ate without further complaint. The soup was actually pretty good, but he didn't say so out loud. "Now what are you doing?" he asked.

"I'm making flatbread," Tassyn said. "Edty, how about gathering some more dry branches for firewood? I will need a hot fire to bake bread."

"Sure, anything for hot bread," he said, cheered by the prospect.

Tassyn knew Edty would have to forage wide of their camp to gather deadwood, the easy close pickings now long gone. "I'm worried about Ollen and Caleeza," Tassyn said to Theon as soon as Edty was out of hearing.

"So am I," Theon admitted, switching from a grouchy tone to a serious one. "They should have been back by now."

"Should I go looking for them? I hate the thought of leaving you alone with Edty."

Theon sighed. "You should do what your heart tells you to do. And don't worry about me; I can take care of myself. But maybe you should wait until after the period of darkness," he said indicating the sun ready to dip below the western mountain ridge. "You will be less likely to miss something in full light."

There was a long quiet during which neither man spoke. Tassyn knew Theon's advice was sound.

"Then I will set out when the sun rises again," Tassyn said.

Theon nodded his head in agreement.

CHAPTER 12

Earth

Standing on the deck of the Alaska Marine Highway ferry *Columbia* as it pulled away from the dock, Melinda could just make out Greg's thin, lithe form covered in rain gear against the persistent rainy mist. He was still waving farewell when a creeping tendril of fog obscured him from her view. She would miss her cousin's humor and support. The farewell she had received from Aunt Adele had been quite different.

"Don't forget to call from time to time..." then remembering Melinda didn't talk... "Well, get a message to us, somehow, if you have problems. I packed you a lunch and some snacks to take with you. You know the food on the ferry will be outrageously expensive."

Thank you.

Melinda's silent, yet "heard" thanks, spooked her aunt a bit. It always did. Even though they had gotten closer, she could sense Aunt Adele's somewhat relief that her unusual niece was leaving. But she sensed a little sadness too.

Like a dreamscape, Ketchikan faded into the mist until only water and cloud-shrouded mountains surrounded them. Melinda was headed into the unknown. Her ticket would take her all the way to Bellingham, Washington ...beyond Alaska ...even beyond Canada. Alaskans would say she was going "outside." The local colloquialism suggested another world, something vastly different from what she was used to. She was going south. Soon she would be further south than she has ever been before. What she would find when she got there she did not know. But it was the direction the key wanted her to go.

Melinda remained standing at the deck railing long after most of the other nearly six hundred passengers had already dispersed to deck chairs in the solarium, private state rooms, or public lounges to pass the time. The trip to Bellingham would take thirty-seven hours and there was no port of call in between. Most of the passengers were tourists at the end of their Alaska trip. Ketchikan had been their last stop and now their thoughts turned toward home.

With her back pack still on her back, Melinda continued to grip the railing, forcing herself to awareness of the significance of the moment as she stared out at the misty mountains. She was leaving her homeland, leaving the Great Northland behind. *I hope the spirits of my people will understand.* She continued to grip the rail long after the ship left the protected channel and churned out into open water. The land disappeared in the fog and fine sea spray, blown off the chop, misted her face. Not until she could taste the salt of the sea on her lips, did she finally move.

Lacking a state room, she searched out an empty deck chair in the solarium, as far from others as possible, and stowed her pack beside her. The warmth and glow of the lights was a welcomed change from the chilly, damp outer deck. Pulling out a book and pretending to read to discourage unwanted dialogue with strangers, she contemplated her future.

For two months she had studied the map tucked away now in an easy to reach outer pouch of her pack. She had located every vestige of remaining wilderness in the northwest corner of the continental United States, planning on avoiding heavily populated areas as much as she could. She had enough money on her to survive for quite a while as long as she camped and ate simply. But soon she would have to decide where to go. Would the mysterious key she carried direct her to a specific destination? She felt certain she would know when she arrived there.

Eventually her mind relaxed to the low strumming of the ship's engine and she actually read the book she held, until her stomach began to growl. Melinda had stuffed a couple of apples and oranges, dried fruit and nuts in her pack, but she would see what Aunt Adele had packed for her first. Upon opening the package she found a small container of sliced ham, some carefully wrapped cheese, bread packed separately in a sandwich bag to keep it from getting soggy, and packets of mustard and mayonnaise. Napkins and a plastic knife were provided to put it all together. There was also a bag of chips which looked to be a little smashed and a bag of chocolate kisses. Melinda couldn't help but smile.

The first twenty-four hours of the cruise went by fairly fast, the last thirteen were painfully slow. She slept, read, and walked the decks. On the second day of the voyage she even treated herself to a cheeseburger and fries in the cafeteria. For the most part people left her alone and the few times someone tried to engage her in conversation, she shrugged, smiled, and pretended not to understand. That doesn't mean she didn't observe others; people-watching helped pass the time. It was fun guessing the relationships among the individuals traveling as a group. Parents with their children were particularly interesting to watch.

As darkness descended ...and it actually grew dark... Melinda tried to catch one more nap before the *Columbia* reached the dock in Bellingham in the morning and she, along with the other passengers, would disembark. The effort was futile. A tight knot of anxiety kept her awake. What am I going to do when we arrive in Bellingham? What should I do? She reached into her jean pocket and cupped the key in her hand.

To her surprise she must have slept after all. Her hand was still gripping the key in her pocket, but daylight brightened the morning. A yellow glow reaching above the eastern hills promised a day of clear skies. On the ferry there was increasing activity around her.

"We dock in thirty minutes," a purser announced, strolling among the passengers.

Melinda jumped up, excitement mounting, as she secured the closures on her pack and headed for the outer deck to watch the approach of their destination. She was not alone. An increasing number of passengers, ready to depart, crowded the railing. A large coastal city spread out along the water's edge like the terminus of a glacier, with Mount Baker's snow-covered peak standing guard in the rear. Between the city and the distant volcanic peak low forested mountains beckoned. Hundreds of colorful boats filled the harbor. With expert skill the huge ferry was piloted to a long pier. Quickly the crew tied up and a gangplank was put in place. The passengers were free to go.

With her pack on her back Melinda disembarked. She moved away from the pier to avoid being trampled and headed aimlessly away from the docks. Soon she was walking down sidewalks past restaurants, hotels, and shops that catered to the busy port area. Shade trees as tall as the buildings lined the streets. She paused in front of a red brick building that looked to be very old.

I need to get out of the city.

The tug of the key felt stronger than it did before. Did that mean she was getting close to her target? Or only closer with still a long way to go? She pulled the mysterious key from her pocket rubbing her fingers over the flat curlicues that formed its unusual shape. Besides the key's pull becoming stronger, it seemed to have also shifted direction a little. The key's pull wasn't directly toward the south, but more toward the southeast. That was good. She didn't want to follow the heavily populated coastline. She would head inland toward the mountains.

Maggie brought the children to the garden to harvest a fresh salad for dinner and to give Vince a bit of peace and quiet to write. It was another beautiful day in an unusually warm Alaska summer. The garden was thriving in so much unexpected sunshine.

"Aaaarrrk!"

"Raven!" Leaf called out in greeting to his feathered friend, abandoning the growth of chickweed his mother had him pulling for the chickens. Raven circled and dive bombed for the children's amusement.

Little brother Rock gazed up at the raven circling overhead, twisting his body to follow its antics. He took a step forward while still looking up, tripped over a row of beans, and fell face down in the dirt.

"Watch where you're going," Maggie sang. She helped her little son up gently dusting him off. Rock was tempted to cry over the injustice of it all, but the situation resolved so fast he managed to contain his protest.

Raven landed high in a tree overlooking the garden. He was wary of getting within targeting distance of the Bradley children. Raven's arrival did not go unnoticed by Keiluk who immediately ran to the base of the tree that kept Raven above the rest. Their four-legged friend was an even greater "must avoid."

Leaf ran up to Raven's tree, joining Keiluk in greeting. Rock decided that making a salad really wasn't his thing and left Maggie's side to follow Leaf.

Keiluk refrained from barking as Leaf had trained her, but kept a close eye on Raven just the same. "It's Raven, Keiluk; he's our friend," Leaf said stroking her thick silky white fur in reassurance. Trusting her master's judgment, Keiluk relaxed ...some.

"What's this, Mommy?" Crystal asked petting the soft, green, fern-like leaves.

"Those are carrots." Before Maggie could react, Crystal grabbed and pulled.

"Is this a good one?" Crystal asked her mother, her little fist full of baby carrots.

"Oh, Crystal, the carrots need more time to grow."

"I'll plant them back," Crystal said, burying them in the dirt.

"No, Sweetie, you can't replant them. How about we wash the little carrots and each of you can eat one and taste how good they are."

"Put them in the basket?"

"Yes, please," Maggie said cheerfully, lowering her harvesting basket so Crystal could reach and drop the carrots in.

"What else do we need for salad, Mommy?"

"Well, we need lettuce, parsley, peas, and zucchini from the garden and tomatoes from the greenhouse. Maggie checked on the boys with a glance; they were playing quietly... that was unusual.

"Is this lettuce, Mommy?" Crystal asked tugging on a young cabbage.

"No, Sweetie, that's cabbage. Come here; I'll show you where the lettuce is."

"What are you doing?" Rock asked Leaf, joining him and Keiluk.

"I'm talking to my friend Raven." Then Leaf whispered secretly to Rock. "I was telling Raven to come back later when Mom wasn't looking and I would have a treat for him."

Raven chortled with pleasure at the prospect.

"What did he say?" Rock asked in all seriousness.

"He said he would. You know, Raven is a very special bird."

"What's special?" Rock asked in wonder.

"Raven can show us pictures of the woods from the air while he flies over it."

"Huh?" Rock tried to imagine that.

"Show him, Raven," Leaf urged. "Show him what you can do."

As though in compliance, Raven flew off the branch, swooped over the garden with a squawk, then circled higher over the forested hills. Soon he was telepathing images to those below.

"Huh...." Rock struggled to understand what he was seeing in his mind. Apparently the images also reached Maggie and Crystal.

"Wow!" Crystal gasped. Maggie looked up startled; she knew where the images were coming from, but not why.

"Leaf, what's going on?" Maggie asked, knowing Leaf must be involved.

"All is okay, Mommy, I just wanted Raven to show Rock what he can do," Leaf explained. As though sensing Maggie's disapproval, Raven's telepathed images stopped.

Vince had also received the messages. "Everything all right out here?" Vince asked rushing out the cabin to protect his family, if necessary. "Why is Raven sending pictures? Is he warning us about something?" He made his way to the garden searching the surrounding woods for an imminent threat.

"Leaf put Raven up to it," Maggie said in way of explanation.

"Oh." Disaster averted, Vince opened his senses to the wonderfully warm mid-summer day. He had been so absorbed in his work he'd failed to notice it before. "Need some help picking vegetables?" he asked, reluctant to go back indoors.

"Sure," Maggie said smiling. "I hope your help is an improvement over some of the help I've had so far," she added for his ears only and gave him a little peck of a kiss. "You can pick sugar peas, Sugar."

"Do I get a kiss for every pea I pick?" Vince asked teasingly.

"We'll negotiate the contract later," she said sending him on his way. "Here's the lettuce," she pointed out to her daughter. "We take the leaves off like this." Maggie demonstrated bending a leaf of Romaine back, tearing it off the head and dropping it into the basket. She placed the basket down between the rows.

"I can pick lettuce," Crystal said tearing a leaf. Torn lettuce leaves wouldn't matter; she had to tear the leaves for salad anyway. The task would keep Crystal busy while she checked the greenhouse for tomatoes.

"We will have plenty of tomatoes in a week or two," Maggie said returning from the greenhouse with only two small ripe tomatoes.

"Maybe we should take the children for a hike," Vince suggested, his calloused hands full of peas.

"Oh, yes!" Maggie loved these family outings. "What about writing?"

"Family is more important than writing, especially on a beautiful day." They carried their bounty to the basket where Crystal still tore away at the lettuce.

"Good job!" Maggie praised. A pile of lettuce leaves covered the bottom of the basket.

"I picked a lot of lettuce," Crystal pointed out.

"You sure did. You did great." Maggie and Vince placed the peas and tomatoes on top the lettuce. "Do you have a knife?" she asked Vince.

"Sure do, what do you need?"

"I want a young zucchini for the salad." Vince pulled out his pocket knife and cut away the zucchini Maggie pointed out as her choice.

With salad harvested and the picnic basket packed, the Bradley family prepared to set off on their family hike. Maggie doused the children's clothing, hands, cheeks, and foreheads with a citronella based insect repellent, even though the mosquito population was low due to a dry summer. Vince checked his rifle; bears were his concern.

"Make noise to let the bears know we are coming," Vince said. He lead them down an old game trail, now turned people trail that used to go through their front yard. After he built the cabin, the bears and moose established an alternative route to avoid humans. The trail, nearly hidden by the height of summer growth, led to their favorite picnic spot on the ridge overlooking the big swamp at the head of the creek.

Bears were Leaf's friends, too. Leaf knew the rifle his father carried was for protection against a charging bear. He could mentally read his father's protective concern. Leaf didn't want anything to happen to his family, but he didn't want anything to happen to his friends the bears either. So he decided to keep watch mentally scanning the woods. Leaf could detect the presence of squirrels, birds, shrews, and voles in the area, but there was no sign of bears.

Numerous wildflowers bloomed in sunny openings along the way. Maggie and Melinda had learned the names of all the flowers together. Now she identified the flowers for Crystal, Leaf, and Rock.

After weeks of little rain, the forest was dry. Even known low spots in the trail had dried out. Yet the foliage was still lush and green. In places the Fireweed, Monk's Hood, and wild grasses grew taller than the children, forming green arches over their heads. Keiluk broke through the tall growth ahead of them. The distance wasn't great, less than a quarter of a mile, and it looked like the twins would make it all the way this time on their own feet.

Hot and sweaty, they arrived at their picnic site. A few mature birch trees shaded the grassy ridge framing the expanse of the big swamp green with summer. Across the vast muskeg the Talkeetna Mountains defined the skyline to the east.

They rested on logs near the fire pit containing the remains of their last campfire. There would be no campfire today; conditions were too dry and the threat of forest fire too great. It was too hot for a campfire anyway. A thermos of cold water was passed around. Keiluk made her way down the steep embankment to cool off in the creek.

It didn't take long for the children to recharge with energy. Vince romped around with the kids, making sure no one went too close to the edge of the ridge where it dropped down to the swamp and creek, while Maggie set up their picnic. She spread out the picnic blanket from the top of the basket near the fire pit where the summer growth was the shortest.

Hearing the shrieks of laughter and smelling the scent of food, Keiluk shook herself off releasing a shower of water and quickly climbed back up on level with her family. The smell of food drew her to Maggie first who instantly protested. "Ugh, wet dog; go away!" Rejected by Maggie, Keiluk joined in the fun with Vince and the kids.

"Lunch!" Maggie called out when all was ready.

"Stay!" Leaf ordered Keiluk a few feet away from the feast. "Sit!" A mental directive accompanied his verbal command. Keiluk sat. "Lay down!" Keiluk dropped down on the grass. Maggie handed Leaf a dog biscuit to give to her. "Good girl," he said rewarding her with a pet and the biscuit.

While they ate, Leaf continued to mentally scan the area for bears. He detected other signatures of life. There were robins, sparrows, and chickadees flittering about in the trees, a moose browsing down on the big swamp, and a fox in the woods across the creek sniffing out a vole for lunch, but no bears.

It wasn't until they were packing up to leave that Leaf detected the mental essence of a bear, still a long ways off, but headed toward them following the ridge. He glanced at Keiluk contentedly lapping up the last crumbs of their picnic shaken out of the picnic blanket. Good, the bear was still too far away for Keiluk to detect. Now was the time for action.

Without alerting anyone to the approaching danger, Leaf drew energy from within. Then formulating a powerful mental suggestion to change direction, he slammed it into the bear's mind. Leaf could sense the lumbering bear's vague confusion, but felt little to no thought resistance. The bear turned around, seeking a different route to his favorite fishing spot on the creek.

After two days of hiking, Melinda reached the Cascade Mountains. It had taken a full day just to clear the sprawling metropolis. Not wanting to draw attention to herself, she avoided the major highways as much as possible. There was no reason for her to hide except for a lack of desire to communicate. When she finally reached woods dense enough to hide her, darkness added an additional cloak of concealment. Hopefully, she was far enough away from any unseen residence not to be disturbed. She couldn't see any lights shining through the trees which was a good sign. Even more importantly, no barking dog broke the silence. More tired than hungry, Melinda rolled herself up in her sleeping bag and fell instantly asleep.

The sun blazed brightly when she woke the next morning stiff, but rested. No one had bothered her ...for which she was thankful. After a breakfast of dried fruit and nuts, she rolled up her sleeping bag and continued on her way. The terrain had become more up and down demanding more energy to traverse. When she came to an intersection in the road, she let the tug of the key guide her direction. A couple of times she was offered a ride by passing motorists, but Melinda could sense the offers were tainted with an underlying hope of getting lucky and shook off the offers. As the day wore on, the terrain became increasingly more mountainous with communities spread further and further apart. She stopped at a marketplace in one little town and bought a sandwich and a bottle of water.

There was only one road to follow now with few places to divert off of it. In some spots it was downright scary with steep mountainside rising up on one side of the road and dropping just as steeply down on the other.

"Hi there! Where're you going? I could give you a ride."

The voice startled Melinda. Lost in her thoughts, she didn't hear the pickup truck driven by a thirty to forty year old woman with a friendly demeanor slowly come up from behind her. With disappointment in her lapse of attentive surveillance of all around her, she turned to face the woman attached to the cheerful greeting. She could read nothing threatening in the woman's offer, just concern for a young woman traveling alone on foot.

Thank you, Melinda spoke silently with her lips, then brought out the pad and pen she kept in a handy pocket on the outside of her pack.

"I'm Melinda," she quickly wrote and showed it to the woman.

"Hi, Melinda. I'm Charlene," she said gazing at Melinda with curious but compassionate blue eyes. "Where're you going?" she asked adjusting the red bandana that held her shoulder-length brown hair out her face. Both Charlene and the sturdy red pick-up truck she drove had a certain rural air to them.

Pulling out her worn map folded to the northwestern states, Melinda pointed to their approximate current position and moved her finger across the map in a southeast direction.

"I see," Charlene said looking at the map but still not sure where Melinda was headed. "Well, hop in; I can take you as far as Wenatchee. You can put your pack in the back of the truck."

They rode in comfortable silence for a while, the windows down letting in the cool mountain air. The scenery was beautiful, even breathtaking ...rivers, mountains, forest, and sky. Much like the mountains back home Melinda thought, but different somehow ...bolder and warmer.

"Where are you from?" Charlene asked after a while.

Melinda could see she would be doing a lot of writing, but she didn't mind. Charlene's vivacious personality was contagious and she had enjoyed little human interaction lately. She just hoped she wouldn't run out of paper.

"Alaska!" Charlene exclaimed, reading Melinda's written response and thinking she certainly looked native. "What are you doing here?"

Melinda had learned that vague, dreamy answers were best for avoiding deeper interrogation. "Looking for something special," she wrote.

"I know how you feel," Charlene sympathized. "A word of caution though, some of these 'someone specials' turn out not to be so special after all. I've had a few 'someone specials' and came out on the losing end of the deal every time. I've decided I don't need them. I can take care of myself," she chuckled.

Melinda had written "something" not "someone," but she didn't make an effort to clarify. She decided she liked Charlene and posed questions of her own to keep up the chatter. "Do you live in Wenatchee?" she wrote.

"For now; I moved back to take care of my aging father. I'm an only child. Mom died a few years ago." Charlene went on to cheerfully share her life episodes while Melinda enjoyed both the landscape and the stories. "You're a good listener," she said a couple of hours later with a grin.

As they crossed the summit and started the long descent back down to farmland and towns, Melinda realized with gratitude how far Charlene had taken her. The key, acquired in a nightmare and concealed in her pocket, assured her she was headed in the right direction. Yet she was surprised its tug had increased only minimally in strength. The object it lured her toward must still be a long distance away.

"Where do you want me to drop you off?" Charlene asked when they reached the outskirts of Northern Wenatchee.

"Bus station," Melinda wrote after some thought. Traveling on foot was just too slow.

CHAPTER 13

Aaia

With the help of the star stones, Traevus and Ilene were able to draw enough energy to teleport Captain Setas and Inventor Sulyan short distances over the difficult rocky terrain. Now the small group was taking a much needed rest after a rather steep climb. Using the star stones meant revealing their properties. Traevus explained their assumption that the Crystalline Landscape, dominating the center of the continent, somehow interfered with their ability to naturally draw usable energy from the elemental forces. But a star stone pushed back against the interference from the Crystalline Landscape, at least within a small radius, making telekinesis possible.

"Really..." Zaloka exclaimed with surprise when Traevus finished expounding on the subject. The near star Seaa illuminated her face with soft milky light. "And how many of these star stones are there?"

"Where did they come from?" Drak asked, his interest whetted.

"This one," Traevus said, holding up the smooth round golden stone he carried, "came from..."

"That's the stone I gave Rojaire and Theon," Sulyan gasped in recognition. The star stone caught Seaa's light as though drawn to it, reflecting the light toward Sulyan, giving him an aura of clarity.

"That's right," Traevus confirmed with obvious surprise. "You gave it to them before they left on the mapping expedition."

"So it proved to be useful after all," Sulyan chuckled pleased with himself. "We can certainly see how it got its name." Of all the colonists,

Inventor Sulyan seemed the most changed by their adventure so far, becoming more social ...and cognizant.

"But how did you come by it?" Traevus asked.

"I found it back home on the beach ...when I was conducting a rather explosive experiment," Sulyan confessed. "It seemed to be an energy source of some kind. I wasn't sure what it did."

"My star stone was found on Earth." Ilene said in a mixture of Aaian and English. All drew their attention toward her.

"That far away...!" Captain Setas rasped in awe.

Ilene pulled out her star stone for all to see. She had made as much effort to learn the Aaian language as she had in conveying her own and had understood enough of the conversation to discern the topic without a translator. After all, as Theon's daughter, Ilene considered Aaian as much a part of her heritance as English.

"So it is possible more of these star stones might be found," Drak concluded. It was then Traevus spotted movement below them.

"By Seaa's light, look who's coming," he announced, standing up for a better view of their teammates trudging up the rocky slope toward them, heavily burdened with freight.

"I told you we would catch up with you," Rojaire bragged dropping his heavy pack with a deep sigh, signaling a rest. Kaylya, Thayla, and Kiril, in need of a rest, did the same. Kiril had just enough strength left in him to choose a place as close to Ilene as he could without raising notice from the others before dropping down.

"There is still a load or two left on the ferry," Kaylya said.

"We can send Kiril for them," Thayla volunteered. Kiril wished he had something soft to throw at her.

Ilene inched closer to Kiril. "I'll go back with you," she whispered softly to Kiril in sympathy.

"You will?" Kiril smiled forgetting about his weariness.

"You made the trip fast. It's a long hike." Not sure he understood, she pantomimed "long hike" with her hands while attempting a telepathed message since she had the star stone, to help get her meaning across.

"It's a long walk," he agreed, not quite sure of the word "hike."

"Yes, it's a long walk," Ilene repeated ...in Aaian ...and then again in English. Kiril stared at her in near disbelief. They repeated the phrase together in both languages until their effort dissolved into laughter.

"We already have more seeds, tools, food, and household items we can carry into the mountains," Rojaire informed the group, "and plenty to eat until we get there. We will also be leaving the shelter in the Cremyn Valley well stocked."

"How much farther do we have to go before we reach this shelter you keep talking about?" Captain Setas asked. Her voice sounded as weary as her body looked.

"Yes," Zaloka added, "I'm starting to worry about Wessid ...lame and all alone."

"He's not lame; he just needed to rest," Rojaire reassured her. "I'm sure he's walking fine by now. There is nothing there to hurt him and food and water is close at hand."

"But you said he was limping."

"We don't have too much farther to go," Rojaire said. "We should be able to see the valley over the next rise." Actually the distance to the shelter in the Cremyn Valley was still great. It was only close relative to the distance they had already covered since leaving Lavender Beach.

It wasn't long before the group was ready to move on. The pace was adjusted to accommodate everyone. The camaraderie of being together lifted their spirits. Kiril and Ilene walked side by side practicing languages. His spirit was so high, he felt he could go on forever. The colonists took turns helping Captain Setas and Inventor Sulyan over difficult terrain, but when the landscape leveled out some, they stoically declined further aid. And Zaloka continued to worry about Wessid.

The period of dark was nearly over by the time the colonists descended into Cremyn Valley. Seaa dipped below the horizon, leaving only distant starlight to light the way when the group finally arrived, startling Wessid out of a deep sleep. Wessid stumbled groggily out of the shelter into an unexpected crowd. "Is everyone here?" he asked surprised by the sudden throng of people.

"Wessid, you're walking," Zaloka exclaimed rushing up to him, relieved to see him up and about.

"Of course I'm walking; I'm not lame."

"Greetings, Father." Kiril noticed there seemed to be a greater closeness between his chosen mother and his chosen father than he had been aware of back in their community. Making a life-altering decision to follow their son probably had something to do with it. Remembering he was the reason they were here, Kiril bowed his head slightly in contrition.

"Greetings, my son." It was Wessid's turn to bow his head, but in respect. "I just wanted to say," Wessid paused searching for the right words, "I'm proud of you."

"Not as much as I am of you," Kiril found himself saying. "It took a lot of courage for you to come with me. Thank you."

"Thank you?" Wessid asked, not familiar with the words.

"A simple expression of gratitude," Zaloka explained. "I think the proper response is "You're welcome."

Kiril realized Ilene must have been instructing the others all along the way. *At this rate everyone will be capable of conversing with Ilene but me.*

A fire was built up and tea served as well as snacks. "I wish I had my flute," Ilene sighed wistfully in otherwise mellow contentment. "I would play us a tune to celebrate." Her flute and pack had been abandoned in the rooms she had been assigned to back in the Community of the High Council.

"I'm sorry," Rojaire said. Her things had been abandoned by his order in an effort to escape before they could be stopped. "I greatly enjoyed your music on our first expedition together. Perhaps Inventor Sulyan here can make you a flute."

"What's a flute?" Sulyan asked.

"It's a musical instrument," Ilene explained.

"Oh, I do enjoy the art of tonal creativity.

With Rojaire and Kaylya translating and Kiril hanging on to every word, Ilene described the basic principles of how a flute produced musical notes. To her surprise, the inventor actually retrieved a stylus and pad and took notes.

Food and drink revived the companions only briefly. Weariness quickly took hold once again. "We will be taking a long rest here," Rojaire told the group. "Get some sleep; we'll have a meeting at daybreak." As they began to make a move, Rojaire spoke out again. "A word of caution when you start strolling around in the morning. There are hundreds, perhaps thousands, of little tree seedlings growing in the area around the shelter all the way upstream to the creek that we will follow to the Crescent Mountains. You will want to avoid trampling on them."

"My trees," Captain Setas rasped, but she was too tired for more.

The women were offered the shelter although there was no threat of rain. The men snuggled into their bedrolls around the fire. "Here, you can have possession of the star stone back," Traevus said extending his hand to Kiril. "It might help you with your communication problems," Traevus grinned. Kiril gladly took back possession of the mysterious golden stone.

Exhausted, the colonists quickly became quiet. One by one, conversations were replaced with sounds of even breathing and the murmur of the river.

The sun rose long before the camp stirred, except for Wessid. Since he was the only one well rested, he took it upon himself to have aromatic teas brewing and porridge simmering by the time the others got up. He was busily making flatbread when Zaloka snuck out of the shelter to join him by the fire.

"It was certainly nice of you to prepare breakfast for everyone," she praised him, helping herself to some tea.

"Well, I am a provider." He smiled at her warmly, but resisted the urge to touch her. Sharing a son did not permit him to be so forward. She was beautiful. The golden highlights in her auburn hair, still rumpled from sleep, matched her gold-flecked eyes, charged with the excitement of their adventure. "What a beautiful morning!"

"It is indeed." Zaloka blew on her tea, her gaze taking in the sparkle of sunlight on the Cremyn River and the deep purple of the Crescent Mountains to the East. Then she noticed the expanse of the valley around her. Amidst the sparse vegetation she had become accustomed to, a hand span high miniature forest stretched out before her. As far as she could see, brilliant touches of blue and orange dotted the coarse lavender soil. The little trees stood out against the sparse pink and yellow foliage that grew naturally in the valley. Suddenly the captain was standing beside her.

"My trees," Captain Setas whispered. Wessid placed a cup of herbal tea and warm flatbread into the captain's hands. She barely noticed. Without another word she hobbled off into her emerging forest.

After the tall one cried out all her frustration and despair, Chiita (the tall one will never get it right) fed Caleeza a broth to help her sleep. It also gave Chiita time to think.

She laid back thinking in her lookout over the valley from the uppermost woven rope hammock level in her tree. She had plenty to think about. Gazing out across the lonely, but fruitful valley, she touched the crystal floss satchel and medallion she wore. According to legend, the satchel and medallion once belonged to a tall one called Vestan. Vestan visited her people long ago, before the great darkness. The satchel and medallion were handed down to her by her father. Chiita's father received it from his mother. Until now she had thought she would be the last to wear them. That may have changed. She gently caressed her abdomen. The encased embryo that had arrived with the girl glowed warmly in her reproductive pouch.

Chiita's ancestors were nearly obliterated during the great rumbling darkness. Food became scare, survival tenuous. Only a few of Chiita's people survived. Food was strictly rationed and even with their reduced numbers there was little to go around. Reproduction was halted and the fertile faintly glowing embryos the females produced were preserved in their shells of translucent stone. These were stored in a sacred place in the mountains to await better times instead of placed in their reproductive pouches. The ordeal stretched over many cycles of seasons leaving the people weakened and in time infertile. Eventually no more fertile eggs were produced.

Very few repositories of the preserved eggs survived the mountains' turmoil. But some did. The preserved embryos were the people's only hope of continuation. Chiita was once one of those preserved embryos. And the tall one brought her another. Does the tall one know where there are more? *Perhaps I can save my people from extinction after all.* Once again Chiita touched her reproductive pouch. *I can't change the loss of my people,* she sighed, *so I might as well concentrate on solving the problems of this new tall one. Maybe she will lead me to more fertile eggs.*

Chiita had picked up numerous images of other tall ones from Caleeza's mind. She felt certain they were in the valley to the east. All the images she could draw from Caleeza's thoughts supported it. Caleeza had to have arrived here in her valley through a warp tube, but of course the warp tube was closed now. For her to return Caleeza to her people, they will have to cross the mountains. It will be an arduous trek, but doable, once the tall one regained her strength; Chiita knew the way. If she helped the girl find her people, she may learn more about where this embryonic stone was found.

But when Chiita finally descended her tree to check on Caleeza, a long sleep later, Caleeza was gone.

Caleeza....

Awakened by the message, a confused Caleeza sat up in her crystal floss bed. Colorful crystal-filtered light spangled her sleeping chamber. Was she dreaming or waking up from a dream? *Pray I'm dreaming for I can't bear captivity again in the Crystalline Landscape.*

"Sarus...?" She rose from her bed.

Caleeza, what are you doing here? Sarus did not project an image of himself.

"I don't know."

You do not belong here.

"I thought you called me. Are you all right?"

I often call your name so that I may remember.

"You do?" Caleeza's heart swelled. Not only did Sarus remember her, but he often spoke her name so he would never forget her.

For you to hear me, it must be you who is in distress, Sarus explained.

It was a strange sentiment, but she found it somewhat reassuring. Did Sarus really continue to watch over her?

How can I help you?

Should she tell Sarus of her troubles? She decided it couldn't hurt. "I found a wonderful group of people to live with in a beautiful valley. And I found Ollen and Traevus from our expedition, but now I am lost and can't find my way to return to them. My friends will be looking for me, but I fear they will never find me.

For the longest, Sarus didn't answer. Caleeza paced around the chamber wondering what to do next. She couldn't stay here. She must get away somehow. Then Sarus spoke in her mind once again.

I will take you where you want to go.

☆☆☆☆

When Caleeza finally began to awaken from her deep sleep, she didn't want to open her eyes for fear of where she would find herself. Was she lying on Chitter's woven mat in the little cave? Or in the Crystalline Landscape on her bed padded with crystal floss? Or back in the colony with Theon and the others in her private stone chamber? She just wasn't sure. She felt with her hands for more clues. There didn't seem to be enough light penetrating her eyelids to place her in the Crystalline Landscape. In fact, the bed felt very familiar. Then she heard someone speak in the main cavern.

"So you are leaving now?" The voice was low, lacking in enthusiasm, as though stating something that both the speaker and the listener already knew and neither were happy about.

Theon... that was Theon!

"Yes, I might as well get started." He had agreed to wait for the next period of light. The wait was over.

Tassyn.

Caleeza tried to jump up and shout out to them, but she was a bit groggy still and only managed to roll on her side and mumble incoherently.

"I hate leaving you with just Edty to help out," Tassyn said for the tenth time.

"We'll be all right," Theon assured him once again. "Just find them."

"I'm right here," Caleeza called out in a whisper, working her way up into a sitting position.

"Did you hear something?" Caleeza heard Tassyn ask.

"In here," she called out louder, wobbly gaining her feet. In an instant Tassyn was by her side offering support, with Theon moving faster than he thought he still could close behind him.

"Caleeza, you're here!" Tassyn exclaimed with more excitement than usual, especially since being "reformed" by the High Council for living the life of a renegade. "When did you get back? Where's Ollen?"

"I was hoping he was here."

"Not unless he snuck in like you did," Theon informed her.

"I didn't sneak in. It's a strange story," she added seeing the confusion on their faces. "I'll try to explain," she sighed. Her stomach growled loudly for all to hear.

"Well, come out on the terrace by the fire. I think Edty has something cooking and you can tell us what happened."

Edty nearly dropped his spoon when the three of them walked out together. "By Seaa's Light," he gasped.

Tassyn led Caleeza to the best chair in the house, after Theon's, and ordered breakfast. "Are you all right? You seem a bit weak. Have you been hurt?"

"I fell down a hole... Ollen and I got separated... He fell into a stream..." Caleeza paused in exasperation. "I hardly know where to begin."

"Now, now, take a deep breath," Theon urged. "We have time."

"Where's Ollen?" Edty asked anxiously, delivering the breakfast Tassyn ordered for her. "Did he run into a bear beast?"

"No, I did. Thanks," she said, smiling to him, gratefully accepting the gourd of porridge and fruit and a carved utensil to eat it with. The men watched cheerfully and waited impatiently as Caleeza had her fill. When she was done, Tassyn handed her a hot cup of tea to wash it down. Feeling better, she was ready to tell her story.

"You and Ollen left long before daybreak, rotations ago, in order to cover familiar ground before sun-up," Theon reminded her gently, pointing out where the story should begin.

"And we did just that; when the sun rose above the eastern mountain peaks we looked out on undiscovered country from our perch on a low plateau." She told them about crossing a large range of grassland filled with kurpers to a forest of angular trees with water flowing beneath them. She described climbing through their tangled branches, seeking a way across the flood, the small crawling lifeform that startled Ollen, causing him to fall into the deepest part of the stream, and his efforts to stay afloat as the strong current carried him away. "It was the last I saw of him."

"Where did you meet the bear beast?" Edty wanted to know after a thoughtful pause.

"Not long after Ollen and I were separated. I made it across the stream safely and immediately went looking for Ollen. I was certain I would quickly catch up with him, but I was wrong. It wasn't long before I came to a waterfall. I feared he may have gone over the falls. But before I could find a way down, I found myself face to face with the bear beast."

"Were you scared?" Edty quivered and whimpered in fear.

"Absolutely terrified!"

"Did it have long sharp teeth and claws?" Edty's voice chattered.

"It certainly did, but it didn't look anything like the bears in Alaska."

"So what happened?' Tassyn asked.

"The beast threatened to attack. I backed away from it and the ground opened up beneath my feet." From here Caleeza was less sure of the validity of her perceived experiences. Real or not, she had a captive audience. She went on.

"The fall beat me up quite badly... I probably suffered a concussion. It was Chitter who nursed me back to health."

Caleeza realized too late she should have led into the topic of the discovery of another intelligent lifeform more cautiously. The three men leaned questioningly toward her.

"Chitter nursed you...?" Theon asked for all of them. "Who's Chitter?"

"Her name isn't exactly Chitter, but it sounded something like that. She lives wherever it was I ended up when I fell down the hole." Her story was starting to sound like a fairytale even to her. She described Chitter in great detail, from her brown flesh mostly covered in brownish orange feathers to her round dark violet eyes. "Chitter could walk upright, she only reached about waist high when standing. She could also lope about on all fours. She could build a fire, cook, weave fibers, and she took care of me when I was hurt." Caleeza realized she never had a chance to thank Chitter for her care.

"So how did you get back here?" Theon finally asked.

"It was Sarus who brought me back," she said to even more stares of disbelief.

☆☆☆☆

Ollen collapsed in exhaustion and despair. The valley had proved vaster than they had ever imagined. He was yet to reach the end of it. He searched for Caleeza relentlessly, refusing to give up. He backtracked to the jungle gym trees where he had fallen into the stream after being startled by the crawling life form and back again to where he had washed up on the streambanks after tumbling down the waterfall. Failing to find her, he followed the river downstream for many leagues, calling her name until his voice gave out. He climbed up every vantage point and searched every depression he could find along the way. Caleeza was nowhere to be found.

Finally the river itself had abandoned him, plunging down into a rocky hole in the mountain. For a moment he actually considered diving in and letting the swift current bash him to death against the rocks. Ollen lay on rocky terrain softened by a carpet of wildflowers and sobbed uncontrollably. He lost Cremyn long ago; now he lost Caleeza. Theon, Tassyn, and Edty expected them back by now. How could he return to the others without Caleeza?

In the end, he felt he had no choice. As a new dawn announced a new period of light, Ollen decided to head back. He could only hope that either he would still find Caleeza on the return journey or she had already found her way home. There may actually be a search party out looking for him. It wasn't much, but for now, it was enough of a thread of hope to get him up and going again.

CHAPTER 14

Earth

"My Boats!" Papa screamed frantically, running up the beach. "What happened to my boats?" he cried gesturing toward the empty water in angry bewilderment. Melinda watched helplessly in terrifying confusion as her father raged on. Nothing made sense and even more frightening, she had never seen her father so upset before. What happened next was even more horrifying than the disappearance of their fishing boat and skiff. Papa became ominously silent, grabbed his chest and slumped to the ground.

"Papa, Papa!" Melinda cried, dashing to his side and throwing her arms around him. "Papa, what is happening?" she cried disparately.

Papa didn't answer; his body was lifeless. Grief overwhelmed her. Then he vanished from her arms. Inexplicably he was gone, body and soul. Grief turned to shock and then to panic as Droclum approached, his evil aura nearly smothering her as he came closer. Melinda screamed with the terror of a thousand nightmares, a silent scream that uttered no sound, no matter how hard she tried.

Melinda thrashed about in her seat, consumed by horror and panic. The elderly woman seated next to her stood up and silently moved to another seat. Gradually the sound of the surf transformed into the noise of the road. Shaken by the relived ordeal, she took in her surroundings with welcomed relief. She was riding on a bus through a dark summer night with a ticket to Denver, Colorado. Not since she had acquired the mysterious key from a very different nightmare, had Droclum haunted her dreams.

Determined not to fall asleep again, Melinda stared out the window at blackness. Occasionally, a grouping of lights denoted a spot of habitation along the way. When they passed through a town, the night lit up with streetlights, gas stations, convenience stores, and closed strip malls. The bus even stopped once at one of these spots of illumination to let a passenger off. Sometime during the night they pulled into a station and switched out drivers. Most of the towns they passed through were small, their illumination brief, before the darkness swallowed them up again. There was no way to tell what the countryside beyond the dark window looked like. As she was carried along through the night, she thought of Aunt Adele, probably alone in her little house since her sons had lives of their own. Did her aunt miss her now that she was gone, or did she embrace her solitude? Strangely, Aunt Adele relished the brief attention from reporters. Recalling her "fifteen minutes of fame" made Melinda shudder.

By contrast, reflecting on the time she spent with her cousin Greg on his fishing boat brought a smile to her face. She chuckled silently as she relived the stealth with which Greg had snuck her out of the house and onto his boat to deflect reporters. It was comforting to be on the water again after so long. She was born to live near the sea. Perhaps she should have returned to her life in Southeast Alaska instead of remaining in the Susitna Valley with Rahlys and Maggie after her ordeal with Droclum. Once again she was a long way from any coastline. It was an almost depressing thought.

Of course, she had lived for years peacefully happy in the Northern Susitna Valley far from the sea, but those years had been bittersweet. Immersion into a loving extended family had been clouded by the horror of events that had severed her from her father and the life they had shared. Her existence continued to be haunted by the essence of Droclum. What she sought was relief. The key tugged at her being with increasing urgency, leading the way. Rahlys had plucked her from Droclum's evil clutches, but as Droclum's essence had repeatedly gloated in numerous nightmares since, Rahlys could no longer hear her cries for help when under Droclum's aura.

Melinda wiped tears from her eyes as she thought about how much she missed the gang: Rahlys, Maggie, Vince, Ilene, Elaine, Jack, Rock,

Crystal, and especially Leaf. Even though they were her friends, she never revealed the key's existence to any of the members of the Order of the Oracle. This was her fight. She would face what lay ahead on her own, with no risk to them.

It was already afternoon before the bus finally pulled into Denver. Stepping out of the restraining confinement was a welcomed relief. Donning her pack, she quickly left the station. She wanted nothing more than to walk. But where to go from here? The unmistakable tug of the key pulled stronger than ever. Cloud cover obscured the sun making it necessary to pull out her compass to determine the direction of the compelling pull from the mysterious artifact. Taking a reading, her concern of overreaching her unknown destination proved unfounded. The key still wrenched her toward the southeast. How much further she had to go, she did not know. Trying to judge by comparing the distance she has already traveled to the relative increase in the strength to the tug of the key didn't help.

Hours later, nothing had changed; she had barely made it out of the city. As far as she could tell, she wasn't any closer to her destination. By the time she reached a state park where she could camp, darkness threatened. Then it began to rain. Melinda quickly strung up a tarp for shelter and crawled under it. After munching on snacks, she took out the map she had purchased along the way and studied it carefully. Her new map covered several states from Colorado south to the Mexican border and east to the Mississippi River. Drawing an imaginary vector from Denver southeastward, took her through several states: Kansas, Oklahoma, Texas, and Louisiana. How far would she have to go? Time would tell. When it became too dark to read the map any longer, she lay in her bedroll deep in thought ...and then deep in dream.

Melinda.

No.

Melinda stood in a raging thunderstorm, drenched in darkness and rain. Sizzling lightning lit the sky, momentarily revealing heavy gray moss and twisting vines in a tangle of unfamiliar trees surrounding a small clearing. Ear-splitting thunder followed the lightning, temporarily drowning out the thrashing of the treetops in the wind. Another blinding flash of lightning, and she saw her new map spread out before her, floating on the wind and pounded by rain.

I am waiting for you.

Terror gripped Melinda's heart. Droclum was near. The putrid essence of his evil sickened her.

Where? Where are you waiting for me? She wanted to scream, but couldn't. Nauseous bile rose in her throat causing her to puke. Another flash of lightning, this time so close she felt the heat and electrical charge. Melinda dropped to the ground screaming silently.

When she opened her eyes, the roar of the storm turned into the patter of gentle rain on the tarp and early morning light seeped into the shelter. Melinda sat up trembling, drenched in sweat. The storm had been a dream, but Melinda knew that Droclum's essence was real. After recovering her calm and dignity, Melinda pulled her carefully folded map from its pouch in her pack. It was dry. Putting the nightmare behind her, she decided to plan her day. But what she saw when she opened the map, brought back the terror of the night trifold.

Burned into the map was a quarter inch hole ...deep in South Louisiana.

Leaf sat up suddenly, awakened from a deep sleep.

"Melinda is in trouble," he whispered in the dark. Rock slept soundly in a tangle of blankets across the room. Keiluk slept undisturbed on the rug by his bed. Outside his window, dusk was turning into dawn over the Susitna Valley. Night was fleeting in the subarctic summer.

Leaf had felt Melinda's terror. But where was she? Leaf couldn't tell. She seemed so far away. To his relief, Melinda's panic quickly subsided, but she wasn't at peace. Something evil was still lurking ...something without form or substance. Would it threaten again? He felt certain it would.

As Melinda's stress eased, Leaf's eyes became heavy with sleepiness. Slowly his head dropped to his pillow and he drifted off to dreamland once more.

Leaf woke hours later to a gloriously warm late-summer day that normally would have gladdened his little heart, but gloom doomed his mood as he worried about Melinda. Even awake he could sense an evil presence following her. Or was she following it? It was hard to tell. The evil essence felt familiar; he had sensed it before faintly coming from the strange flat metallic object Melinda kept hidden in the lining of her jewelry box. If the thing was evil, he should get rid of it.

After breakfast, Leaf snuck into the girls' room. Melinda's pretty blue jewelry box still stood on the dresser by her bed where she left it. He opened the lid of the box and felt under the torn lining at the bottom for the secret object. It wasn't there. Melinda must have taken it with her.

"Mom, where is Melinda?" he asked when he rejoined the others.

"Well sweetie, she's living in Ketchikan."

"Where is Ketchikan?"

"It's in Southeast Alaska. Just a minute, I'll show you."

Maggie brought out an Alaska map, spread it on the table, and then caught a glass of water the twins knocked over, clambering up the same chair to see. She whisked the map away before the flood reached it. Vince jumped up for a towel to mop it up with after moving his own work to safety. Once the table was dried, Maggie laid out the map again. She showed Leaf, Rock, and Crystal where they lived on the map, and then moved her finger across the map to Ketchikan. "And Melinda lives here," she said after her finger crossed a large area of blue. Leaf was still confused. The map didn't look anything like the woods outside.

"Is it far away?"

"It's pretty far away," Vince said. He took note of Leaf's obvious disappointment. "Maybe one day we can take the ferry and go visit her," he added as consolation.

One day would not be soon enough; Leaf was ready to take action. Melinda was in trouble and he was going to save her. It never occurred to Leaf that others would consider this an impossible mission for a little boy.

Using the controlled chaos that prevails in a household with two-year-old twins as cover, Leaf snuck off to the garden with Keiluk in search of Raven. To find Melinda, he would need help. "I'm going to call Raven," he warned Keiluk and gave her an affectionate scratch behind her ears. "Remember, Raven is our friend." Keiluk tended to get worked up when Raven made an appearance.

Then standing under the tree by the garden where Raven liked to perch, Leaf closed his eyes and raised his little arms in concentration.

Drawing energy from the elemental forces that abounded in the very air around him, he transmitted a mental call to Raven.

Raven heard the call. It roused him from a perfect nap in his favorite tree by the bears' popular fishing spot along the creek. The murmur of the stream and the warmth of the summer sun had unexpectedly lulled him into slumber. Shaking himself awake, he realized there was something strange about the message. It hadn't come from Rahlys, but from the little guy, Leaf. Should he answer the summons? What kind of mischief could Leaf be into? From what little he knew, the possibilities were limitless. Well, there was only one way to find out. Raven sprang into the air spreading his shiny black wings and headed upstream.

Soon Raven circled over the Bradley's garden and landed in the tree with Leaf and his dog below. "Aaaarrrk!" he complained loudly although he really didn't have anything else to do.

"Raven, you came!" Leaf cried excitedly. "Here, I brought you something."

That's more like it, Raven thought, catching the dry crusty remains of a peanut butter and jelly sandwich Leaf tossed up to him in his beak. While he munched down his treat, Leaf explained the situation.

"Something evil is after Melinda." He did his best to share with Raven what the evil haunting Melinda felt like. We have to find her, Raven, before anything bad happens to her," Leaf pleaded with his bird friend.

"Aaaarrrk!" Raven agreed.

"We'll need some food for the trip," Leaf said wisely and rushed to the garden. Helping himself to its bounty, he filled one pocket of his jeans with peas and the other with little carrots. "I guess we're ready to go," he announced.

Taking Raven and Keiluk by surprise, Leaf teleported the three of them down to the railroad tracks at the foot of the trail. Leaf didn't know if the railroad tracks went all the way to Ketchikan, but he knew they went a long ways.

Deposited in mid-air, Raven frantically swooped up into flight just before hitting the ground. He landed in a nearby tree and shook out his feathers to regain composure. Keiluk barked in confusion, then sniffed and paced to compensate for the lack of security inherent in a sudden change in scenery.

"It will be Keiluk's job to look for danger on the ground and your job to watch for danger from the air," he told Raven.

The little guy can be a real nuisance sometimes, Raven thought, but he decided to do the best he could to help keep him out of trouble. Raven flew a short distance down the tracks and landed in another tree to wait.

Having surveyed the area and finding nothing alarming, Keiluk returned to Leaf's side and patiently waited for further orders. "It won't be long before Mom and Dad and Aunt Rahlys will be looking for us. If they find us, they will try to stop us from going," he told Keiluk. "And Aunt Rahlys has the crystal."

To prevent that from happening, Leaf drew energy to create an invisible shield that he hoped would prevent detection from Rahlys and the Oracle of Light. He knew how to do it. He had learned the basics from Warrior Quaylyn. Quaylyn had concealed a whole traw playing field from detection from the air.

When all was set, Leaf and Keiluk started walking toward Ketchikan.

☆☆☆☆

"Where's Leaf?" Maggie asked after getting the twins settled with a box of toys.

"I saw him go out the door with Keiluk a few minutes ago," Vince said, engrossed in his writing. He didn't look up from his work.

Maggie took a quick glance toward the twins ...still playing quietly... and stepped out onto the porch, looking for Leaf. When she didn't spot him immediately, she headed out toward the garden, certain to find him there, but Leaf and Keiluk weren't in sight.

"Leaf!"

Maggie called and waited repeatedly, listening for a clue to their location. All she heard was the soft rustle of birch leaves in the breeze and the birdsong of robins and sparrows in the grasses and trees.

"Leaf!" she called even louder, transmitting her voice on the breeze.

"Leaf! Keiluk!" she shouted with greater concern. When there was still no answer, she searched down the trail calling, and by the creek (even though that was a forbidden place without an adult.) No Leaf and no dog. Getting frantic now, Maggie rushed back to the house and stormed in.

"I can't find Leaf and Keiluk!"

"Huh? What do you mean you can't find them?" Vince asked pulling his concentration away from the novel he was writing.

"I've looked everywhere ....the garden, down the trail, along the creek."

"They can't be far. I'll find them," Vince spoke with certainty. He rose from his work, stretched, and headed out in the yard. "Leaf! Where are you?"

Sensing drama, Crystal and Rock abandoned their toys, seeking to become part of the attention. It was another unusually beautiful summer day so Maggie herded the kids outside.

"Leaf!" Vince continued to call. Receiving no answer, he extended his search, fanning out further from the house.

"Is Leaf missing, Mommy?" Crystal asked.

"Yes, do you know where he went?"

"No," Crystal said with a pout, unhappy about Leaf taking off on an adventure without including her. Then Maggie glanced at Rock for help, but Rock just shook his head. It was obvious he knew nothing.

"Leaf!" Rock and Crystal called out, imitating the adults as they wandered around the yard.

"Contact Rahlys," Vince called out to Maggie, heading down the hill. "I'm going to check along the creek." The creek was the most dangerous place they could be.

By "contact Rahlys," Vince was referring to Maggie's ability to reach Rahlys telepathically, especially if she was under stress. Their closeness as friends when Rahlys took possession of the crystal probably had a lot to do with it. The talent extended only to connecting with Rahlys and no one else, despite all Quaylyn's efforts to improve on this achievement.

"Stay right here in the yard with me," Maggie instructed the twins anxiously, and then focused on reaching out to Rahlys.

Rahlys... Maggie called out mentally with mounting fear for Leaf's safety.

Rahlys was enjoying the warm summer day with sketchbook in hand. Her interest in the Bradley vegetable garden provided her with all the vegetables she needed, so she concentrated her gardening effort at home on flowers she and Maggie had started from seeds. Hanging baskets graced all the buildings including the woodshed and outhouse. Pots of plants in full bloom lined the edge of her southern facing porch. But her real pride and joy blossomed from the crescent shaped flower garden she planted outlined with stone around the birdbath. It was this she was sketching when she heard the faint whisper of her name tickling her mind.

Please, Rahlys, please hear me.

Maggie, what's wrong?

We can't find Leaf. Is he with you?

It was not a bizarre question. A much younger Leaf had teleported over to visit Rahlys without telling anyone before they could get across to him that he couldn't be allowed to do that because they worried about him.

No, he's not here. I'll come and help you look for him.

Rahlys immediately set down her sketching and joined Maggie and the twins in the Bradley yard. Vince came into sight once again along the creek, obviously empty handed.

"Anything...?" Maggie called down to him anyway.

"No," Vince said coming up the hill.

"Is Keiluk with him?" Rahlys asked. Maggie nodded her head. That at least was reassuring.

Rahlys drew energy from the elements around her and reached out mentally seeking Leaf's familiar signature. To her surprise he wasn't anywhere close by. She gradually expanded her search, but still couldn't locate him or the dog. Something was wrong.

"Where is he?" Maggie asked in near panic when Rahlys said nothing.

Without answering, Rahlys summoned forth the Oracle of Light. The crystal appeared hovering in the air, spinning slowly, and reflecting multi-colored light in the sunshine. She focused on the crystal and gave her command.

Seek and find Leaf and Keiluk.

The Oracle took Rahlys on a 'journey.' The search for Leaf and Keiluk began close, but quickly extended outward until eventually it spanned the globe.

"Well...?" Vince asked when Rahlys opened her eyes.

Rahlys feared to give her answer.

"I couldn't find them."

CHAPTER 15

Aaia

The journey from the Cremyn Valley to the Crescent Mountains had been arduously slow, even with the help of the star stones, but fortunately uneventful, which was just the way Rojaire liked it. Although it may have been wise to leave some of the settlers behind, at least for a while, the colonists were adamant about sticking together. Rojaire warned them of the difficulty of the passage through the mountains before setting out, but no one wanted to stay, even with adequate shelter and plenty of food.

There was far more in food and supplies at the shelter than they could carry in one load or even in two considering what lay ahead. Rojaire, Kaylya, Wessid, Traevus, Ilene, Kiril, Thayla, and even Zaloka carried packs a third their own weigh filled with tools, utensils, rope, rechargeable power crystals, kitchen ware, seeds, food, water, and useful supplies ranging from soap to paper. Drak and Sulyan insisted on carrying lighter packs that were also stuffed full. Captain Setas' small frame was deemed too frail to bare more weight than what she could eat and drink. Once they were settled in the hidden valley, a pack team could eventually return for the luxury items left behind.

They started out following the Cremyn River north for several leagues to its confluence with an unnamed creek flowing out of the east. This remarkable beginning took them through the largest swath of newly planted forest on the continent. With great care they threaded through the hand span high forest of young trees, not wishing to trample a single one. Captain Setas was so taken by the results of the tree planting venture, Rojaire expected her to change her mind about leaving the Cremyn Valley, but he did not take into consideration her desire to reach Theon.

A long period without rain had shrunk the little stream flowing into the Cremyn River leaving a wide gravel trail of dried riverbed for the colonists to walk on. They followed the smaller stream east all the way to the Crescent Mountains. Only in a few places along the way was the stream squeezed tight between its banks forcing the colonists to take to the hills. Regardless, frequent rest stops had to be called. Still, the mountains continued to loom ever closer and shortly before the next period of darkness, they reached the beginning of the underground passage. Rojaire called for a rest stop.

"I'm not looking forward to going underground," Captain Setas moaned easing her weary body down on soft grass.

"There is no other way," Rojaire said. "It will be hard, but after seeing you make it this far, I am sure you can do it." Rojaire's encouraging words perked up morale throughout the group.

"Will we be crawling on our hands and knees?" Inventor Sulyan asked pulling out the hollow reed he carved on, Ilene's flute, when there was down time.

"For the most part, no. There are a couple of tight spots of short duration. The worse spot is one area that slopes steeply down where we have to make a precarious connection from the lava tube to a cavern through a hole in the wall." Kiril knew the place Rojaire alluded to and shuddered. "We have a plan Traevus and I will share with you when we reach that point."

"I can carry on my back anyone who fears they can't make it," Thayla boldly offered. Traevus didn't doubt that for a moment. He couldn't help admiring her strength and endurance. She was fascinatingly terrifying. The group ate and rested as the sun set and the sky darkened into night.

After their final rest above ground, Rojaire led them into the first lava tube. Here it was always night and darkness reigned and despite his lecture about conserving energy, a string of sun charged crystal powered lamps followed.

The first part of the nocturnal journey proved easy despite the occasional pile of rock debris that littered the tunnels. Here the lava tubes ran fairly level and the correct route through the labyrinth was well marked. Then suddenly a tremor ran through the ground under their feet, loosening particles of crumbling rock that rained down upon them. With abated breath, everyone paused anxiously waiting for more. Ground tremors were the last thing they needed now that the colonists had entered the passage through the Crescent Mountains. Fortunately, the tremor quickly subsided and all was quiet. For the longest, they continued on in silence, listening to the mountain.

"I don't like it in here," Captain Setas croaked, breaking the silence.

"I don't either," Inventor Sulyan agreed.

Ilene would have joined in with the plaintive, but she didn't want to appear cowardly in Kiril's eyes. In the light of their lamps she could see that others shared her unease. Kiril, on the other hand, showed no concern at all for crumbling lava tube walls. All he could think of was arriving at the fabulous secret valley and what a surprise it will be for Theon, Ollen, Tassyn, Caleeza, and Edty when they all showed up.

They passed through several junctions where lava tubes connected, but Rojaire always knew the way. As much as Rojaire would have preferred to keep going, the weaker members of his team showed mounting signs of fatigue. Eventually he had to call for a period of rest.

Besides worrying about a cave-in, Rojaire had a different concern coming up altogether. They had reached the point in the passage where the floor of the lava tube began sloping downward. This downward trend would be gradual at first becoming frightfully steep before they intersected with the cave system that would take them a long way through the mountains. Some of the people he led were not as limber and sure-footed as he would like. He didn't want to take any unnecessary risks and even took some precautions before leaving the Community of the High Council. Aware of this tricky spot in the route, Rojaire had come prepared. Based on mountain climbing technology he had seen on Earth, Rojaire had Inventor Sulyan design a couple of rock anchors for the trip in his workshop. At the time, he would never have guessed that Sulyan would then surprise them by joining the colonists.

Rojaire got them moving again as soon as a few began to stir. The trek went well until the floor of the lava tube more noticeably started to slope downward. This was going to be tricky. It was time to call a rest halt while he detailed his plan to the others.

"The path we are following is going to get steep," Rojaire warned.

"You call this dark tunnel a path? It's a death trap is what it is," Captain Setas fumed. The revered matriarch didn't like this part of the journey at all. She was going to like what was coming even less.

"How steep? Up or down?" Inventor Sulyan asked with uncertainty.

"The lava tube takes a frightfully steep dive down. It's so steep, if you slip and fall, gravity and momentum may take you away," Rojaire informed them solemnly. "We need to put in a safety net."

"I'm starting to have a distinct dislike for the underground," Drak mumbled.

"What did you have in mind?" Kaylya asked to bring the discussion back to solutions.

"Here's the plan." He pulled a rock anchor out of his pack to show them. "After we get everyone as close to the cavern entrance as we comfortably can, we will find a place to anchor a rope to the rocks using this. We have lots of rope; we'll put it to use."

"Are you sure that's going to hold us?" Drak asked worried.

"Sulyan made these for us and Traevus, Kaylya, and I tested them in the mountains on the Main Land. When we reach the point where you feel uncomfortable, Traevus and I will continue on down to the mouth of the cavern driving in anchors and feeding out rope as we go. Once we are there, we will secure the other end of the line in the cave. Then, Traevus will remain at the cave entrance at the receiving end of the line while I return and guide you down one at a time."

"What about me?" Kiril asked. He felt that having made the passage before with Rojaire and Traevus, without a safety rope, should recommend him for an active role.

"Kiril, I want you to be responsible for the others until everyone has arrived safely. You will be on the last trip." It wasn't exactly what he had in mind, but it did give him a sense of responsibility.

"Yes, sir."

After going some distance with the rock under their feet only gradually adding gradient, things suddenly changed considerably. "How much further do we have to go?" Zaloka quivered, staring down the sharply sloping way ahead of them.

"We'll stop here," Rojaire said and pulled a rock anchor out of his pack.

"I'll finally get to see this thing put to use," Inventor Sulyan said with a chuckle.

"Let's just hope it works," Rojaire said looking for the best place to wedge it in. There were plenty of cracks and rock protrusions, but much of it crumbled away easily. He needed something substantial to anchor to. Traevus held a light on him while he worked. Several steps further down the sloping lava tube he found the secure anchorage he was looking for and drove it in. After frequent tugs, giving it all his weight, he was satisfied. "Ready, Traevus?" The two men tugged together as hard as they could. The anchor held. "Let's go." Rojaire and Traevus paid out the rope as they descended, enjoying the extra security of a line. It wasn't long before the men seemed to drop out of sight. Only the movement of the rope noted their progress.

"We have to go down there?" Zaloka sighed with dismay.

"Don't worry, Zaloka, I won't let you fall," Thayla promised her. Nothing seemed to faze Thayla. For Thayla every moment was a welcomed challenge which she fearlessly faced. Kiril wondered if all her people were like that.

"If anyone is going to protect her, it will be me," Wessid said good-humoredly and put an arm around Zaloka to calm her. But Kiril could detect the unease in Wessid's voice.

"I've done it before without a rope; with a guideline it will be easy," Kiril assured them. He turned toward Ilene to offer her personal assurance. In the light of their lamps he could see all the color in her face had drained away. "It will be all right," he added softly. Ilene actually smiled for his effort.

They sat quietly and waited in the light of their lamps for Rojaire's return. Only Thayla seemed willing to extinguish her light to save energy. Then Kiril turned off his lamp to set an example; Drak, Wessid, and Captain Setas followed suite. They tried to relax as much as they could.

It was some time before they spotted a light returning; Rojaire was on his way back. They stood up waiting for him to reach them. "How was it?" Kiril asked.

"Good, the rope is anchored at the other end and Traevus is waiting at the mouth of the cave. Captain Setas, you're first. I'll go ahead of you in case you lose your footing. You're going to hold on to the line as you go. Ready?"

"Yes, 'Captain' Rojaire." she said with great respect. Rojaire knew Setas calling him "Captain" was the highest honor she could bestow. He nodded appreciatively.

"Be brave," Inventor Sulyan called out to her as Rojaire led Captain Setas to the guide rope. Only after they could be seen no longer did the group sit back down to wait. It seemed a long time before Rojaire returned, but return he did.

"Captain Setas made it fine; it just took a while. Zaloka you're next."

"I'll be glad when this is over," she admitted.

Time dragged on, but eventually it was Inventor Sulyan's turn, then Drak's, Ilene's, and Kaylya's respectively. When Rojaire arrived for Wessid, Kiril spoke up. "I don't need help reaching the caves. I can make it on my own, save you a trip."

"I'm with Kiril," Thayla said. "We can go together. He can show me the way."

Rojaire considered their proposal carefully. "All right, give us enough time to arrive then follow the line down. Make sure you maintain a grip on the rope," Rojaire emphasized. Thayla and Kiril watched Rojaire and Wessid recede into the darkness.

"So how's the romance going, Little Proton?" Thayla asked to lighten the mood once they were alone.

"Great!" Kiril declared with more certainty than he actually felt.

"Are you sure?" Kiril blushed. "Earth sounds like an unusual place, I wouldn't mind seeing it for myself." The distant world often crept into conversation since so many of their group have actually been there including Rojaire and Kaylya, as well as Theon and Caleeza.

"Do you really think that's very likely? I mean, we're all renegades now, aren't we?"

"Anything is always possible, Little Proton. Don't ever forget that!"

"So do you expect to return to Twaka someday?"

"No," Thayla answered emphatically without hesitation.

"Why not?" he asked boldly, surprised by her answer. It was his understanding, Thayla was some kind of warrior princess on her world.

"I was quite young still when my parents sent me away to a warrior training camp, far from any cities or settlements, for breaking rules of etiquette and decorum at the royal court. I was written off, then and there, as expendable."

"You a rebel; imagine that!"

"It's not like I would be missed. I have four sisters and two brothers, all very ambitious, who have long been in intense competition for succession to the throne."

"Warrior training camp seems to have agreed with you," Kiril observed.

"It turned my life around. For the first time I was happy. I thrived on the tough training and discipline, excelling in the martial arts. I also enjoyed the freedom of wide open spaces. When I returned to the royal court after my training, I found life at the palace unbearable. Its lack of substance and conniving pettiness were maddening."

"So you became a warrior," Kiril said, indicating the deadly blade she always carried. He'd never seen her use it. "Aren't your talents being wasted here?"

"Are they? I think that remains to be seen. At some point someone may need to protect your puny hide." Kiril didn't have a response.

"Anyway, when Kaydra, Aaia's mentor to Twaka, needed a body guard, I saw my opportunity to escape."

"But why did you decide to join the colony?"

"Why not? I needed space to think and this sounded like a grand adventure. Why are you here, Little Proton? Shouldn't you be in school?"

"I don't need the Academy," Kiril said with disdain. "I am fulfilling my destiny. I'm where I'm supposed to be, recording Lynnara's new history." Thayla didn't challenge his answer and the two became quiet.

"I guess we can start to descend," Kiril said after what he hoped was enough time.

"You go first; you're leading the way."

"I'm supposed to be last," he reminded her.

Thayla didn't argue; she grabbed ahold of the guide rope and started down. Placing both hands on the line, Kiril followed close. It quickly became apparent that Thayla was as sure-footed as she was self-assured. Kiril fell further and further behind as they descended, making him feel increasingly less like a leader.

"Careful, take your time," she kept instructing him as she lithely sped on ahead. "I can see a light ahead," Thayla called back to him after some time.

Then the mountain began to rumble.

Both Thayla and Kiril paused as the rumble grew menacingly louder and drew ever closer. "Ground tremor!" Kiril gasped just before the mountain began to shake. "Hold on," he shouted as much to himself as to Thayla. Bits and pieces of tunnel wall crumbled before their eyes, raining down rocks large and small. Much of the debris, driven by momentum, continued on down the steep decline forming a rock stream.

Kiril tried to move forward, but was repeatedly knocked off his feet, the weight of his pack nearly pulling him down into the flow of debris as he clung on desperately to the guide rope. Just as the tremor seemed ready to ease, it intensified. "Ah!" Kiril screamed as a boulder dropped out the ceiling and slid pass him. No one heard him over the din. Then suddenly he was moving. Not understanding what was happening at first, he looked at his hands, but his hands were still firmly attached to the line. Then with horror he realized the problem; the upper end of the rope was no longer attached to the tunnel wall. Kiril frantically struggled to regain footing, but the intense shaking, the resulting rock slide, the choking dust, and the burdensome weight of his pack defeated all his efforts.

"Hold on to the rope!" Rojaire and Traevus shouted out to him as he passed by the opening to the cavern. Unable to stop his momentum, Kiril slid on ...down the maw of the tunnel. Then he went airborne. In freefall, he dropped pass Thayla, visible in the glow of her headlamp, dangling from a taut rope. Then he came to a jolting halt that nearly ripped his arms out of his shoulders and knocked his head lamp off his head, disappearing in the void below. Finally the rumbling and shaking ceased, a stream of rock continuing to trickle down from the brink of no return long after the shaking stopped.

"Help!" Kiril cried out in pain and stress. His hands felt like they were on fire, burned from the friction of the rope and slipping. Looking up, he could see a pinpoint of light above him, marking Thayla's location. Was she really that far away?

"Kiril, are you alright?" Thayla shouted down to him.

"Yes...no! I can't hold on," he shouted back, the rope slipping a little through his hands.

Then he heard her shout up to a murmur of voices almost too distant and faint for him to hear. "He's down below me."

"Hold on," she shouted back to him. "Grab the rope with your legs to help alleviate the strain." Kiril wrapped his body around the rope squeezing hard, but despite all his efforts, more rope inched through his grasp.

"I can't hold on!" he shouted back.

"Drop your pack!" she instructed, but Kiril couldn't release his hold enough to do so.

"I can't!"

"Hold on," she called down again. "Don't you dare let go of that rope, Little Proton. I'm going to climb up and then we will pull you up." Her use of the nickname she had given him calmed him some.

Then Thayla began her climb. The rope jerked with her efforts, each tug sending a jolt of pain searing through his body. Kiril gritted his teeth, struggling to hold on. The light above barely seemed to move. After what seemed like an interminable among of time, the light moved off, leaving Kiril nothing to focus on.

Slowly, but skillfully, Thayla climbed up out of the abyss. When her head appeared over the lip of the drop off, Rojaire and Traevus, anchored to ropes, reached for her and pulled her to safety.

Kiril's body screamed with pain; he couldn't hold on much longer. Any moment now he feared he would fall to his death. He closed his eyes to the darkness to concentrate. Then he remembered his star stone. Why hadn't he thought of it before? Kiril focused intently on the cavern he'd visited before with its veins of quartz and gold, willing himself there.

"Where's Kiril? Is he hurt?" Zaloka asked anxiously.

"He's struggling to hang on; we have to haul him up," Thayla said.

"Everyone grab ahold of the rope," Rojaire ordered, "and we pull together."

But when they grabbed the rope it came easily. They were too late.

Zaloka and Ilene collapsed into each other's arms, Zaloka screeching in grief.

"It's all right, Mother; I'm here," Kiril said in the cavern beside them, then sank down to the cavern floor his heart pounding.

A roaring cheer erupted all around him.

The first ground tremor stirred deep beneath Mt. Vatre, radiating out to the Crescent Mountains. It did not go unnoted. The essence of what had once been Sarus, now the conscious awareness of the Crystalline Landscape, sensed a minor irritation. Something evil and faintly familiar that had long been dormant was awakening. A thick, dark plume of smoke rose high above Mt. Vatre's collapsed caldron. To learn more, Sarus concentrated energy along the inner edge of the mass of crystals encircling the volcano.

The second tremor started as a low rumble, quickly growing in intensity. The mountain shook, spewing ash and sending shock waves through the Crystalline Landscape, shattering crystals as Sarus perceived the essence of Droclum awakening. The shock waves spread out far and wide across the continent's interior, reaching beyond the Crescent Mountains and the continent's coastline all the way to Alaia Island, shaking Captain Setas' deserted cottage constructed of living trees. Hidden away in her workroom, in a drawer of relics she had combed off the beach, Droclum's wand glowed momentarily with energy, then went dormant again.

☆☆☆☆

"Oh...!" Theon moaned, as the ground lurched violently knocking him off his feet, his left side landing hard on the stone pavilion. The ground continued to shake nearly drowning out his curses; there was nothing he could do, but ride it out. At least he was out in the opening where rocks couldn't fall on him. Finally the tremor subsided. "Ah..." Theon moaned, followed by a string of words Edty lacked the cultural background to understand, but this time Edty heard him and came running from the perimeter of the camp.

"Oh, no, oh, no...," Edty whimpered. He had promised Tassyn.

"Ah...." Theon's face contorted in agony with any movement he made.

"What do I do? What do I do?" Edty begged for guidance. It was obvious, even to Edty, that Theon had fallen and was in lots of pain ...a horrible development. Even worse, Caleeza and Tassyn left a rotation ago to search for Ollen. Caleeza had argued the "No one ventures out alone." rule and won. Theon and Edty were alone.

"Help me up. Where's my staff?" Theon grimaced between breaths.

"Up...? Staff...?" Edty asked in a panic frenzy, nearly tripping over the staff. "Here it is."

But all efforts to move Theon proved too painful for him to bear. Theon felt certain he had cracked some ribs, if not broken them all together. It was probably best to move as little as possible. In the end, Edty made him as comfortable as he could where he lay. He placed padding under his head and stuffed grasses under him to get his body off the unforgivingly hard stones. At least he was out of the cavern in case of an aftershock.

It could take a long time for Theon to heal. Meanwhile he would be exposed to the elements, so after infusing Theon with as much strong pain-easing tea he could get down him. Edty set about constructing a temporary shelter of sticks and grasses around Theon. Then he pressed their star stone in Theon's hand to help him draw whatever healing energy he could. It was their last star stone. Caleeza had confessed to losing the one she and Ollen had taken with them.

Edty devoted all his time and effort to Theon's care. When Theon slept, Edty gathered the herbs he needed to make Theon's tea, prepared nourishing foods for him to eat, and heated stones by the fire to place beside him to keep him warm.

"Edty," Theon called from his tented shelter after waking from a long sleep.

"I'm here," Edty answer deferentially, appearing in the opening to the tent.

"Would you be so kind as to look in my chamber by my sleeping area for my journal?" Theon asked politely.

"Yes, sir." Edty knew the book Theon was asking for. He also knew it was actually Kiril's journal, but preferred not to mention that. The first in longevity thought about Kiril nearly as much as he thought about his daughter on Earth.

"Are you hungry?" Edty asked delivering the book.

"I'll eat after a while," Theon said holding the journal unopened in his hands, waiting for Edty to leave. Sensing he had been dismissed, Edty left to heat up some food.

Theon had done a lot of thinking confined as he was. He wasn't likely to get much better. There was no healer. How long did he want to live like this? He leafed through Kiril's journal reading excerpts about tree planting, declarations of Lynnara's independence, spelunking, lost expedition members found, and the discovery of new life forms. The writing, far from merely factual, exceeded Theon's expectations with warm insightfulness and brilliant details, all written with the bright-eyed expectations of youth. It saddened him he would never see the boy again. *I hope you're staying out of trouble.* The boy had an impetuous nature that could easily get him into trouble.

Reading about the expedition he and Kiril had shared, Theon thought about another expedition; one he had shared with his daughter Ilene ... how he longed to see her again. Tears blurred the words on the page.

"Time to eat," Edty announced, entering the tent with a hot gourd of soup. Theon covered up his tears with activity, gingerly sitting up as Edty put woven mats in place in preparation to eat.

"Edty, do you think Rojaire will ever return?" Edty froze. It was a question he might ask, but it was frightening coming from the mighty Theon. Edty understood it was his turn to be strong.

"Nothing will prevent Rojaire from returning and Traevus and Kiril will be with him; that I truly believe," Edty said. Such a decisive statement from Edty struck Theon as odd. It went against his usual indecisive nature.

"In that case, I hope Ollen brings back Kiril's map," Theon said softly. "I promised it would be here when he got back."

CHAPTER 16

Earth

Melinda had no doubt Droclum's evil essence had burned the destination on the map with a lightning bolt, showing her where to go. Baton Rouge was the closest town name she could read along the singed edges of the hole burned into her map. It was a long way to go. *Droclum will never cease to taunt me until I face him, but then what?* Resolving to end this ordeal as quickly as possible, Melinda took a bus from the park to the Denver airport. At the airport she bought a plane ticket to Baton Rouge, Louisiana.

It was a bold move for her to make. Melinda had only flown in a small seaplane before, in Southeast Alaska, once, when she and Greg flew from Ketchikan to Papa's boat, The Taku, broken down and moored in a secluded bay where Papa waited for the part they were bringing in. It had been an exciting experience seeing her world from up in the air.

This plane ride was very different. During the flight, she contemplated with dread what might lie ahead. *What am I rushing toward with wings?*

Stepping out of the airport in Baton Rouge, Louisiana, the heat and humidity hit Melinda like an ice cube entering a hot sauna. The intake of heat took her breath away, the air seemingly too hot to breathe into her lungs, making her gasp for air. A dozen steps from the door sweat covered her skin. The midday sun blazed hotly directly overhead, offering little in the way of shade anywhere. By the time she reached the highway, her clothes were wet with sweat.

From the highway she looked for landmarks ...mountains, hills, anything that could be used for a point of reference. There was nothing; the land was decidedly flat shimmering in heat that made everything seem to vibrate. The key in her pocket tugged strongly. She headed south the key relentlessly urging her on, the strength of its pull confirming she was closer to her destination.

It took most of the day to hike through the city. She trudged on, despite the stifling heat, taking every opportunity to rest in shade whenever shade presented itself. How did these people survive in such heat, she wondered?

Eventually suburbs thinned into farmland and farmland into wetlands. Looking at the landscape, Melinda feared it was going to be difficult to find a suitable place to camp free of snakes or worse. Finally the sun lowered to the horizon bringing some relief from the heat, but the cooler air enlivened the mosquitoes drawn to her blood for nourishment. As darkness fell, Melinda found herself entering another little town. When she came upon a small rundown motel at the edge of town, she rented a room for the night.

Wasting no time getting started in the morning, she headed out early into moist warm air that promised another hot day. It was obvious when she stepped out it had rained during the night. Whether it was because she had been too tired to dream, or because the evil force driving her was satisfied with her progress, she had slept soundly through the night undisturbed by rain or Droclum.

The streets and pavement quickly steam dried in the sun, adding to the humidity. By mid-morning she reached a bridge crossing the Mississippi River. *Should I cross the river or continue on this side?* At a safe distance from the traffic and road, Melinda held the key enclosed in her hand, stretched out her arm, and turned slowly. Gauging by the tug on her arm, she needed to continue south crossing the river. Cautiously she headed for the bridge.

The river was wide and traffic on the bridge loud and steady. Melinda felt anxious walking the narrow edge with the deep muddy current of the Mississippi flowing below on one side and trucks and cars whizzing by inches away from her on the other. With steady focus forward, she finally made it across, glad to put some distance between her and the traffic.

As Melinda continued south, sugarcane fields and swampland became regular features of the landscape, and communities became smaller and smaller. To avoid attention, especially on the outskirts of small towns where everyone probably knew everyone else, she decided it would be best to move away from the road. While no car was passing to see her, she jumped the deep ditch along the side of the road and ventured into the nearest field. The sugarcane grew tall and could easily conceal a person; but the air was stifling hot and the leaves cut her skin. Suddenly she jumped back in a silent screech. A terrifying sight, a snake, a real live snake lay stretched out before her. Long before Melinda regained her composure, the snake quickly, and just as silently, slithered away, but her heart pounded in her ears long after. So much for hiking through the fields.

She exited the sugarcane field, glad to be out in the sun again, onto a headland that bordered yet another cane field. Beyond the cane fields, trees grew. To Melinda's relief, a breeze picked up, bringing in clouds and cooling things off some. She picked her way carefully through the headland grasses looking for snakes, and headed in the direction of the distant trees. By the time she reached the edge of the woods, a cloud momentarily veiled the sun and a low distant rumble of thunder played overhead. Rain would cool the air, but what could she do for shelter?

She spotted a muddy track cutting through the woods a short distance away and made her way to it. Melinda stepped into the edge of the woods and soon stopped short. The tangle of fan-like foliage, woody spires, vines, and moss-draped trees took her back to her dream when Droclum called her. The realization gripped her heart with horror. *This is where Droclum's essence is taking me.* She didn't want to go on. Fear chilled her spine. Turning around, Melinda made a dash for the openness of the headland. The opposing tugging jerk of the key in her pocket and the pull on the blood in her veins made her nauseous. A few more steps and nausea nearly brought her to her knees. Fighting the sickness, Melinda continued running against the tug of the key toward the road. She didn't make it far before nausea doubled her over, empting the meager contents of her stomach.

When Melinda recovered somewhat, she stood and changed direction, walking back toward the mud track through the woods. To her relief, the illness eased, but she would have to face whatever horror waited for her. She could not turn back if she wanted to.

The rough cut through the trees looked recent and reminded her of a logging road. Trees and brush had been cut down and old boards had been brought in and deposited on the muddy track to help support whatever vehicles were passing here ...and it led to whatever the key was luring her toward.

Melinda cautiously followed the rough cut through the dark woods, now dreading what she would find. The sky darkened as the thunderstorm moved closer. A brighter flash of lightning forked through the lowering clouds followed by a louder, longer rumble of thunder and even a few large drops of rain fell. Still the storm held off, biding its time and increasing its theatrics with even brighter flashes of light and louder booms of thunder.

It was Melinda's first experience with a tropical thunderstorm, not counting the one in her nightmare marking her map, and with each flash and crash she crouched low to the ground, closed her eyes, and covered her ears. The sky grew darker. She didn't want to go on. Soon nightfall would add to the darkness, and she certainly didn't want to get caught in these forbidding woods after dark, but there was no turning around.

Then she came up with a compromise. She couldn't turn around and go back, but she didn't necessarily have to continue forward either. Why not make camp here? There was no one around to stop her. To her surprise, by the time she had constructed her tarp shelter, the storm had moved on with all its fury unspent and the clouds had scattered to let in the last rays of the sun before it dropped below the horizon for the night. There was no way she was going to sleep. Using wood that had been used to strengthen the road, Melinda built a fire.

Along the railroad tracks in Alaska's Susitna Valley, Leaf and Keiluk arrived at the tree where Raven perched, at which point Raven flew off again to reconnoiter up ahead. He soon sent Leaf images of a work crew on the tracks coming his way. The workers would stop and question a boy and his dog by the tracks. Deciding it would be best not to be seen, Leaf led Keiluk away from the railroad tracks through tall late summer foliage down to the bank of the Susitna River. Keiluk sniffed circles around Leaf, chasing scents of shrews, voles, and fox, bear scat and moose droppings, and numerous other intoxicating smells that had crossed their path. The silty river flowed by, whispering words of caution as boy and dog walked along its sandy bank.

Seeing Leaf and Keiluk leave the railroad tracks, Raven joined them down by the river, landing in a nearby tree to watch their progress. When they came to a rivulet of clear, fresh water flowing out of the hillside making its way to the river, they paused for a drink. Feeling hungry, Leaf pulled the little carrots he had harvested from the garden out his pocket. Dusty and somewhat wilted, they no longer looked as appetizing as they did before. Hoping to revive them, he swished them in the cool water rinsing off the dirt and giving them new life. Then finding a shady spot by a weathered log dropped by the spring flood, he sat down to eat, sharing his meager bounty with Keiluk and Raven.

"Sorry I don't have more to offer," he apologized to his friends, placing a carrot a comfortable distance away for Raven after feeding a carrot to Keiluk. "I guess we should keep moving," he said when all the carrots were gone.

☆☆☆☆

"What do you mean you can't find him?" Maggie cried, panic constricting her throat. "You think he's...," the thought was too unbearable to utter.

"No," Rahlys hastily assured her.

"You can find anyone you want. So where is he?"

"I don't know. I believe he has put a shield in place preventing me from detecting his whereabouts. In other words, he doesn't want to be found."

"But why?" Vince asked. "Why would he hide?"

"I don't know," Rahlys said, repeating the words again. "Did he have anything special on his mind this morning before he disappeared?" Rahlys knew that Leaf was an independent thinker despite his tender young age and if he had decided to take some action, nothing would stand in his way.

"He asked about Melinda," Vince informed her. "He wanted to know where she lives, so Maggie showed him where Ketchikan is on an Alaska map."

"Oh, no," Maggie moaned. "He couldn't be headed for Ketchikan ... could he?" Maggie asked incredulously.

"Well, maybe."

"You really think Leaf went looking for Melinda? But that's impossible." No sooner than he said it, Vince realized that nothing was quite impossible when it came to Leaf. "But why? Melinda has been gone for months. Why would he go looking for her now?"

"Maybe he thinks she is in some kind of trouble," Rahlys offered. *Maybe I need to check on Melinda and make sure she is not in trouble,* she added to herself, but she decided to do so away from Maggie and Vince. She didn't want to add to their stress.

"But how would he know if she were in trouble?" Maggie asked, not thoroughly convinced.

Rahlys gave Maggie a sympathetic glance. "Melinda and Leaf have always been closely connected. Physical distance matters very little. You underestimate Leaf's abilities. Regardless, he can't be far," she added, hoping to console her. "He has to be able to visualize a destination to go there. The furthest Leaf could have maybe gone would be to your place in town," Rahlys reasoned.

"This is what I have always feared would happen, that he would one day vanish and we wouldn't be able to find him."

"At least Keiluk is with him," Vince said taking his wife into his arms to comfort her, but the stricken look on his face revealed his own painful anxiety.

Crystal and Rock's cheerful giggles at play jarred incongruently with the sharp worry consuming the adults. "We'll find him," Rahlys said taking charge. "I'll go to town and check with Jack and start looking for Leaf from that end. But he's probably following the railroad tracks," Rahlys offered. "So Vince, you can take the four-wheeler and start on this end. Also alert Grumpy George in case he shows up there. Maybe he will help with the search. Maggie, you and the twins continue looking for him here. He may return on his own." Rahlys knew she couldn't tell Maggie to just sit and wait.

After Rahlys left, Vince held his wife a little longer, then started up the four-wheeler. Maggie stared down the trail long after he vanished into the summer brush. For the longest she continued to stand there unmoving, drenched in stunned anxiety. Eventually she pulled herself together, reminding herself she still had two small children to take care of and led the twins indoors to make them some dinner. Even though she had no appetite, the children still had to eat.

Immediately Crystal and Rock carted themselves off to the boys' room which served as their main playroom. Maggie headed to the kitchen where she mechanically sliced up an apple and constructed cheese sandwiches, frequently pausing at her task to wipe away tears from her moist cheeks with a dishtowel.

In the playroom, Crystal put down the toy robot and turned to Rock. "We need to go and look for Leaf," she said with all seriousness.

"Okay," Rock agreed, easily led by his sister.

Distracted by worry, Maggie did not notice when Rock and Crystal slipped out the door. When their plates were finally ready, she took them into the family room and called the twins to the table to eat. When they didn't answer her call, she strolled to the playroom to gather them, but the twins were not there. She looked in Crystal's room.

"Crystal! Rock!" she called walking through the cabin, a new panic shattering her confused mind. When her search turned up empty, Maggie rushed out the door screaming wildly. "Crystal! Rock!" she shouted out at the top of her lungs. Still no answer.

Maggie dashed about madly crying and screaming. Then finally catching the tiniest hint of movement, she dashed down the trail. "Rock! Crystal!"

"We're right here, Mommy," Rock called back as his mother caught sight of them. Sobs of relief gushed over. Rushing to them, Maggie grabbed them both into her arms and held them tightly.

"We were just looking for Leaf," Crystal explained. Maggie broke down in uncontrolled weeping as she continued to hold on to them, unwilling to ever let them go. Rock and Crystal, sensing her need for release, let their mother cry it out.

☆☆☆☆

Rahlys teleported to the backyard of Vince and Maggie's town abode, a secluded corner hidden from view by alders and fireweed. When she knocked on the door, there was no answer. Jack wasn't home, and if Leaf was there, he wasn't answering. Grasping the Oracle of Light in her hand, she tried again to detect Leaf's essence, but still without success. Could Melinda really play in Leaf's disappearance? It's time to find out.

Rahlys focused on Melinda, reaching for her familiar essence, so minutely touched by Droclum. When she didn't find it, she extended the reach, beyond the state, and even beyond the country. Melinda was undetectable. The realization stunned her. *Melinda doesn't have Leaf's ability to throw up a shield. Something is preventing me from detecting her. Something is wrong.*

Rahlys felt the need to talk to someone, but she didn't want to further stress out Maggie or Vince. Detecting Jack's presence at the gift shop with Elaine, she walked straight there.

"Rahlys!" Jack greeted with delight when she entered the shop. "What brings you to town?" Elaine was busy at the cash register helping a customer. "Is something wrong?" he asked noting Rahlys' agitation.

"Oh...," Rahlys didn't know where to start. "Can we go somewhere to talk?" she asked. Jack would make an excellent soundboard to share her thoughts with.

"Sure... let's step out into the glorious sunshine," Jack suggested.

"Yes," Rahlys nodded in agreement.

Jack led her to a nearby picnic table, warmed by the sun. "I take it something has happened," he said opening the dialogue.

"Leaf is missing," she blurted out.

"What? But you are the Guardian of the Light. Can't you do ... whatever it is you do... to find him?" Jack asked.

"It's not working this time?"

"Huh?"

"I think Leaf has put up a shield to prevent me from finding him."

"Now why would he do that?"

"Again this is speculation, but Vince and Maggie said he asked about Melinda. I think Leaf has detected Melinda is in some kind of trouble and he is going to her to help. I can't find Melinda either."

"I didn't know Melinda could do the shield thing."

"She can't."

"Leaf is shielding Melinda, too?"

"No, I don't think so. Something else is going on here."

"Wow," was all Jack could say at this point. A powerless man from Earth, he had seen many wonders. Kaylya, from across the galaxy, had been like a daughter to him. Then his immersion into the Order of the Oracle had opened up another world. Suddenly he had an idea. "The painting upstairs," he said getting excited over the possibility. "Elaine regularly enquires about Ilene's whereabouts. Maybe it can locate Leaf for us."

After helping Jack up the stairs by drawing on a little magic, Jack unlocked the door. Rahlys didn't make an issue of it, but she was a little surprised that Jack possessed a key to Elaine's living quarters.

As soon as they entered the apartment, the hologram crystal emerged from the painting on the wall by the door. The hologram portrait of the Oracle of Light recognized Rahlys as the artist who rendered it into being. It twirled about the Guardian of the Light in greeting.

"It certainly seems to like you," Jack said offhandedly closing the door. Rahlys just smiled.

"Please, where is Leaf?" she asked the hologram, not wasting any time. Just as quick to respond, the radiant hologram went into action, zinging across the room in a comet blaze of light, sizzling out a reply.

ALONG THE RIVER!

As usual, short of yes and no questions, the hologram crystal's answers were vague. "The Susitna River?" she asked for clarification. The hologram sparked.

YES.

"North or south of town?"

NORTH.

"Thanks, Jack," Rahlys said turning to him. "You were a great help." Then giving him a quick peck on the cheek, she disappeared.

Vince.

From the landmark big rock on the bank of the river not far from the foot of their trail Rahlys reached out to Vince connecting with his mind.

Vince, Leaf is along the river.

Rahlys detected Vince relaying the information to Grumpy George.

"We can use my riverboat to search," George said.

"The sun is starting to set," Vince pointed out, eyeing the sky. "And some clouds are moving in. Although it was still summer, night had already started its slow return.

"We still have time," George reassured him. The two men left the railroad tracks, turning their four-wheelers toward the river.

☆☆☆☆

Along the river under blades of dark clouds slicing up the summer sky, a blazing sunset of yellow, orange, red, and salmon silhouetting the mountain in deep purple reflected off the water. Leaf knew it would eventually get dark for a while, but then the sky would lighten again for another long Alaska summer day. Leaf wasn't worried; he could always make glow globes.

But Leaf was hungry. He missed out on Mommy's lunch and now he's missed dinner too. There were fish in the river he could draw out and he could easily make fire, but the fish were Leaf's friends. Instead of fish, he tried to fill up on berries. Keiluk found a fish carcass left by the bears in the brushes beside the river and shared it with Raven who took his portion up in a tree where he held it against a branch with one claw while he tore it with his beak to eat it.

Leaf was also tired and looked for a comfortable spot to take a nap. He chose a grassy spot away from the river under the shelter of some trees and lay down. After checking out the area making sure all was well, Keiluk curled up to her young master to keep him warm and safe. Raven roosted comfortably overhead in one of the trees. Soon the three companions slept peacefully.

☆☆☆☆

After connecting with Vince, Rahlys summoned Raven. If Leaf had shielded himself, and Keiluk too, against her, perhaps Raven could succeed where she couldn't. Hearing Rahlys' summons, Raven shook himself awake. He glanced down, turning his head, to see Leaf and Keiluk sleeping below him. Then Raven took off heading north, following Rahlys' compelling call.

Leaf had covered quite some distance for such a little fellow Raven realized flying over it, but soon he spotted Rahlys on the big rock by the river. "Aaaarrrk!" he called out, his deep throaty cry shattering the evening stillness.

I need your help to find Leaf. He's somewhere along the river. Rahlys informed him.

Circling overhead, Raven immediately telepathed images to her of Leaf and Keiluk sleeping in the woods.

Can you take me there? Please!

In response, Raven flew off following the river heading south. After a distance, he paused, flying circles, until Rahlys teleported to the riverbank below. After repeating the sequence a couple times, Raven led Rahlys to the spot where Leaf and Keiluk were sleeping.

"Aaaarrrk!" Raven squawked in surprise. The boy and dog were no longer there. Rahlys and Raven could see the indention in the grasses where they had been, but Leaf and Keiluk were gone.

☆☆☆☆

More than four thousand miles away in the Louisiana woods, darkness had long ago closed in. Sitting by her campfire, Melinda had an increasingly difficult time keeping her eyes open, adding wood to the fire and swatting mosquitoes the only things keeping her awake. But it had been a long day, and eventually she lost the battle. As her eyelids closed, storm clouds moved in.

A flash of lightning struck the brush road followed by an explosion of thunder. Melinda bolted awake, screaming silently. Beside her, a section of the roadway burned brightly, bellowed by Droclum's breath.

Melinda.

His voice felt so close, Melinda looked around expecting to see him. She stood for a better vantage point, but still she could see no one.

Leave me alone. Melinda shivered in the warm night. *Go away.*

Droclum's wicked laugh chilled her heart.

You're almost there. Follow me.

The powerful tug of the key compelled her forward. She tried to resist, stepping back, but resistance proved painful. Taking another step back, she buckled up in agony.

Come.

The message boomed in her head.

"No!" Leaf shouted, materializing suddenly before her with Keiluk by his side. The burning road lit his youthful countenance, stern with determination, his red hair aflame with firelight, his emerald eyes glowed with intensity. Keiluk barked momentarily in confusion, but sensing she was out of her league, quieted with Leaf's touch.

"Leaf," Melinda gasped, nearly inaudible. "Help me."

The whispery sound barely escaped Melinda's throat. Leaf had never heard Melinda speak before and ran up to her.

"Melinda you spoke," he said amazed, putting his arms around her. His touch helped ease the pain.

"Leaf! What are you doing here?" she gasped.

Before Leaf could answer, a shattering boom of thunder accompanied another blinding flash of lightning that set another section of road on fire.

"Follow!" a voice boomed.

"Don't go," Leaf begged.

"I have to," Melinda cried, her whole body shuddering with the strain of resistance.

"Then I will go with you."

Clutching each other tightly, they followed the burning road, Keiluk close behind them.

CHAPTER 17

Aaia

Leaving Theon in Edty's care had been extremely difficult for both Caleeza and Tassyn. Theon's frail longevity and Edty's simple mindedness were a frightening combination. But Caleeza needed to find Ollen. She and Ollen had both lost someone to the continent. Ollen had buried Cremyn on a hillside in the Zayla River Valley. Caleeza had lost Sarus to the Crystalline Landscape, but now they had each other.

Caleeza was leading Tassyn through the jungle gym forest above the rushing water of the stream, when the ground tremor passed through. They managed to hold on tightly while the trees swayed. Fortunately the stout branches were able to sustain their weight. When the swaying finally stopped, several of the crawling life forms came out to investigate. Having been warned of their existence, Tassyn had enough presence of mind to knock one of the strange tubular creatures rushing toward him away, causing it to rear up on its hind end and change direction. When it collided with one of its own kind, it too did the rear end pirouette and the pair ran off, disappearing again in a tiny hole in the tree branch. It wasn't long before all the little crawling life forms had retreated.

Touching ground on the other side of the stream, Caleeza led Tassyn toward the growing sound of the waterfall. They advanced cautiously, not wanting to fall through any openings in the ground that may be concealed in foliage. They reached the waterfall without mishap and gazed over the edge of the cliff. Gauging her distance from the edge, Caleeza searched for the opening she had fallen through. She covered the area over and over, even tearing back the foliage that revealed nothing but solid soil and rock.

"I met the bear beast right here," she repeated time and again with growing frustration as Tassyn watched for a reappearance of the beast. "I was backing away from the animal when I fell through an opening in the ground. It was here. I'm telling the truth," she said, starting to doubt herself.

"I believe you," Tassyn assured her. "Some things are just inexplicable." For Tassyn much of Caleeza's life seemed shrouded in mystery. She claimed she had vanished in an energy field from the Crystalline Landscape, appeared on Earth, and eventually returned with Sarus's help to the land of crystals. Her sojourn to Earth had supposedly been confirmed, but the existence of Sarus as a spiritual part of the Crystalline Landscape remained a mystery. "We need to continue our search for Ollen," he finally convinced her.

Tassyn and Caleeza carefully picked out a safe route down the rocky cliff, dislodging a few loose stones along the way, to the bottom of the waterfall and searched the area. "Ollen, where are you?" they called out from time to time. Only their echo, bouncing off the hills, came back. Where would he have gone after going over the waterfall? Had he been injured, or worse, in the fall? So much time had passed since they had been separated. Even more puzzling in Caleeza's mind was the disappearance of the hole she had dropped down, leading her to Chitter. Had something similar happened to Ollen? On a positive note, there was no sign of the bear beast.

Caleeza and Tassyn covered all the ground that she and Ollen had traveled, and beyond, without finding a trace of him. "Maybe we should leave the stream and search inland," Caleeza suggested after they had covered a great distance. Tassyn thought about it before speaking.

"I think Ollen would follow the stream ...to look for you ...looking for him." At least he hoped that was the case. "He would also want to see where the water flows to," Tassyn added. The stream would have to eventually, somehow, make it out to the sea, he reasoned. They continued following the stream for some time in silence.

"Perhaps we should consider making camp," Tassyn suggested after they had trekked many leagues without resting. The sun had already dropped behind the mountain ridge. Soon they would be entering another long period of darkness, lit only by Seaa and the more distant stars.

"Alright," Caleeza finally relented. The low rocky hillside that followed the stream most of the way, curved away from the bank here, opening up into an area of low brush and small trees. It would provide a good sheltered spot for camping. They dropped their packs a short distance from the stream in the shelter of the trees.

"Look!" Caleeza cried suddenly, excitement mounting. "There's been a campfire here before," she said rushing up to the bits of charred wood surrounded by stones. "And there's his pack! Ollen is here." Evidence was clear.

"That's a positive sign," Tassyn agreed. "He must be around here somewhere. His pack is here so he will be back," he assured her.

"Ollen! Where are you?" Caleeza called out, half expecting him to reveal his presence. There was still no response.

"I'll gather wood for a fire," she said disappointed. "If I sit and rest first I might not want to get back up."

Tassyn smiled; he felt just as exhausted. "I'll help you. It won't take long to gather enough firewood to make tea." While scouring the ground for dead wood, Tassyn looked up toward the hillside, noting an anomaly. A large swath of the growth on the hillside looked like it had been torn away. "I wonder what happened over there?" he said dropping the wood he had collected by the fire ring and walking in that direction.

Caleeza automatically followed him. "The ground tremor must have triggered a landslide."

Upon arriving at the location, it was clear there had been a recent slide. A jumble of rock, dirt, and uprooted brush with wilted leaves formed a tangled mound at the foot of the hill. Sticking out of the pile, partly covered with debris, lay a human body.

☆☆☆☆

Kiril's survival of a precarious situation unified the spirit of the colonists even more. Together they would make it. No one doubted their survival as a group depended on their collective efforts, and their individual survival depended on the sound thinking of each and every one of them. The celebration though was short lived as Rojaire and Traevus explained there was a long way yet to go before they would be above ground once again.

"My main concern is there could be more ground tremors," Rojaire said. "The sooner we get through the underground passage of caverns and lava tubes the better."

"Well, I'm all for reaching fresh air; let's go," Captain Setas croaked and donning her light pack, she ambled onward. "I assume we go this way," she called over her shoulder.

"That woman sure has spunk," Kaylya said with admiration, attaching herself to her own heavier pack.

In many ways, the passage through the caverns proved harder going than in the lava tubes. There was no clear path to follow. Most of the string of caverns were wide enough to be considered spacious and the ceilings high enough to stand in, but occasionally it was necessary to crawl through narrow spaces, taxing the colonists even more. The irregular cave floor presented endless obstacles and challenges, but offered beauty as well. Veins of gold, crystal, and gemstones reflected back the light of their lamps.

Finally after having pushed the group to their limit, Rojaire, just as tired, called for a rest. "Get some sleep," is all he said. After a meal of dried foods, the weary travelers extinguished their lamps and slept.

It was another ground tremor that rudely woke them up. Fortunately the tremor didn't amount to much, but since they were now awake, they decided as a group to push on.

"I can't wait to see the light of day again or even the light of night," Drak said working his way around stalactites and stalagmites that formed a barrier of columns.

"Is it day or night in the world above us?" Zaloka asked wondering. "I've lost track of time."

"By my calculations, it is still light out," Inventor Sulyan said.

"How do you figure that?" Wessid asked with interest.

"Well, you see, I've developed a device," Sulyan said pulling it out of one of his numerous vest pouches, "that measures increments of time and according to this, the sun should be setting about now."

"A clock," Ilene said after Kaylya's translation.

"We have similar devices on Twaka," Thayla added.

"But the sun was setting when we entered the underground passage," Ilene said amazed. "It seems like we have been down here longer than that. Has it only been six days?"

"No, dear, it's only been one," Zaloka corrected after Kaylya's translation.

"She meant Earth-days," Kaylya explained. "A day on Earth is very short."

"This is the last cave," Traevus announced encouragingly when they entered the watery cavern at the end of the line. "The rest of the trip is by lava tube."

"I hope that's good news," Captain Setas moaned, dropping her pack and easing her tired body down on a mineral encrusted rock.

"We are closer to our destination. The news you might not want to hear is this; we have to climb up before we can go forward," Rojaire informed her turning and pointing to a jagged sloping rock wall. "But that will only be a minor inconvenience."

"I'm guessing we will be making good use of the rope again," Traevus grinned.

"We went down before," Setas said after some thought. "Up actually sounds encouraging."

"I want to be on the pulling end this time," Kiril said, causing everyone to laugh.

After a long, much needed rest listening to the babbling brook that flowed through the cave, Rojaire sent Kiril and Traevus up the side of the cave. They took one end of the rope with them to their connection with the lava tube that would eventually lead them out. With the agility of a mountain lion, Thayla followed them up to help pull. Ilene, Zaloka, and Kaylya looked questionably at the steeply terraced stone.

"It's not as hard as it looks," Rojaire said. "But if you would like the extra security of the rope, that's fine. I don't want anyone falling."

"I say we go for it," Zaloka said, challenging the other women. Ilene and Kaylya readily agreed and immediately they started up.

"Well, I can do it if they can," Drak said with what he hoped sounded like confidence. Not letting the women get the best of them, Wessid and Drak climbed up behind them. Soon all five of them were safely in the lava tube. That left only Rojaire, Captain Setas, and Inventor Sulyan.

Rojaire turned to Captain Setas. "Once again you're first," he said when the others called down saying they were ready. Taking her pack, he picked up the rope securing it around her waist. "This will help you up; I'll be going with you, showing you where to place your hands and feet, to help steady you." Setas nodded her understanding.

"Alright, start to pull her up ...slowly now," Rojaire called to the others above them. He need not have worried. They made surprisingly easy progress; Captain Seta was stronger than she looked. "Good job," Rojaire said to both Setas and the pulling crew, handing her to waiting, out-stretched hands and depositing her pack.

"I think I can make it up on my own," Inventor Sulyan said when Rojaire came back down to tie him in.

"Good, let me take your pack then. You can grab the rope if you need to." Not wanting to hurt Sulyan's pride, Rojaire stayed back a ways on the ascent. Half way up he paused, watching with respectful admiration as Sulyan successfully made the climb to the top, the pulling crew giving him a hand up into the lava tube.

"Crystal shards!" Kiril exclaimed when Rojaire joined them after returning for his own pack. "We're almost there." He could hardly contain his excitement when they started on their way again. There was still quite a ways to go, but Kiril rushed ahead. His anticipation of returning to the secret valley surged so high, he could barely keep from running.

But he didn't get very far before a cave-in of the lava tube blocked his way.

☆☆☆☆

Caleeza and Tassyn carefully, but rapidly, removed debris partially covering Ollen's body. A mass of dried blood caked one side of his head and face. His right leg lay askew, obviously broken and multiple contusions as well as superficial lacerations covered his body. "He's still alive," Tassyn assessed, detecting a pulse.

"Ollen, can you hear me? Wake up," Caleeza begged, gently stroking the less damaged side of his face. "You hold on, Ollen. You hear me? Tassyn and I are going to take care of you. You are going to be all right."

"Should we try to move him?" Tassyn asked cautiously.

"We can't leave him here," Caleeza cried. "If only I had a star stone, I could tell more." She continued to search for injuries. "I can't tell if he's bleeding internally."

"Let's splint the leg and make a litter of sorts to move him," Tassyn suggested, taking action. When they finally got Ollen's leg splinted and Ollen moved to the shelter of the trees, darkness had fallen. Tassyn made quick work of building a fire and putting water to boil.

By the light of the campfire, Caleeza cleansed and bandaged his wounds with bits of clothing from their packs. The worse visible damage, besides a broken leg, was the side of his face and head. When she washed away the caked dried blood on his face, the cuts started bleeding again, but to her relief they were not very deep and she easily stopped the bleeding. The gash on his head was deeper and swollen. Hopefully his skull was not fractured.

"If only I still had the star stone," Caleeza moaned again. "If he dies it will be my fault."

"You need to stop blaming yourself," Tassyn said handing her a hot cup of herbal tea.

"Thank you," she said, taking the cup. The simple, Earth-born expression of gratitude had become commonplace in the colony. Tassyn and his associates had once been a threat to the expedition she and Sarus once led. A lot had changed. Now Tassyn was a corner stone of strength in their tiny community.

"It is no one's fault. We found him and we're with him. That's what is important now. We need to accept what has happened and do what we can." Caleeza's logical mind said Tassyn was right, but her heart spoke differently.

She was a healer, but there was little she could do without healing herbs and the ability to draw energy from the elemental forces. The plants growing around them may have healing qualities, but they were unknown and untested. The foliage here resembled that growing in Chitter's valley. It was unfortunate she hadn't stayed with Chitter long enough to learn the formula for her healing tea.

After taking a few sips, she placed the cup on the ground and took Ollen's hand in her own. His hand felt cold against hers, warmed by the teacup. She touched his cheek, even tried to open an eyelid. "Ollen," she whispered. "Can you hear me?"

For the first time a low moan answered her. Tassyn rushed to join her by his side.

"Ollen, it's me, Caleeza. Can you hear me? Give us a sign if you hear? A grunt will do." There was another moan, louder this time with a hint of movement in his face ...then a gentle squeeze of her hand.

"He squeezed my hand," she told Tassyn jubilantly. "We need to get some liquid in him as soon as possible. First, some water. Then there's some of the tea we give Theon in my pack."

"I'll take care of it," Tassyn offered, anxious to do something to help.

"Listen to me, Ollen," Caleeza continued. "Tassyn and I are here to take care of you." Another gentle squeeze of her hand conveyed he understood.

"Caleeza." The soft word coming from his lips was barely audible, but distinct.

"You are going to get well. You have to," she whispered in near tears close to his ear.

"Why?" he breathed closely.

"Because you are the love of my heart," she said so only he could hear. But he was sleeping again. She continued to hold his hand until Tassyn brought the water.

"I'll cool the tea some and put it in a water container to make it easier for him to drink," Tassyn said, handing her the canister of water.

"Good. Ollen, can you hear me? Do you think you can drink some water?" Caleeza coaxed, rousing him back awake. Ollen stirred.

"Should I hold him up to drink?" Tassyn asked. "I don't want to hurt him."

"Ollen, can you open your eyes?" Caleeza asked. Subtle movements of the eyelids indicated an effort to comply. Then slowly they opened. Tassyn and Caleeza glowed over his success.

"Ollen, Tassyn here. It's good to have you back." A hint of a smile twitched the muscles in Ollen's face.

"Tassyn," he acknowledged.

"Can you move your fingers and toes?" Caleeza asked. He did so, grimacing some in pain. "Good. We're going to try and lift your head and shoulders a little to help you drink. If it hurts you too much, let us know and we will stop. Are you ready?"

"Yes," he answered softly.

To their relief, the maneuver went well and Ollen drank some of the water and eventually most of the tea. Soon he was resting comfortably and Tassyn and Caleeza moved to the other side of the fire to talk.

"So what do you think?" Tassyn asked when they were seated.

"There are a lot of positives; he regained consciousness, he can move his extremities, he recognizes us, and he seems to understand what we say ...he even spoke. How he does between now and the next sunrise will tell us more. Regardless, a broken leg will take some time to heal."

"Once he is stable and recovering, we could try carrying him with a litter," Tassyn ventured. "Progress would be slow, but eventually we would get him there."

"Should we somehow get word to Theon and Edty letting them know we found Ollen?" Caleeza asked.

It was a long way back to the settlement. "I think it's more important we stay together," Tassyn said after some thought. "You and I need to carry Ollen. Edty wouldn't be much help and Theon can't be left alone. They will just have to wonder what happened to us for a while longer."

☆☆☆☆

Kiril gazed in stunned disbelief at the wall of rock between him and ... everything. Theon, Ollen, Tassyn, Edty, Caleeza, his longed-for valley, his treasured map, and his lost first journal ...all were on the other side. He was still staring at the jumbled mound of rock blocking the way when Rojaire and Kaylya caught up to him.

"Oh, no!" Kaylya cried in dismay.

Immediately Rojaire dropped his pack and started climbing up the rock pile. Some of the stones shifted under his feet causing Kaylya to gasp in fear of his safety as she watched him climb. From the top of the pile, he carefully dislodged stones, sending them tumbling down to the bottom of the heap.

"How does it look?" Traevus called up to him.

"Not good," Rojaire called down, looking over his shoulder to see more of their team arriving to the bad news. "It's blocked as far as I can see with the headlamp."

"Do we have to go back?" Captain Setas crooned in despair.

"That's what I'm trying to find out." Rojaire shifted position, climbing laterally across the rock mound to get another view. After a few moments he offered more encouraging news. "I might see an opening on this side. Kiril, bring up the star stone. I want to try something."

Kiril quickly climbed up the rock pile with the star stone he, Traevus, and Rojaire shared. "Do you think we can make it to the other side?" he asked hopefully. "I tried to teleport to the opening to Kurper Valley, but it's still too far away," he admitted.

"You did, huh? Don't you think you should say something before attempting a stunt like that?" Rojaire said turning to the task at hand. "From this angle I can't see anything behind that large boulder but darkness," Rojaire said, pointing it out to Kiril. The boulder in question touched the newly exposed ceiling. Was it the pillar holding up the ceiling against further collapse? It did look like there was only dark emptiness beyond it.

"I could crawl up to the opening and see?" Kiril offered.

Rojaire considered. "It could be dangerous. If the wrong rocks are disturbed, the ceiling could come down and crush you."

"I'll be careful," he promised.

"Okay, but I want you to go easy," Rojaire relented. Kiril was smaller and more limber than he was. "Try not to disturb anything you don't have to. When you are certain you can see through to the other side, teleport yourself there. Then return for the rest of us," he added just in case.

Kiril gave Rojaire an apologetic nod and started up.

"Be careful," his mother begged. Rojaire was surprised Zaloka didn't object outright.

All discussion ceased as the colonists anxiously watched with baited breath as Kiril climbed up and away while trying to avoid disturbing the rock base as little as possible. When he finally reached the perceived opening, he shouted back jubilantly. "I can see the lava tube on the other side." Then what little they could still see of Kiril suddenly disappeared. Moments later he appeared again among them. "We can teleport across."

Rojaire eased back down. "Okay, transport Ilene with you to the other side so she can see it, then the two of you can start relaying us over.

"I...I...I can't teleport," Ilene stammered.

"Loan me your star stone," Traevus suggested. Ilene gladly complied and Kiril took Traevus to the other side. Soon they were back ready to transport two of the colonists beyond the barrier. They made quick work of it, barely pausing between trips. Only Rojaire and Wessid remained behind the cave-in when the mountain began to rumble.

CHAPTER 18

Earth

Rahlys rushed back to Elaine's living quarters above the gift shop and pounded on the door. By now Elaine had closed shop and was home. Jack answered her anxiously demanding knock.

"Rahlys."

She didn't give him the opportunity to say more before turning toward the portrait of the Oracle of Light. The holographic image flew out the painting.

"Where is he?" Rahlys urgently demanded of the ghostly image as soon as she barged through the door.

"Where is who?" Elaine asked from the sofa, her tired feet propped up on a cushion on the coffee table where Jack had been massaging them.

"Leaf! He's gone! Raven showed me where Leaf and Keiluk were along the river, but they were no longer there," she explained to Elaine and Jack.

Both Jack and Elaine gasped in horror.

"Where's Leaf?" Rahlys asked the hologram crystal twirling around her. The softly glowing projection zinged across the room sizzling out an answer, the words filling the air around them.

IN LOUISIANA.

"What?" Jack asked in astonishment. "How can that be?"

Rahlys ignored him. "Where's Melinda?" she asked. The answer was the same.

IN LOUISIANA.

"Where in Louisiana?" Rahlys shouted, losing patience. The elusive crystalline image responded to her mood by rapidly blazing out an answer.

BY THE OLD OAK TREE.

The answer jolted Rahlys. "Oak tree...," Rahlys whispered.

Only one oak tree loomed supreme in Rahlys' mind. It stood majestically by an old dilapidated house in the Louisiana swamplands.

A teen shooting, sensationalized by the media, had revealed a cache of stolen goods there, including a titanium laser-cutting machine that had mysteriously disappeared from a science institute in Baton Rouge. Months ago, Rahlys had stealthily visited what had to have been Brakalar's hideout. Although Brakalar had been captured, the rune-covered chest containing the Rod of Destruction had not been recovered. Rahlys' search of the property had failed to locate it. In her mind, Rahlys struggled to connect Melinda and Leaf to the site.

Droclum ...Droclum's touch had tainted Melinda's essence. Rahlys had seen the key to the chest sinking into the stones of the ruins of the Temple of Tranquility on Aaia. For this reason, she had allowed herself to believe that the Rod of Destruction was safely enclosed in a locked chest with no key. Had she been duped by an interstellar ruse? Could Melinda somehow have the key ...a key that has led her to the deadly weapon?

"I have to go," Rahlys cried out before disappearing without further explanation. Elaine and Jack stared dumbfounded at the empty space Rahlys left behind.

"Do you have any idea what that was all about?" Elaine asked confused.

"Barely; the implications aren't good." Jack sensed his little buddy Leaf and Melinda were in a lot of danger and there was nothing he could do. He hated feeling so useless. Jack made a move for the kitchen. "You keep your feet up; I'll see about fixing us a little something to eat.

It wasn't long before there was another pounding at the door. This time Elaine got up to answer it and Vince and Grumpy George surged into the room. She didn't really know Grumpy George but could guess who he was. Jack rushed from the kitchen. It was Vince who riveted their attention.

"Leaf...," was all Vince managed, his face contorted in agonized desperation as he fell in Elaine's uncertain embrace, nearly knocking her over, dwarfing her with his mass.

"Leaf is missing," George filled in. "We have been searching the riverbank by boat, but we didn't find him. We were hoping Rahlys had more information."

"Well maybe," Jack added cautiously. Was bad news better than no news at all, he wondered? "Here, come sit down and we can try to figure this out." The three of them helped Vince to the sofa where he collapsed, trembling uncontrollably.

"It's my fault," Vince confessed, struggling to pull himself together. "I should have helped him embrace his abilities instead of ignoring them. Maggie too. It's no wonder he doesn't trust us."

☆☆☆☆

In the dense Louisiana darkness eerily lit by Droclum's fires, Leaf and Melinda clung tightly to one another. They had only taken a few steps forward, before Melinda halted. "You have to go home, Leaf. You can't come with me." Her voice was low and whispery, vibrating on vocal cords that had gone long unused. Melinda loved Leaf and couldn't bear to put him in danger. She would have to face Droclum alone. "Go, now," she added with strained force." But Leaf was undeterred.

He reached out with heightened senses enhanced by a drawing of energy from the elemental forces. He could detect the powerful evil signature looming ahead, more like an essence than a presence that relentlessly drew Melinda to it. He could feel the pull of the strange object, the key, she carried in her pocket.

"I have to stay and protect you," he answered fearlessly. "You are going to need my help."

"You're only five years old."

"Five and a half."

Melinda stared at him with incredulous wonder, his youthful face fixed with determination in the dying glow of the burning road. She stooped down to meet him at eye level, gently held his little bony shoulders in her hands and pleaded. "Leaf, I love you more than anything. You are so sweet, so perfect ...so wonderful." Sobbing tears broke up her words. "I can't let anything happen to you. It would break your parents' hearts. It would break my heart." Before she could say more, another impatient bolt of lightning struck the board road ahead of them shattering the night.

"Follow!" the disembodied voice boomed in their heads like an explosion of thunder.

"Give me the key!" Leaf said. "I can get rid of it; take it far, far away."

"What?" Of course Leaf would know about the key she realized. He could probably sense it. "No, Leaf, I can't. It's bad, evil ...tainted with the essence of Droclum. It's connected to me." How could she make Leaf understand? "I have to find out what this key unlocks and face up to it, whatever it is. Please, go home," Melinda cried desperately.

"No, I'm here to protect you." Leaf wasn't convinced she had it right, but he didn't say anymore.

There was nothing Melinda could do; she had to be strong and take the lead. "Okay, but stay behind me and do what I say." She stood up, forcing herself to take fortitude from her inner strength. She straightened her shoulders and bravely held her head high. *I will not let Droclum win. He has stolen enough of my life. It is time for his ultimate defeat, never to exude his corrupted essence on this world again.*

"Then let's go," Leaf said having read her thoughts.

They started off again toward the next cindered spot on the planked roadway and the still burning strike ahead. Intently focused, Leaf allowed Melinda to take the lead as she had requested, following at a respectable distance.

When they passed the site of the last lightning strike, they faced only darkness. Leaf produced a glow globe sending it up to light the way. Before long, the board road came to an end, depositing them in a clearing where nothing grew. Something must have been here that was now gone leaving behind the bare ground. Was that the reason for the plank road?

A more natural flash of lightning, much brighter than Leaf's glow globe, briefly lit the area outlining the large sprawling branches of a giant tree. Across the clearing stood a small crumbling brick and concrete structure. As they drew closer, Melinda's heart raced in recognition. It was the same clearing she had stood in when Droclum burned the location onto her map. They had arrived. Now what, she wondered trembling?

As though in answer, the wind began to swirl around them quickly growing in ferocity. The trees moaned and thrashed their branches in the howling maelstrom. Lightning forked around Melinda and Leaf blinding them with sizzling light illuminating the surrounding trees. With one arm around Keiluk, Leaf gaped in horror at the unnatural storm while Melinda stood frozen in place. A sense of unbounded evil permeated the air. Keiluk sensed it too, and howled in warning.

"Come!" Leaf screamed above the din tugging on Melinda's arm, "We have to get out of here!" Keiluk barked, aggressively backing Leaf's plea, but Melinda remained transfixed, unresponsive to his desperate urgings. Leaf tried teleporting them away, but the wind continued to howl and lightning flashed ever closer electrifying the air. Keiluk howled again.

Leaf looked around. The brick and masonry rubble and ruins of the old cistern several feet away was the only semblance of shelter. "Melinda, over here!" Leaf cried above the turmoil that drowned him out, all to no avail.

Boom!

The ear-deafening explosion shocked Melinda out of her trance. Leaf, Melinda, and Keiluk dove for the deepest recess of the crumbling masonry structure, their hearts pounding with terror. It was questionable protection against the raging evil.

"Leaf, are you all right?" Melinda pleaded suddenly aware of their danger.

"Uh huh," Leaf nodded nearly paralyzed in fear. "What happened?"

"It must have been a lightning strike."

Daring to look back as they huddled together Leaf saw lightning still coruscating over the centuries old mighty oak now split in half down the middle. "Wow!" Leaf gasped. The wind continued to rage and lightning danced about, seemingly unsatisfied with the sacrifice of one tree.

Then Leaf's senses were hit by an overwhelming flow of putrid evil the essence of which made him gag. The unnatural storm that continued to rage did nothing to staunch the dark flow of energy coming from the old oak tree ripped open by the lightning strike. Flashes of light limned the shattered branches of the monolith illuminating a mysterious object covered with glowing designs of some sort. It was obvious to Leaf the nauseating flow of corruption emitted from the exposed object.

"Melinda, we have to get out of here," Leaf groaned fighting back the nausea. But Melinda didn't acknowledge him. Keiluk licked Melinda's face hoping for a response, but Melinda did not react. Instead she eased out of the hole in the tumbled down masonry of the old cistern and walked slowly, silently into the storm. She headed toward the glowing object wedged in the split trunk of the tree across the clearing.

Leaf jumped up and grabbed her arm. "Melinda, what are you doing?" he shouted over the turmoil of the storm. "We have to get out of here. That object is evil; it wants to hurt you," he cried. Melinda neither responded nor attempted to shake off his pleading grasp. Unwilling to give up, he tried again teleporting her away, but the stream of evil defeated his efforts. Melinda continued inexorably to advance toward the tree.

"Melinda, no!" Leaf cried desperately tugging on her arm. Keiluk joined the effort grabbing her shirt with her teeth and pulling back. Nothing stopped her forward progress. "Melinda, please, stop! It's evil; it wants to destroy you," Leaf pleaded over and over again, tears streaming down his face. Realizing Melinda couldn't hear him, he moved in front of her and tried to push her back. "Melinda, stop!" but his small frame did little to slow her down. The object in the tree had control of her; she was under its awful influence.

Somehow he had to stop her. When mere physical force failed to impede her progress he drew strength from the elemental forces whirling furiously around them. With greater force he pushed back, but to his horror the pull from the vile object proved stronger. Trying again, he drew in more and more energy in a desperate effort to overcome the powerful pull on Melinda. But she continued to slowly plow forward, pushing Leaf ahead of her and dragging Keiluk behind her, getting ever closer to the glowing object. Then, still in a trance, Melinda pulled out the key she had harbored for so long. A dark tentacle of corruption oozed from the object in the tree connecting with the key in Melinda's hand compelling her on. All seemed lost.

But Leaf could not give up. He would never give up. Melinda meant everything in the world to him. She was more than a big sister; she was his best friend. "Melinda, I love you," he cried. "Please stop. Please."

Still Melinda advanced drawing ever closer to her demise. Leaf's body tensed with effort as he continued to draw strength, his little form trembling with the load. The surge of energy coursing through his body blocked out the rage of the storm, leaving only the rage in his heart fighting against the destructive force threatening to destroy his world.

CHAPTER 19

Aaia

At the center of the continent Mt. Vatre rumbled spewing putrid darkness that blocked the sun as crystals tinkled and shattered in the grumbling quakes. The essence of Sarus, fused with the Crystalline Landscape, drew on the power of the Crystalline Landscape. What awakened Droclum from his long slumber in the bowels of the mountain? Sarus reached out to find the source of the disturbance. His ethereal reach extended beyond his domain, beyond the island continent of Lynnara, beyond the Golden Sea and the Main Land, beyond Aaia and the great void between planets and solar systems, across the galaxy to a tiny distant world positioned on a radiating arm on the opposite side of the spiral galaxy.

Droclum has awakened; of that Sarus was certain.

The mountain rumbled; the ominous rumbling distant at first as shockwaves traveled toward them. Rojaire and Wessid, still trapped behind the cave-in, exchanged worried glances as once again their world began to quake. The shaking intensified and the ceiling began to disintegrate. "It's all going to come down," Wessid shouted, stating the obvious.

Then Traevus arrived. Wasting no time, he quickly grabbed ahold of them, or they desperately grabbed ahold of him, and in a flash teleported them away to relative safety. They quickly joined the others, already on the move. The ceiling wasn't as crumbly here, but rocks and dust rained down on them. The tunnels would not hold up much longer.

Rojaire instantly took charge. "People, let's move it ...quickly." The group began to surge forward. "Kiril, Traevus! Use the two star stones to move the slowest out," Rojaire shouted. "Traevus, you have Sulyan and Setas. Kiril, take Drak and Zaloka. Quickly!" Wasting no time, Kiril and Traevus grabbed on to their charges and soon had them far ahead, teleporting them in short leaps toward the longed-for exit to the little valley.

Rojaire rushed the rest of the colonists along. "Everyone move it. We are in great danger." The colonists picked up speed as the lava tubes continued to disintegrate. The light of their lamps barely pierced the roiling dust. Then suddenly the quake subsided. "Keep moving!" Rojaire urged when the group started to slow down. "It may not be over yet." No sooner were his words spoken when the rumbling started up again quickly building in intensity.

"Run!" Rojaire shouted.

The intense shaking knocked Ilene off her feet. Without breaking stride, Thayla lifted her with one arm setting her upright once again on the run. Then up ahead Kaylya screamed. A large boulder had her pinned to the floor. Thayla and Rojaire stopped to help her. "Keep moving!" Rojaire shouted at the others as rocks rained down around them.

"My foot is caught," Kaylya grimaced in pain.

Rojaire and Thayla crouched beside her. "We will get you out," Rojaire reassured her, then turned to Thayla. "We need to find something we can use as a lever." There were no trees in the lava tubes to provide a stout pole. Thayla unstrapped her hefty blade and scabbard and wedged them under the boulder. "It won't be strong enough," Rojaire told her. Thayla glared at him defiantly.

"You underestimate the strength of Twakan steel. Get ready to pull her out." With a warrior's grunt Thayla heaved and groaned nudging the massive stone. "Now!" she grunted with effort giving it her all.

Rojaire grabbed Kaylya around her chest from behind and pulled. Kaylya cried out in pain as Rojaire dragged her out and Thayla let the boulder drop back in place. They didn't have much time; the lava tube continued to crumble around them.

"Can you walk?" Rojaire asked.

"I don't know."

Before Rojaire could lift Kaylya up into his arms, Thayla had her blade strapped on. "I've got her; let's go," she said throwing Kaylya over her powerful shoulder.

Rojaire didn't argue. It occurred to him that if they made it out alive the underground passage would be forever closed, isolating the colonists in the lush hidden valley, from the outside world. He hoped they would be so lucky.

The final distance seemed endless. Once again the quake subsided. Rojaire and Thayla, still carrying Kaylya over her shoulder, fought their way through, over, and around obstacles. There was no sign of the rest of the colonists. Barring a mishap, the others should already be free and safe. Every step forward without seeing them offered increased hope everyone made it out.

"I can carry her for a while," Rojaire offered.

"I've got her." Thayla trudged on indefatigably.

"Maybe I could try to walk," Kaylya said tired of being a burden.

"You would only slow us down," Thayla said plowing forward.

"We are almost there," Rojaire added.

Thayla sniffed. "I smell fresh air."

As the first tendrils of fresh air reached their dust-clogged lungs the mountain lurched violently. Both Thayla and Rojaire were thrown to the rock-strewn floor of the lava tube, forcing Thayla to drop Kaylya. Struggling back to their feet, they grabbed Kaylya on either side forcing her upright, throwing her arms around their shoulders. Supporting each other against the onslaught of the tremor, they stumbled forward. The lava tube disintegrated around them.

Finally they made it around the final bend to face the gaping hole in the side of the lava tube that led to the open valley below. Spotting them, Traevus and Kiril teleported up to them. They grabbed the group and quickly whisked them down into the valley to safety just moments before the lava tube collapsed behind them shutting down the underground passage forever.

Sarus watched Droclum's pent-up fury being released on two worlds. He drew heavily on the tremendous store of energy in the Crystalline Landscape and produced a powerful shield to protect the field of crystals from destruction. But there was little he could do for the rest of Aaia ...

or the distant world. All his efforts to calm the erupting forces had done little to mitigate it. All he could do was watch.

Sarus watched shockwaves ripple through the mountains and valleys reshaping parts of the continent's landscape. He watched as the shockwaves reached the Lynnaran coast line and crossed the Golden Sea sending ripples across the water to Alaia Island. He watched as Alaia Island rumbled and shook till it broke apart and sank beneath the water sending out a wave to wash Lynnara's shore, lifting up and carrying Captain Setas' ferryboat far inland up the Zayla Valley. And he watched as Droclum's vile, evil essence emitting from the rune-covered chest containing the Rod of Destruction pulled Rahlys, Guardian of the Oracle of Light, toward her destruction.

CHAPTER 20

Earth

Rahlys arrived in a raging storm eerily lit by Leaf's powerful magic. Melinda, under Droclum's control, held out the lost key drawing her to the exposed rune-covered chest. The chest glowed menacingly in the once mighty oak ravaged by the unnatural disturbances around them. Already a dark evil misty tentacle reached out from the chest toward Melinda's out stretched hand. Between them Leaf, rigid with effort, fought valiantly, the elemental forces burning through him, a stoic warrior for good against the overwhelming forces of evil. Keiluk growled frantically, her teeth firmly gripping Melinda's clothing in an effort to pull her back from the menace.

Rahlys called forth the Oracle of Light and drawing heavily from the elemental forces thrust herself between her loved ones and the rune-covered chest. Bright light emanated from Rahlys' body and the spinning crystal directly over her head flooding the clearing with radiance. With the release, Leaf collapsed unmoving to the ground. Stepping over Leaf's limp body Melinda advanced forward. Seeing Leaf drop, Keiluk let Melinda go. She lay by her master's side whimpering her concern.

Rahlys forcefully blocked Melinda's forward progress. "Melinda, stop. Give me the key," she shouted over the maelstrom.

Melinda's young face remained expressionless. She gave no sign of recognition. In a tug-of-war Melinda pushed back strongly against Rahlys, reaching for the rune-covered chest containing the Rod of Destruction.

Rahlys wanted desperately to turn to Leaf's aid, but she couldn't let Droclum's essence claim Melinda. His evil had to be contained. She had rescued Melinda from Droclum's clutches years ago in the underground caverns. She had to prevent her from reaching the chest to save her again.

"Sorcerer Anthya!" boomed Droclum's voice from the filament, recognizing the crystal as the embodiment of his arch rival's powers.

The crystal blazed brilliantly, powerfully in response, illuminating the smoky dark tentacles emanating from the chest. "Melinda!" Rahlys called out again, straining to free her from the compelling draw of dark energy reaching toward the key. "Melinda, give me the key."

The tendrils of evil streaming from the chest tugged ever harder on Melinda and the key she held in her hand. Rahlys fought back, but Droclum's hold was stronger. She had to separate Melinda from the key.

Rahlys grabbed hold of it and yelped in pain. "Melinda, let go of the key," Rahlys gasped struggling for control. Melinda's only response was a momentary pause in her push to join chest and key. Apparently Melinda was impervious to the pain or felt no pain at all. Her face remained blank and empty of expression as she maintained her hold on the key.

"Melinda, let go of the key," she repeated gritting her teeth in resistance to the burning sensation in her hand and the effort to maintain the spell holding Melinda back. It wasn't enough. Somehow she had to gain control of the key and prevent it from being drawn to the chest. "Anthya help me," Rahlys gasped.

The crystal brightened even further emitting a high pitched whirling sound.

"Rahlys," hissed Droclum's essence.

To Rahlys' surprise, Melinda suddenly let go of the key leaving it in her possession. With the release of the key, Melinda seemed to awaken. Her eyes blinked, then focused. Finally recognition; her lips moved.

"Rahlys?" she whispered.

Rahlys didn't have time to contemplate Melinda's softly spoken word. It took all her strength and concentration to continue her hold on the key.

"Melinda, check on Leaf!" Rahlys screamed out. She couldn't give her attention to the two young people she loved. To save them, she had to defeat Droclum once and for all. Melinda turned, saw her little brother lying unconscious a short distance away, and dropped down beside him.

Rahlys held fast to the key; the effort draining her. "Help me," she pleaded to the Oracle of Light. "How do I stop this?"

"You cannot stop me. I will have what is mine," Droclum hissed.

"I must stop you," Rahlys cried out desperately.

When Rahlys felt she could hold on no longer, the crystal whirled blindingly bright, seemingly merging with Rahlys, giving her guidance. With the crystal's help, she drew increasingly more power and began to weave a containment spell, a layer at a time, first around the key and then around the chest.

"No!" Droclum howled with a piercing shriek.

Rahlys continued to weave. The process was slow and exhausting, but the dark smoky forces coming from the chest weakened with each glowing layer of the containment she wove.

Droclum's shrieks became an echo and then a whisper.

Finally with a dazzling flash of light from the crystal, the key went dormant and the chest went dark. In that same instant, the storm stopped raging and all became quiet under a starry night sky.

Rahlys staggered then quickly became steady. The crystal, its brilliance now a soft glow, twirled slowly before her. Immediately she turned her attention to Melinda and Leaf. Leaf had regained consciousness with Melinda embracing him in her arms and Keiluk licking Leaf's face to urge him back to strength.

Rahlys dropped down beside them.

"Is it gone?" Leaf asked timidly.

"Yes. We did it," she assured him.

Rahlys, Melinda, and Leaf shared a hardy embrace, tears of joy and relief staining their faces. Keiluk jumped about with jubilation. All her people were safe.

"Melinda can speak," Leaf announced wide-eyed.

"Yes, I know. I heard her."

"I'm sorry I didn't tell you about the key," Melinda said, her head bowed in contrition.

"It would have helped," Rahlys said, "but you were probably compelled not to. It's all right," she added gently and smiled giving Melinda another reassuring hug. "Everything worked out in the end." For the longest, they just sat there in the quiet dark snuggling together with the softly glowing crystal for light.

"Ready to go home?" Rahlys asked after a while. When they nodded in agreement, Rahlys secured the chest and key for the journey. "Everyone is worried about you two." Keiluk barked. "You too," she added rubbing the dog's thick soft white fur and scratching behind her ears.

Rahlys called the crystal to her hand and in an instant they were on their way home.

CHAPTER 21

Aaia

Finally the shaking stopped. Regaining his feet, Rojaire rose to assess the damage. First he counted heads. To his relief, all were present and accounted for, but his companions were almost unrecognizable covered in dust and blood as they were, some moaning from injuries. Sulyan stumbled about bleeding profusely from a gash to his head. Thayla grabbed him gently. Rojaire jumped in to help.

"Where are we?" Sulyan asked, his eyes glued shut with blood.

"We're safe. Sit here my friend," Thayla urged easing him down next to Kaylya.

"Yes, sit with me, Sulyan," Kaylya said soothingly. Except for her foot, Kaylya appeared to be alright. Ilene quickly joined them to assess Sulyan's condition.

"I'll check on the others," Rojaire said. Traevus and Kiril joined him.

"Let me take a look at your head wound," Ilene coaxed taking her water canister and a cloth from her pack to wash away the blood.

"Ilene, is that you?"

Ilene smiled; voice recognition was a good sign. "Yes, let's see what's under all this blood."

"If you can tend to him, I'll see who else needs help," Thayla said and with an affirmative from Ilene moved away. She found Wessid and Zaloka trying to calm Drak who was obviously in a lot of pain with a broken arm.

"Oh, Thayla..." Zaloka began pleadingly, but needed not say more. Thayla immediately took charge. Apparently her warrior training had included tending to the wounded. Traevus admired her all the more.

"Looks like a clean break. We need to splint that arm." Thayla looked around for something to use as splints; only grasses grew in the little enclosed valley. Drak moaned.

"He's in a lot of pain." Zaloka's face was tense with worry and concern.

"What's the situation here?" Rojaire asked checking in on them.

"We need materials to make a splint," Thayla updated him. "I have a short blade in a thin hardwood case that will work for one side. We need something else." Then Thayla thought of the reed flute Sulyan was making for Ilene.

By now Ilene had cleansed and bandaged Sulyan's head and face and he could see again. Sulyan readily agreed and Ilene retrieved the unfinished flute from his pack and brought it to Zaloka, ripping what must have been a tunic to wrap the arm and tie on the splits.

"What can I do to help?" Rojaire asked.

"When we're ready, you can help hold him still while I set the bone," Thayla said. "We could use some grass for cushioning,"

"I'll cut some," Kiril volunteered and stepped away to do so.

"I wish we had something to give him for the pain," Ilene said.

"You do," Traevus said walking up to Ilene. He placed the star stone he had borrowed in her hand. "You can help relieve his pain."

Ilene still felt inadequate and poorly trained despite the brief intense training she had received from Councilor Anthya at the Academy. Hesitantly she caressed the smooth golden stone with her fingers. If her ability was strong enough, it would allow her to draw soothing energy to transmit to Drak. Could she do it?

"I will try," Ilene said with gentle hope.

Soon Kiril returned with an abundance of cut grass. With everything needed assembled, they were ready. Ilene sat by Drak, placed her hands on Drak's head and focused. Drawing on her own strength and the natural energy around her, she sought to block the pain receptors to the brain and send a flow of tranquil warmth. With eyes closed and focus intense, she could feel the warm flow of healing energy through her arms and hands. Soon Drak's arm was set and splinted, and Drak was resting comfortably.

Rojaire took stock of their situation as gray clouds moved in. They were fortunate to have made it to the valley alive and until another way out was found they were here for good. Most of the colonists suffered only superficial cuts and bruises from falls and falling rocks, but one of his crew had a head injury, another a sprained foot, and yet another a broken arm. They still had to go up a steep uphill climb over the cut and down the other side to the larger valley. Then there was quite a ways to go to reach the settlement camp. *How will I get them there? And how have the others fared since Traevus, Kiril and I left them a season ago.* He was anxious to find out.

"Now what?" Captain Setas croaked as spry as ever.

"We rest, eat, and hold a meeting," Rojaire said.

Long before the caverns caved in, Edty and Theon had moved their camp out on open ground by the fire pit and Theon's crude branch chair. Kiril's journal was safe and Edty had rescued the rest of their meager belongings. Theon reassuringly touched the familiar weight of the journal hidden away in his tunic.

The ground had finally stopped shaking, but now it was threatening to rain. From his chair, Theon directed Edty in building a shelter cuddled in a thicket of trees. Edty covered the lean-to pole construction frame with woven mats of large thick rubbery leaves in varying shades of purple and green. Their make-shift beds, woven mats stuffed with grass, were already in place. As Theon's cramped old hands struggled to weave he reflected over the abundance of the color green in the valley's foliage. On Earth nearly all the foliage was green, except for seasonal changes, but on Aaia green was rather scarce, except in their special valley. For some reason Theon found this comforting. And as always when he was in a reflective mood, he thought of his daughter Ilene half a galaxy away. He shed a silent tear and wiped it away.

"I think we're done," Edty announced having finished attaching all but what Theon was still working on into the construction of a waterproof door to keep out the rain. On cue the first drops of rain began to fall.

"Are you ready to go in?" Edty asked taking the unfinished woven mat from him and laying it aside.

"Yes, sure," Theon said glad to be done with his shaky effort at weaving. Tenderly Edty helped him slowly stand. "And thank you," Theon added sincerely.

"It is my pleasure to serve," Edty said softly.

Tassyn, Caleeza, and Ollen hadn't showed up. Theon began to doubt he and Edty would ever see them again, but he wouldn't say that to Edty. He also suspected that the underground passage, the only way into their valley probably collapsed during the quakes. Hopefully their friends were not trying to reach them at the time. Either way, Theon doubted they would ever see Rojaire, Traevus, and Kiril again. He didn't share this dismal thought with Edty either.

"Why do you call it Kurper Valley?" Wessid asked.

Rojaire, Traevus, and Kiril told the story of finding the little silvery grass eaters in the valley when they first arrived. "Theon crushed one in the head with a stone and we cooked up the meat," Kiril exclaimed.

"Meat? You have been eating meat?" Zaloka asked.

"It's a common practice on Earth," Ilene said in her father's defense.

After much discussion over several possible options the colonists voted unanimously to stay together although they did agree to lighten their packs by leaving behind some nonessential items in Kurper Valley to be retrieved later.

The nourishing rest and surging rush from having survived so much already seemed to invigorate them. Sulyan was speaking coherently. Ilene looked tired from expending so much healing energy, but was eager to continue on. Drak with his arm in a sling agreed. He seemed comfortable enough, thanks to Ilene. Kaylya's sprained ankle didn't seem as bad as they had feared and with her foot carefully wrapped walked with only a slight limp. They would make her a cane when they reached wood. Meanwhile the others were willing to give her a hand. They also had a couple of star stones. Ilene was using one to aid in pain control for her patients. Traevus could use the other to aid those who needed help up the cut and down the other side to the promised valley.

Thayla summed it up for them. "Let's see this valley you've been telling us about." Over the duration of the journey Thayla had truly become one of them.

The crossing over the cut to the promised valley proved difficult, but went smoothly. Even with the heavy clouds limiting the distant view from the top, what they did see impressed them. Wessid took Zaloka's hand and whispered, "I think we made the right choice."

"I agree," she whispered back.

Entering the forest below, they halted long enough to cut Kaylya a walking stick, then moved on. They hadn't gone far before a ferocious beast appeared suddenly before them roaring and baring sharp teeth. Zaloka screamed in terror, no doubt having second thoughts about coming here after all.

"It's the bear-beast!" Kiril announced matching the life form standing in front of them to the large claw prints they had seen before.

"Bear? That's not a bear?" Ilene corrected. It looked more like a cross between a dinosaur and a dragon.

Rojaire reached for Kaylya's walking cane to use as a defense weapon which she willingly surrendered. Waving the staff and shouting, he tried to drive the animal away. Whatever it was, bear or dinosaur or dragon, it didn't seem intimidated by their greater number.

"Stand back," Thayla shouted taking over. The warrior awakened, she drew her great blade and charged the beast with a spine-chilling war cry that sent the beast running, dragging its spiny tail behind it. That was the last they saw of it.

"What a woman!" Traevus praised respectfully.

Then it began to rain; soon drenching rain poured down. Before the rain began, the colonists, covered in blue-violet stone dust from head to boots, appeared to be a homogenous race. A shortage of available water had made it impossible for them to wash up. As the rain washed the dust away a wide range of skin tones and fabric colors emerged. By the time Rojaire and his colonist reached the river, just as fast as the cloudburst came in, it glided away over the mountain. Soon the sun drenched the valley in steamy warmth.

"Our camp is on the other side of the river," Rojaire informed them when they stopped to rest. "We will follow the river for a while before crossing; we still have a ways to go. Eventually we will come to a shallow rocky ford where we can cross."

"I could run on ahead and let the others know you are coming," Kiril volunteered, his patience with the group's slow pace wearing thin.

"No, we stay together," Rojaire said without hesitation. "We are too close to take unnecessary risks now; besides, we want to arrive together." The rest quickly agreed.

The period of darkness was quickly approaching. The sun had already disappeared behind the western mountains after having dried up the day's rain. Once again Theon sat in his chair near the campfire reflecting on his life while Edty put on water for tea. At first Theon thought the voices he was hearing were in his head, but before long Edty heard them too. Standing up, he gazed into the gloomy distance and soon he could see a group of people making their way toward them. It couldn't be Ollen and the others returning; they were coming from the wrong direction.

"Theon, I do believe we have company, lots of company," Edty gasped. What would constitute as a lot of people to Edty he wondered?

Theon reached for his walking staff and stepped forward for a better look. Edty was right. A large group of people were approaching. To his surprise, nearly a dozen people were headed their way.

"It's Rojaire!" Edty shouted nearly dancing in place. "And look, there's Kiril and Traevus."

Theon said nothing, too overcome with emotion to speak. Rushing up to him he saw Kiril and, dare he believe, his daughter Ilene.

"Greetings Theon and Edty, I told you I would return," Kiril shouted gleefully.

"Oh, Father; I've missed you so much," Ilene cried, nearly knocking Theon off his feet if not for Kiril adding his support. Tears streamed down Theon's face. He raised his aged hands to her face and tangled his fingers in her hair to assure that she was really there.

"Ilene, my dear daughter, welcome."

Ilene looked him over carefully concealing her shock over how much he had aged. He seemed so frail. She gently probed his condition.

Kiril could read her concern even without a star stone. "Here sit down," he said, gently guiding Theon back to his chair. "Crystal shards, it's good to see you again." But before he would sit, Theon reached into a pocket of his tunic and pulled out the purloined journal.

"I kept it safe," Theon said handing it to him.

Kiril accepted it calmly nodding. There was no further exchange of words over it. None were needed; all was understood, their bond of friendship unbreakable, or so Kiril hoped. Theon did not yet know that Ilene was the love of Kiril's heart. Kiril tucked the journal under his arm and helped Ilene ease Theon down into his seat. Edty stood fixed in place, overwhelmed by the crowd.

"How did you survive the underground passage through all the ground quakes?" Theon asked. "Who are the others? Did the High Council send them?"

"Greetings, Earth traveler and Edty." Once again Theon was shocked by an unexpected presence as Captain Setas stood before him in all her diminutive form.

"But, my lady, what about your ferryboat?"

"I do believe my sea-faring days are over."

"Greetings, Theon and Edty." Rojaire said stepping up to them. "As you can see Kiril, Traevus and I have returned with colonists as promised and no, the High Council did not send them. I am fairly certain we are no longer recognized by the High Council as Accepted Ones. It hardly matters anymore; the underground passage is sealed. We barely got out alive and some of us are injured. One thing is for certain; we are here to stay." Then Rojaire brought Kaylya forward. "I would like for you to meet Kaylya, the love of my heart."

"You found her?" Theon asked in surprise.

"Yes, thanks to Rahlys and the Oracle of Light."

"Greetings, Theon. It's wonderful to finally meet you," she said taking his hand in hers. "I've heard many stories about you."

One by one the others were introduced.

"Zaloka is my chosen mother and Wessid is my chosen father," Kiril explained introducing them. "And this is Drak?"

"The map maker?" Theon asked.

"That was my great grandfather," Drak clarified. "I'm just the map keeper."

"And Inventor Sulyan?" Theon gasped in surprise recognizing him.

"Greetings, Theon. It is my pleasure to serve."

"And this is Thayla from planet Twaka," Traevus introduced with obvious admiration.

"Greetings, Wise One." Thayla bowed in deference to Theon's great age.

"Where are Ollen, Tassyn, and Caleeza?" Traevus asked when all had been presented.

"We don't know," piped up Edty.

"It's a long story," Theon said taking a deep breath before getting started. But before he could begin to tell it, the colonists heard a distant shout in the growing darkness. All turned their gaze to the north as the shout repeated.

"It's Tassyn," Edty cried and forgetting his fear of the dark rushed toward the shadowy figures in the increasing darkness. "Tassyn!" they could hear him shouting as he ran.

"It looks like they're carrying something," Rojaire said. "They may need help." Putting aside their own weariness from the long journey just completed, he and Traevus headed out to meet them. Caleeza and Tassyn carried a makeshift litter bearing Ollen, conscious and obviously in pain from all his injuries and the jostling he must have endured on the way. But he rallied when he saw Rojaire and Traevus again.

"Did our boy Kiril make it back too?"

"He certainly did," Rojaire assured him, "and we brought a few more along with us. Let's get you back to camp so you can meet them." Edty and Traevus quickly replaced Tassyn and Caleeza carrying Ollen.

"What happened?" Rojaire asked as they walked along.

"He was crushed in a rock slide triggered by a ground shake," Caleeza explained.

"Where did it happen?"

"A long way from here." She paused and turned to him. "This valley is a lot bigger than we thought."

"I take it, life here hasn't been exactly uneventful since we left."

"Looks like you have stories to tell, too," Caleeza said nodding toward the waiting throng of people, some apparently with injuries of their own. The throng of people parted for them and Edty and Traevus carefully placed the litter down by the fire. There was a chorus of greetings and introductions as well as a barrage of questions.

Ilene probed Ollen's condition while Caleeza sat anxiously by his side. She didn't detect any life-threatening damage to any vital organs. "He's going to be alright," Ilene reassured Caleeza. "But it will take a long time for him to fully recover." Ollen assured them that even though he was badly beaten, he was not defeated.

"He can have my bed in the shelter," Edty offered.

"You and Ollen were members of the lost expedition," Ilene suddenly realized. "You were on Earth. I was part of the expedition looking for you."

"Yes, I was on Earth with Maggie and Vince and the children," Caleeza confirmed. "I learned so much from them."

Ilene felt a pang of homesickness at the mention of their names. *Is my mother alright? Will I ever see her again? I wish I could let her know I am happy.* It was true Ilene realized. She had adventure, new friends, and she felt useful. She had never been happier.

"I wish I could see how the children have grown."

"You can; I brought pictures." Then she remembered that the pictures were in the pack she had abandoned. While Ilene and Caleeza spoke of their friends in Alaska, Tassyn walked up to Edty now tending the fire.

"You did a good job, Edty, of taking care of Theon and taking charge of the camp while we were gone," Tassyn said after looking over the place and talking to Theon. "I want you to know I'm proud of you."

The praise was almost more than Edty could bare. His best friend Tassyn was back and Rojaire, Traevus, and Kiril were back, and Tassyn was proud of him. He never felt so important before.

The colonists kept the fire fed from Edty's well stocked woodpile, ate till they were full and exchanged stories long into the period of darkness. Ilene and Caleeza tirelessly checked on their patients. Finally they were all together, some in better shape than others, but together. It was enough for now. As Rojaire, with Kaylya by his side, listened to stories and drank Caleeza's healing teas, or so she claimed, he almost let himself relax for a bit. The hard work would start after they rested up.

When Kiril described how Thayla battled off a bear-beast, Caleeza described her own run-in with a bear-beast to a new captive audience.

"Somehow I was transported to what I think was a different valley." When she described her encounter with Chitter, Drak jumped up excitedly forgetting about his arm, winced in momentary pain, then pulled out the crystal floss map he carried.

"Did she look like this?" he asked unfolding the map and turning on his lamp for her to see. On the edge of the map he pointed to what could have been a drawn portrait of Chitter.

"That's incredible," Caleeza gasped. "It looks just like her."

"Probably an ancestor of hers. The portrait was drawn by my great grandfather." Everyone wanted to see it.

"You just verified my story."

"You just verified that a representation of the intelligent life form my great grandfather encountered, but kept secret, still lives."

"Chitter was alone," Caleeza emphasized. "I didn't see any others."

"Explain again how you went to this other valley," Wessid asked confused.

"I can't explain it," Caleeza lamented. "All I can say is I fell into it."

"It sounds like some kind of portal," Sulyan said speaking up. "Perhaps the bear-beast creates it; uses it to travel between the valleys."

"So how did you return to this valley?" Wessid asked, trying another angle.

"Sarus brought me back." Which opened a discussion on the fate of Sarus, leader of the lost expedition, and the Crystalline Landscape.

With Ollen and Theon comfortably resting in the shelter, an exhausted Ilene curled up in her bedroll by the entrance and fell into a deep sleep. Kiril covered her with his cloak, then sat by the fire. Most of the colonists were already sleeping. Across from him Tassyn, Rojaire, and Traevus talked on softly. They were the last ones up.

"Ollen believes there is another way out of the valley," Tassyn said gazing into the fire. "The flood of water we crossed going through the jungle gym trees going north was down to just a trickle by the time we crossed on the way back. Something must have shifted from the quakes. Where we found Ollen, the stream disappeared into a cavern in the mountain. Ollen says if we followed where the water went we might find a way out the valley, possibly a route to the sea."

By Seaa's light the men continued to talk long into the period of darkness. Kiril opened his recovered journal and turned the pages to a blank sheet. "THE FIRST COLONISTS" he wrote across the top of the page. Then he began listing their names in pairs like in the stories of life on Earth. Kaylya and Rojaire, Caleeza and Ollen, Captain Setas and Theon, he chuckled at that. Wessid and Zaloka, Thayla and Traevus, Ilene and Kiril, his heart swelled at the thought. That left Edty, Tassyn, Drak, and Inventor Sulyan. They were sixteen total from three different worlds. A low number to build a sustainable colony, but Kiril had no doubt the colony would succeed, at least until they could find another way in and out. They would work hard together to make sure everyone was fed and sheltered. They would make things from the materials at hand and the valley, still mostly unexplored, would provide. They would live and multiply. They would make their own life decisions without interference from the High Council.

After carefully putting his journal away, Kiril continued to sit for a long time by the dying embers of the fire dreaming of the future.

CHAPTER 22

Earth

ANTHYA APPROACHES.

The message was not unexpected. The close friends and members of the Order of the Oracle were gathered to see Melinda off to a new life on a faraway world. "She's almost here," Rahlys announced. Anthya was coming to retrieve the rune-covered chest containing the Rod of Destruction and Melinda was going with her.

Melinda's decision to go to Aaia had not been made lightly. On Anthya's world she could be true to herself. She would not have to hide the truth about her past; in fact she would tell her story to the High Council. She would not have to explain years of absence now that she had regained speech; it would be impossible to do so without betraying Rahlys and the others. The secrecy of the Oracle of Light had to be protected. And the media attention she had received already put her at risk of being recognized. By going to Aaia she would literally disappear from the face of the Earth.

"Leaf, stay where I can see you," Maggie called when Leaf ran momentarily out of sight around the corner of the cabin.

"I'm right here," Leaf sang in response, his head popping back into view. The motherly stress of recent events had pushed Maggie over the edge in protectiveness. The twins she kept close by her side.

Then Councilor Anthya appeared suddenly shimmering in silver and gold in the bright autumn sunshine. "She's here," Leaf sang running up to join them.

"Greetings Sorceress Rahlys, guardian of the Oracle of Light, Warrior Maggie, Warrior Vince, Warrior Elaine, Warrior Jack, Warrior Melinda, Warrior Leaf, New Person Crystal, and New Person Rock. The High Council of the Crystal Table wishes to congratulate you on your success.

"Greetings Council Anthya; you are always welcome," Rahlys answered for all of them. "What will the High Council do with the Rod of Destruction? Will we be safe?"

"It is our belief that Droclum has now been truly destroyed."

"What can you tell us about my daughter Ilene?" Elaine asked.

"And my adopted daughter Kaylya?" Jack added.

"I cannot tell you how they fair for Ilene and Kaylya left with Rojaire for the Devastated Continent, now renamed Lynnara, against the High Council's wishes along with others. We no longer have contact with them. And we can no longer reach Limitation Island. To find out why that is so would require the construction of a sea-faring vessel and a long hard sea journey to investigate," Anthya explained.

Jack and Elaine knew that Ilene had arrived safely to the special valley and reunited with her father. While she wished her daughter home, it surprised Elaine to discover she found it somewhat comforting knowing Ilene was with Theon and she was happy. Jack and Elaine did not share with Councilor Anthya what they knew through the crystal hologram.

Anthya took possession of the rune-covered chest and the key, both carefully shielded. "It is time to say good-bye," she said turning to Melinda.

Melinda gave Jack and Elaine a final hug, and then Rahlys. "Will you come and visit me, Rahlys? Quaylyn and I will be waiting for you."

"I can make no promises. You take care."

"You too."

Wiping a tear from her eye, Melinda hugged Vince and then held on to Maggie tightly for a while. Maggie had been thrilled to get Melinda back and was having a hard time letting her go again. Then it was on to the twins and Leaf. Saying goodbye to Leaf proved the hardest of all. They had been through so much together despite Leaf's young life. She held him in her arms reluctant to let him go. Would she really never see him again?

"I don't want you to go."

"Leaf, I will never forget you. You will be in my heart, my thoughts, and my dreams forever."

"On day when I'm a great warrior I will come and protect you," Leaf vowed boldly while his little body shook with sobs, "and we will go to the Devastated Continent to see Ilene and Kaylya."

"You are already a great warrior, Leaf. Even Councilor Anthya says so. But right now Crystal and Rock need you more than I do."

"When I'm grown up, I will come, you will see."

Melinda couldn't argue with that. "I will miss you," she said wiping the tears from his sweet little face.

"It is time," Anthya said gently. Nodding in agreement, Melinda joined her.

Then before Melinda could even look around one last time at the world she was leaving, they vanished, gone to a distant world on the far side of the Milky Way Galaxy.

www.ingramcontent.com/pod-product-compliance
Lightning Source LLC
Chambersburg PA
CBHW070631310726
48982CB00001B/252